Unsettled Scores

Kel O'Connor

ISBN-13: 978-0-578-95354-0

For the bridesmaids

Chapter One

AMY STUART HIT the pause button on her phone and the quiet drone of the ventilation system replaced the sound of screaming guitars and thumping bass as the music ended. The beat echoed in her head and she set off, prowling around the shadowy training gym, her movements as fluid as a dancer's. A high kick sent the first punching body swaying on its base. Twirling away, she flicked the knife in her hand towards the second dummy, not stopping to see if it made contact. The dim lighting almost obscured the rope that was next in her path. It would be easier to tuck and roll underneath, but Amy instead executed a gymnast's flip over the waist-high obstacle. Easy wasn't fun.

She had just pivoted sharply to her right when the overhead speaker crackled. "Suit up. Garage in ten."

The voice belonged to her team leader, Del, alerting them they would leave for their op in ten minutes.

Panting from exertion, Amy stopped to pick up the knife from the padded floor. Her hand closed around the handle, wanting to stab it into the dummy form she'd missed. Actually, she wanted to repeatedly slash the inanimate object. Two things kept her walking towards the locker room: she didn't have time to waste, and her boss would question the violence.

After almost three years of overwhelming numbness, the last few months of intense anger felt equally alarming and invigorating. At first, she had reveled in the sharp emotion, using it to hone her fighting skills. Lately, though, she found it difficult to reign in her feelings. Workouts only ended when she collapsed. Sleep eluded her while furious thoughts ran through her head. What she needed was a real-life challenge, she thought.

Luckily, she had a job that allowed her to work out her frustrations on unsavory characters, so tonight's op was heaven sent. Her steps bounced as she hurried to grab her gear, eager to get underway.

WAITING WAS TORTURE, but it was part of the gig, she consoled herself later. On this op, her job was to take down anyone who fled the building that housed Thompson Enterprises. Anyone who wasn't one of her DAG teammates, that is. She crouched behind a row of leafy bushes, her muscles coiled, ready to pounce. Her body zinged with electricity, eager to kick some ass.

Slowly and without a sound, she straightened one leg and then the other before resuming her watch. It wouldn't do any good if her legs cramped up if someone ran by. Even though her gun was holstered on her hip, she preferred not to use it. Gunshots had a way of attracting attention, and that was the last thing DAG wanted. She flexed her hands and stretched her neck, her eyes never leaving the front entrance to the two-story structure of chrome and glass.

While the building had modern lines, to Amy it looked like someone had added windows to a toaster. She could imagine that the façade was blinding in full sunlight. The design screamed, "I'm so impressive, you must avert your eyes!" Pretentious and overdone, much like the company founder and CEO, Timothy Benson. The toad brazenly let it be known that he owned the formula for a bioweapon. A gas that could take out an entire building in seconds. Rumor was, Benson was about to sell to a terrorist group.

Thompson Enterprises officially produced vaccines. DAG agents were here to steal the bioweapon formula and all information relating to the potential buyer.

Data Acquisitions Group was formed when two of the founders, Daniel and Peter, left their positions as CIA agents after busting, and immediately befriending, the brilliant hacker, Malachai. Their combined talents allowed them to take black ops contracts from the government and become quite wealthy, playing by their own rules. There was even a legitimate part to the business that handled background checks for businesses. Amy had been part of the elite field team since her life had blown apart three years ago, and she loved it. Meting out justice and kicking ass . . . what more could she wish for in a job?

Whoever planned this landscaping had no clue about

security, she thought, and rolled her eyes. The hedges were thick, too close to the building, and currently shielding Amy from anyone who might look outside. Tonight, the moon was only a tiny sliver in the sky, a bit of luck that helped conceal them. At least the slight autumn breeze kept her cool. DAG's combat gear was black, flexible, and light. It was the knit cap hiding her blonde hair she hated. It was stifling, and it felt like a thousand fire ants attacking her scalp while sweat matted her hair.

According to their intel, it was about to be a shift change for the six guards, who should be clustered in the back security office. Six was a small number, but the team always came prepared for a fight. Well, the others came ready for defensive actions; Amy longed for a fight. She yearned to have someone to pummel. If she were being truthful, she yearned to pummel her teammate, Mick. Even if it was only one hit. She could lay him out with one punch, she knew she could.

Lord, she needed to talk to Peter and ask for a reassignment. Her malice towards Mick was no better than it'd been four weeks ago, when he had banished his girlfriend, Kit, to God-knows-where. While she hadn't known her long, Amy considered Kit a friend. They had an awful past in common. That's why Mick's betrayal was so personal to Amy. Yes, a lunatic was after Kit, and a new identity far away made sense. However, Kit had wanted to stay with Mick. Instead, he broke her heart, rejecting her when she'd needed him the most.

The anger that chafed at her being was a drastic change from her former demeanor. While it was thrilling to feel more alive, emotional anesthesia had been easier for work. It had kept her mind clear. Thanks to her co-worker, all she saw now was red.

Fucking bastard, Amy thought again for the millionth time. Mick had been with DAG less than a year, and she'd been impressed with the Brit until he tossed Kit aside. He'd survived a horrific prison sentence after being caught as a spy in Iraq. Despite that, he seemed put together and had incredible skills with numbers and locks. His quiet and intelligent demeanor meshed well with the team.

Which meant her animosity toward him could be deadly. She made a mental note to go straight to Peter when this op was completed.

INSIDE THE CEO'S office, Mick held a small black box up to the safe, watching the digital numbers fill the reader. He straightened to his full height to stretch some tension out of his back. The muscles protested, and he welcomed the small twinge. He preferred physical pain over the emotional anguish that had set up house inside him. Thank heavens he was back at work and staying busy. Less time to dwell on his despair.

Time bore down on him. His part should have been over two minutes ago, but triple protocols protected the safe. He felt rather than saw Mateo return to the room. *Damn!* The man was light on his feet!

Mick envied that. He was too tall and too broad to be stealthy. Mateo moved like a ghost, while Mick considered himself to be more of a rhino. Well, perhaps not – he didn't stomp or lumber. Hadn't Kit once referred to him as a giraffe? A sharp pain squeezed his chest, and he pushed the emotion away. *Don't think of her*, he ordered himself; *you're on the job!* Later, he could again wallow in his pain. Tonight, his team and many more were counting on him.

"What's taking so long?" Mateo whispered. "I have everything we need from the server."

Just then, the safe latch clicked open. Mick sighed with relief, and then he swept the contents into a drawstring bag he'd pulled from his pocket. In the dim light, he saw wads of cash, papers, and two external drives fall inside before pulling the top closed.

Mateo saw the drives, too. "Fan-fucking-tastic."

If what they required wasn't on the download, the information would be on the drives. There had been no time to comb through everything and find exactly what they needed, so Mateo's job had been to download it all and then wipe the server. Too bad for Thompson Enterprises. They would have to begin from the ground up – everything from payroll files to toilet paper purchases were now in DAG's hands. Mateo had left an added gift of a nasty virus that Malachai had concocted. It would fry every PC within the hour.

"Thirty seconds." Del's warning was sharp in their ears. Soon, half the guards would clock out, and the other half would take up watch.

"Mission complete. Headed out." Mateo's whisper came clearly through everyone's earpieces.

The rest of the team went on high alert. Whittaker was hidden outside at the back entrance, meanwhile Archie was off to the left. They, plus Amy, had each exit point covered, just in case. Since they finished on time, the original withdrawal plan was in place. Mick and Mateo would depart through the side door, furthest from the security office.

AMY WATCHED AS two shadows emerged from the inset doorway. One tall, one slight – Mick and Mateo. She stood, ready to return to the lake where Archie had landed his plane and get the hell out of here.

She could hear distant traffic noise; then all hell broke loose, starting with a high-pitched alarm. A thrill zinged through her, so sharp it amazed her that sparks didn't fly from her fingers. She bent down, ready to sprint, and had no clue she was smiling.

The security guards, equipped with night vision goggles, spilled out of a side door. Amy shook her head at the way they announced their presence with a roar. *Obviously not well-trained goons*, she thought, and charged into the fight. *Lucky for me!*

She laid low the first attacker by merely flicking her high-powered flashlight in his eyes. He fell upon the grass with a cry, his eyeballs momentarily fried. She really could have done that to the rest of them, but by damn, she wanted to fight.

The punches, leg strikes, and tackles felt glorious. The thick body armor the goons wore meant that she had to be accurate in her aim. The dim moonlight made it difficult, but that made her even happier.

The desire to become a cop had hit her in middle school. She couldn't remember what inspired her, but the urge only grew stronger as she aged. She researched and found she had all the requisite attributes except for one: her size. She was of average height and lean build, which, combined with her innocent looks, made it difficult for her to gain respect. So, she trained. Along with playing softball and running track in high school and college, she'd studied martial arts and taken any classes that focused on self-defense. By the time she entered the academy, she'd taken down any man who came at her.

She joined a tangle of people near an oak tree that towered over the sidewalk. She could barely distinguish her teammates among the goons, now that they had abandoned the ridiculous goggles. She pulled one back with force until his head connected with the tree trunk. The thudding sound made her grin. He fell to the ground, unmoving.

Before she could turn, she was pinned against the tree. The man's breath smelled like fish, and his knife was cold against the side of her neck. Amy calculated how she could move without getting sliced open. Before she could act, Archie's voice came through. "Heads up, A!"

One of his wickedly sharp knives landed in the bark beside her cheek, so close that a sliver of wood stung her forehead. Damn, now she would have to apologize for snarking at him for flipping the damn things when he was bored. His accurate aim had just saved her.

She pulled the knife out and pushed her arm back, catching the goon in his thigh. Of course, he cried out. Loudly. She turned to see him on the ground, bellowing, clutching his leg.

There must have been some unspoken communication between the goons, because two of them suddenly tried to grab her. She ducked and danced around them, punching out with the knife when she could. It made contact at least twice. One goon let out a high cry, while the other only grunted.

"Move out!" Del's order sounded in her ear.

She followed her teammates, looking back to make sure there were no goons left standing. Soon, she joined Mick, Del, and Archie in the plane, while Mateo and Whittaker took off in the car they'd stashed nearby.

Besides being a pilot, Archie was the only person who consistently beat her in pool. He was also better with knives, but she'd been practicing. *Obviously not enough*, she thought blackly, remembering her poor aim in the training gym.

Mateo was the newest agent. Unlike the rest of the team, he'd been a legit criminal. Daniel loved to recruit from prisons, but most of the rookies hadn't committed hard crimes. Not Mateo, though. He'd worked his way up to the high echelons of a large drug gang operating on the East Coast. Amy often wondered what caused him to become a double-agent, but he was too tight-lipped to make that common knowledge. Peter, Malachai, and Daniel knew and trusted him, and so did she. Somehow, Malachai had discovered Mateo was a computer whiz in the making and was teaching him all the ways to hack.

Rounding out the team was Del. She was their group leader, a former Army medic whose iron control was legendary. Nothing fazed her, and she had a wicked wit. Amy adored her, and she considered Del her closest friend. Her post was on top of a nearby building. As team leader, she ran logistics, kept the time, and made alternative plans on the fly.

Actually, Whittaker was the last member of the team. *Ugh.* He normally stayed out of the fray, out of laziness or fear of getting hit in the face. He was Peter's nephew, and that was the only reason they tolerated him. He had yet to endanger anyone by the way he cut corners, but the rest of the team were extra careful around him. His spiteful personality did little to help. Amy was grateful she wouldn't be crammed into the small cockpit with him this time.

As much as she disliked water takeoffs, she couldn't fault Archie for his skills. The Cessna Corvalis TTx belonged solely to him, and her name was Darcelle. He was a skilled pilot, but sometimes it seemed as if he purposely chose the more dangerous path. She wouldn't be surprised if there had been a private airport available nearby, and Archie had passed it over for the lake. She understood how he wanted to challenge himself. It wasn't as if any of them ever felt unsafe in his care. By the time she belted in next to him, they were up and away.

"Shit," Mick's voice came from the backseat. "I think I'm bleeding on your seat, Archie."

Luckily, Del was seated next to Mick. Archie flicked on the light so she could haul out the first aid kit. Del served as their emergency doctor, thanks to her background. While major surgery was beyond her skills, field triage was her specialty.

"Fuck. You're paying for the cleanup, Yankee."

Archie's expletive was loaded with concern. Knowing him, he could be equally worried about Mick's wound and Darcelle's leather upholstery.

Amy looked back to see Del pressing gauze on a section of Mick's lower back. Mick was silent, his face pale, his jaw set against the pain. His black compression shirt had contained much of the blood, so the cleaning bill for the plane would be minimal. Darcelle was Archie's treasured possession, and Amy could see momentary dismay on his face.

While Del assessed the injury, Archie radioed the rest of the group, found them safe, and headed for the highway. Mateo was busy uploading the data they'd stolen while Whittaker drove. They would regroup at headquarters, and Amy didn't want to bet on who might arrive first. Whittaker drove like a wild man, while they would still have a short drive from DAG's private landing site.

Mick hissed in pain from the second-row seats. If anyone had to be injured, she was glad it was him. *I'm such a bitch*, Amy thought with little concern. She could blame it on the adrenaline loss, if she felt guilty later.

"Need any help?" she asked, forcing concern into her voice.

Del peeked under the gauze she'd applied. "Nah. Looks like a four-inch slash. Not too deep. Needs stitches, though. I can take care of that at the office."

"Happened at the end," Mick said through gritted teeth. "Fuck. Thought I'd tagged all the knives. Guess I miscounted."

Amy whipped back around in her seat and stared out

at the dark night. *Oh, shit.* The grunt. That had been Mick, not a goon. *Shit.*

Her horror seeped away, replaced by satisfaction. *Karma, baby. This one was for you, Kit!* She certainly hadn't done it on purpose. She would never harm a teammate, no matter what degree of bastard they were.

Yeah. She was a bitch. She needed to talk to Peter right away. But first, she needed advice.

"Can we talk?" Amy kept her voice low, even though they were alone in the ladies' room at DAG headquarters. Since Del knew Peter best, she wanted her friend's input before she approached him.

Del nodded. "Give me a sec to clean up, and I'll meet you in the conference room."

Amy looked away as Del pulled off the bloody surgical gloves she'd used to finish Mick's stitches. She wasn't squeamish, just guilty.

"I'll make tea," she offered. A great excuse to leave the restroom, plus it would keep her busy.

Amy paced the small room until Del arrived. Once they sat down, she kept her hands in her lap under the table so she could fidget with the plain silver ring she wore.

She swallowed a knot of apprehension as she waited for Del to sweeten her tea and sit down. She wouldn't be happy with Amy's request. They were the only two women currently on the DAG covert squad. They worked well together, and every time someone left, it took months for the team to function at peak again. Surely, though, Del would realize that having Amy around Mick was a worse threat to the team's unity.

Amy grasped the ceramic handle on the sturdy cup before looking Del in the eye. "I need you to answer as the team leader, not my friend. I want to ask Peter for a reassignment," she blurted.

Del had just taken a sip of her drink and choked a bit. Amber tea sloshed out onto the glass tabletop as she set the cup down with a thud. "What? Why?"

Amy sighed and leaned forward. "It has nothing to do with you. It's Mick. Rather, my feelings towards him. I want to beat the shit out of him."

Del looked back at her in stunned silence. Amy had confided her feelings surrounding the aftermath of what had happened to Kit, Mick's former girlfriend. That wasn't news to Del. That Amy still felt this strong weeks later was.

"My anger . . . is dangerous," Amy admitted with a grimace. "He's an easy target for it. I need some time off to get myself under control."

Del nodded and reached across to grasp her hand.

"So, this is about Claire and Chris, too," she stated. "Is this the next step of grieving? If so, isn't that good?"

Amy frowned, looking down into the depths of her tea. Her niece and brother-in-law were always a sore spot. When Amy's sister had committed suicide, her husband had blamed Amy and forbade her to see their daughter, Claire. The blame was all on Amy, and a part of her understood Chris's reasoning. But another part of her was furious. Claire was all she had left of her sister. The proclamation had driven a wedge between her and her parents. While they didn't blame Amy, they'd been forced to choose between her and Claire at holidays. Their granddaughter needed them in ways that Amy, as an adult, didn't. So, she stepped back. She was happy they shared a powerful bond. Happy, and oh-so jealous.

All she had left was subterfuge. Every few months, she would visit Atlanta and spy on Claire. It wasn't hard for someone like herself to find out what school Claire attended, what soccer fields she played on, who her friends were. Amy watched. She would blend in with the other mothers at award days and soccer games, disguised so that Chris wouldn't recognize her. It usually went without a hitch, and Amy could return to her regular life knowing that Claire was healthy and happy. Until her visit last month.

Chris had brought a date to the soccer game. He'd never done that before. And by the looks of how they'd interacted, this woman wasn't merely a date. That idea was confirmed as Amy watched Claire approach them with a frown. The girl stood in sulky silence as her dad spoke about the game. She wasn't close enough to hear, but he kept gesturing to the field. Probably congratulating his daughter on her goal, judging by the smile on his face. When the woman agreed, Claire turned on her heel and stalked off toward the field house.

Chris and the woman were crestfallen. Not wanting to feel any sympathy toward him, Amy turned to watch Claire disappear into the building with her teammates. She was crying. That broke Amy's heart. Claire was unhappy, and there was nothing she could do to help her. She could sympathize with the girl's feelings. While she knew it had to happen eventually, she was still furious that Chris had moved on from the memory of her sister. By bringing the woman here, it was apparently serious, and he seemed to want her to step in as Claire's mother. *How dare he.*

Amy had returned home and spent hours at the gym, trampling anyone who was brave enough to volunteer. When she was calm enough to talk, she'd met Del and unloaded. But none of that made her any less angry. Then Mick betrayed Kit, spraying accelerant on the fire that was her fury.

"I want to ask Peter for a reassignment," she repeated. "Working in the legitimate side for a while would give me time to have regular therapy sessions. Plus, no Mick or bad guys to be accidentally injured," she finished with a fake chuckle.

Del sighed, and Amy watched her turning solutions over in her head. The plan made sense. DAG had a public side that conducted in-depth investigations for businesses and the government. Background checks, security clearances, things that were all above-ground and legal. The black-ops side obtained information by less legal, and sometimes violent, means.

"Until I get this under control, I'm a danger to the team," Amy pronounced, and Del reluctantly nodded.

"You have my support, then." Del squeezed her hand. "Just promise to come back."

Amy laughed, a genuine laugh, and returned the squeeze. "Where else would I go?"

AMY HAD TURNED down Del's offer of moral support during her meeting with Peter. She was second-guessing that decision now as she sat with her boss in the small conference room. She'd rather have met with him in his office, but Peter had selected the location. In his office, he would've sat behind his desk; here they sat beside each other, like colleagues.

She pushed her long hair behind her ears and looked out onto the sunny DC day. If it hadn't been for the vapor rising from the cars traveling down on the street, she might have thought it was summer. Normally, she loved days like this, bright and cold. Perhaps she could enjoy it after she got through this meeting.

"I want to be reassigned," she blurted.

Peter raised his eyebrows, more in response to what she said than how. He was used to the abrupt, straightforward way she communicated. While it wasn't the most professional form of dispatch, no one in the organization ever chastised her for it. In fact, she suspected it was the facet of her that Daniel liked the most. Zero filter, zero bullshit.

"I assume there's a good reason?" Peter asked.

The team often shared their ideas of what Peter and Daniel were like back in their CIA days. The collective conclusion was that, while interrogating, Peter had been the smooth, by-the-book spy, and Daniel had been, in turns, the good guy or the off-the-wheels wacko. Even now, Peter remained calm, showing the right amount of concern, which she knew was genuine.

"I need to get my head together. I'm too angry," she forged on. "Things are tense with my family. And after what happened with Kit, I can't keep working with Mick."

Peter leaned back in his chair. His only show of surprise was a slight raise of his eyebrows, causing his forehead to wrinkle. Amy waited, forcing herself to appear relaxed when all she wanted to do was fidget, or get up and pace. She doubted he would fire her, but there was always that chance. Nothing at DAG worked if they couldn't operate as a team.

"I would say it's been good to see you more energized and involved the last few weeks." He smiled wryly. "But it sounds like you're telling me the pendulum has swung too far."

Amy sighed, nodded, and tapped her foot. The carpet was far too plush for Peter to hear her fidgeting.

"You know –" He paused, and grimaced. "There's much more to Mick's story than you know."

So many caustic replies ran through her brain, but she decided that a simple shrug was best. Let him play the diplomat – he excelled at that. She didn't care. Only a complete bastard walks out on his girlfriend after she'd been raped. Whatever Mick said or did in her hospital room had broken Kit's heart. Amy had been there to bear testament to the aftermath. Even Chris, who she hated, had not reacted like that. To his credit, he seemed to do everything right after Amy and her sister were abducted. He had showered Audrey with love, affection, comfort, stability, and had insisted she keep up with therapy.

Silence now filled the room, and she clenched her jaw to keep from speaking. She despised waiting, but Peter needed proof that she was serious. To be honest, guilt nudged at her. Surely, he was disappointed in her.

That thought stung. She pulled on her poker face and stared back out the window, again dismembering Mick in her imagination.

"OK." Peter's voice interrupted her mental hate-fest, and she wanted to sag in relief. "I'm impressed and thankful that you know your limits. However, I'm afraid you would find the legit side tedious."

Her heart sank. He was right. She knew it, but what was the alternative?

"You want me to quit?" Panic made her voice rise, but she felt more confusion than fear.

"Of course not!" Peter frowned. "I don't want you to leave out of boredom, either."

Amy slumped, trying to find an alternative. She could survive a short while in an apathetic position. It was better than endangering anyone on the team, after all.

"How about working as a contractor?" Peter offered. "I could assign you cases that can be worked solo. Tell the team I've assigned you a long-term undercover op."

Amy smiled as the enormous weight sitting on her chest instantly evaporated. Like the rest of the team, she'd been recruited by Daniel. Yet it was Peter who had added a special rider to her employment contract without batting an eye. Somehow, he understood her need for justice on a level no one else did. One day, she hoped to find out why.

This offer was better than she'd imagined. A way to stay in the game that wouldn't disappoint her friends, while also keeping her away from Mick the bastard. While she would never hug her boss, she reached out and squeeze the hand that lay on his armrest. Peter smiled and squeezed back.

"Of course, this comes with the stipulation that you see Ella regularly," he added.

Ella Fisher was the therapist for DAG. Everyone on the team had to meet with her at least four times a year, per his or her employment contract. If they wanted more sessions, the company covered it. Dr. Fisher's practice dealt exclusively with government-contracted groups, so she understood their special requirements and the need for strict confidentiality.

"Already started," she assured him as they stood. "I can continue with video calls when I'm out in the field."

Amy was hotheaded, a bit egotistical, but she knew her limits. The only reason she was alive today was the fact that she'd been paired with the perfect psychiatrist after her rape. God, it had been excruciating, but also necessary. She lived every day with the guilt that Audrey hadn't had the same good fortune. Her sister had bounced around between a dozen doctors before quitting therapy altogether. If only she had found the right person to talk to . . .

As always, guilt smothered her when she thought about Audrey. Even now, years later. She brushed it away and concentrated on the present.

"Thanks again." She stood and shook Peter's hand.

"Let me know when you're ready to come back, Amy. Your spot will always be open."

Amy swallowed the tears that threatened to flow at his words. She nodded and left the room quickly, shutting the door behind her. She strode down the hallway to Del's office, cursing Mick in her mind. *Fucker*. Why did he have to come and mess up her life?

THE FIRST FEW weeks of contract work were precisely what Amy needed: two different assignments requiring her to travel and work undercover. Clandestine operations always helped clear her head. Pretending to be someone else required concentration and practice. So, even in her off-time, she forced herself to think like her new fake personas.

Violet the Administrative Assistant fretted over her houseplants, not an estranged niece. Amy enjoyed living in Canada as her Violet identity. The accents and food charmed her. That op ended too soon when she discovered who had been paying off a governmental staffer.

Emily the new Vice President focused all her animosity on the former VP who had quietly been arrested for embezzlement, instead of on a tall, British co-worker. She loved the view from her new persona's high rise Chicago apartment. Thankfully, her current persona was close to her own age, so she didn't need to bother with much of a disguise, so all she had to deal with were a brown wig, a pair of glasses, and a couple of pricey suits.

Over time, her daily workouts became less angry and more productive. Her nightly sleep increased by two hours. So far, it seemed that she and Peter had found a suitable solution to her issues. Standing in Emily's office, she took one last look around in satisfaction. In addition to stealing money, the former VP had also stolen data. This particular data concerned a top-secret government contract. While that data had been recovered during his arrest, Amy had been sent to find out how it had happened and if any cohorts existed. But the ass-hat had acted alone.

Overall, the last three months of solo work had paid off. She felt almost ready to rejoin the team. Ella, her psychiatrist, agreed. Four to six more weeks, and Amy should be centered enough not to stab Mick a second time.

Since she had a three-day break before her next assignment, she supposed she should head back to DC. Check in on her apartment. Have dinner with Del, as long as Mick wasn't mentioned. Maybe invite Archie, and find a game of pool.

RATHER THAN RELYING on DAG or her friends, Amy hailed a cab at the airport. A massive storm had resulted in delays, and she was too tired to be social. After a stop to collect her mail from a box leased under a fake business account and turning off her elaborate security system, she was home. The old building was in an area that had yet to be gentrified. While the eight apartments it housed had electric heat and gas, even cable TV, there was no central A/C or modern appliances. Dishes were washed by hand, although for Amy, that usually comprised of just coffee mugs and the utensils she used to eat takeout. Her dirty clothes were dropped off at a local laundry; she rarely had time to do them herself.

But despite all the inconveniences, she loved her apartment. After a recent data breach at work, all agents had had to relocate for their safety. Amy had happily left behind a sterile duplex after finding this gem. The original window frames held years of nicks and gouges. The water pipes rattled, the sound familiar and soothing. The scuffed wooden floors popped when you stepped in certain places. Something about the long history of the place charmed her. It endured despite not being cared for properly. Endured, no matter how many tenants came and went.

She often wondered about the people who'd looked out her same windows. Her imagination didn't extend to making up stories about them. She hoped that this space had given them the same feeling of refuge. And hoped they'd treated it better than she did.

Just like the duplex, she had yet to really furnish it. It contained only the necessities. There was a worn leather couch and an end table with a lamp and whatever pile of paperwork was most recent. A secondhand bookcase held everything from ammunition catalogs to a basket for her keys to a tangle of old computer cables. There was even a small stack of paperbacks near the bottom, books she had read years ago. Now, she used audiobooks to while away the hours she spent traveling. One corner held a large fake plant, a gift from her mother, who knew a living one would die of neglect.

The bedroom was better furnished. The bed, shoved against the wall, made room for the two desks and all her computer equipment. While she wasn't the advanced tech-head Malachai was, she wasn't a novice. None of the DAG team were. In fact, new guy Mateo was proving to be a natural, despite not growing up around technology.

Booting up the computer, Amy pulled off her shoes and flopped on the unmade bed. The banded stack of her missed mail was thin. What bills she had were set to paperless auto-pay. She flipped through the junk mail, trying to decide what to order for dinner. It was so late; her top three restaurants were closed. That meant either pizza or Chinese, neither appealing at the moment. Were there still lasagna leftovers in the freezer? That might do. She needed to tackle shopping tomorrow and stock the kitchen. Her laptop alert dinged as she started compiling a grocery list.

Amy logged into the secure site and downloaded the data as she waited for Del to answer at the other end. A chime told her the call connected, and she was surprised to see Peter's face on the screen, not Del's.

"There's some activity in Atlanta," he began.

She couldn't imagine what Peter was like as a friend. As a professional, he used as few words as possible, although he always strove for professionalism. While she usually preferred her conversation blunt and concise, she could have used a warning this time. She slid into the chair and pulled herself closer to the desk, her stomach now a bundle of snakes.

DAG had eyes and ears all over the globe. Part of the employment agreement that Amy had negotiated was that she was kept apprised of any chatter that had to do with The Duke, his gang, or any of his major associates. Peter had kept his word. So far, no leads had panned out in a way that would bring down the drug dealer. Amy was patient, however. Revenge is best served cold, blah, blah, blah.

Without waiting for a response, Peter launched into the details. "There's a charity that ships shoes to needy children. They were spot-checking a future shipment and found drugs. Joshua's Vision is well known and respected in Atlanta. They want the investigation to be discreet. Luckily, someone suggested DAG. The heroin they found was 10% starch and 4% inositol."

Amy sat up straight, energy bouncing through her veins. That percentage was The Duke's signature. It couldn't be a coincidence, since The Duke was one of the largest drug dealers in that area. He was also the key to her plan of retribution.

This could be it. What she had waited for. Excitement made her dizzy, and she shook herself in order to focus.

"I can leave tomorrow."

"No." Peter shook his head, and she gritted her teeth. "Our contact within the charity is out of town until the third. I stressed how important it was to keep to their schedule and not cause suspicion since the affected shipment doesn't go out for another three weeks."

Amy's mouth flattened into a thin line. She knew her boss was right, but she wanted to go now, damn it!

"You'll be posing as an auditor from Superior Generosity, the top philanthropy-rating website. You will have access to everything, including the shipping warehouse. Our contact is the foundation's lawyer. He'll pick you up at a private airport and take you to the rental car agency. Del is sending details on your hotel and car, plus all the intel we have."

Amy nodded, still too keyed-up to speak. How awful was she? Thrilled to be getting a chance to have another crack at the demons that destroyed her family? If she could get The Duke, then he would have to hand over Ajax. This could lead to everything she'd hoped for.

Underneath the desk, she flexed her fingers in anticipation. Yeah, she may be cold-blooded, but bastards deserve to fall.

"Amy." Peter's tone brought her back to the present. She was surprised to see concern in his eyes. "We'll be behind you every step. You won't hesitate to call for help. Understood?"

"Yes, sir. Understood," she replied with a sure voice.

Peter nodded one last time, and the connection went dark. The computer emitted a different tone, letting her know the email from Del had arrived. She hoped the location was close to Claire. Driving from one end of Atlanta to the other was a bitch that could take hours if the traffic was bad. There was no way she would give less than 100% to this op, but she hoped she could squeeze in a few sightings of her niece while she was there. Thoughts of the girl caused a familiar ache in her chest that was always followed by a blast of white-hot hate for her brother-in-law.

But right now, she needed to focus on her job. She had a week to study the background for the charity. First food, then homework.

Chapter Two

"WELL, HELLO, DARLIN'!" Archie greeted Amy as soon as they were both strapped into the cockpit. "Long time, no see!"

"Hey! I've missed you, too." Amy was genuinely happy to spend time with Archie. He was affable, fun to hang out with, and always kept his cool. Teaching her knife-throwing was also a bonus.

The fact that his hair had grown past his ears gave her a pain. Too much time had passed since she'd last seen him. *Fucking Mick*, she thought again. She shook her head, physically throwing away the thought of him. This op could be the break she'd waited for, and it demanded all of her concentration. Plus, she wanted to enjoy this time with one of her favorite guys.

She sat quietly while he communicated with the tower at the private airfield, and then took off. Once they were at cruising altitude, Archie launched into questions. Thankfully, they concerned her new op, and not Mick or why she'd been on solo assignment so long.

"What's new and exciting in the Atlanta heroin

trade?" he drawled.

Amy chuckled dryly. "It's hard to believe how much it's grown since I lived here. I mean – it's always been a major scene, but there's more of a battle for the city's trade than exporting. New gangs are trying to push out the old guard with cheaper drugs and violence."

"Cut with fentanyl?" Archie guessed, and she nodded.

"Yeah. OD fatalities are through the roof, so the long-time users are still loyal to the older gangs."

"One of the oldies is a contact, right?" Archie asked. "The basketball granddad you told us about?"

"Papa G." Amy smiled wryly. "He looks like a grandfather you might see at any YMCA. He started selling pot at fourteen and moved up to dealing heroin by the time he was eighteen. He's been at this for over twenty years. He has long-time Dominican suppliers that give him primo product. While he's in it for the money like every other dealer, he sees it as his duty to have an excellent product that helps people manage their emotional pain."

"Whatever lets you sleep at night?" Archie snorted.

"I know." Amy sighed. "But he's always helped where he could by getting the newer, violent gangs out of the area."

"Do you have a meet set?"

She nodded. "Tonight. Papa G and The Duke have a truce, as long as each group stays in their own territory. They've split the Bluff right down the middle."

"The Bluff?"

"An area downtown that is the most depressed and

drug-ridden. Stands for 'better leave you fucking fool.' There's a corner where more heroin transactions occur than anywhere else in the US."

"Damn!" Archie exclaimed. "I'm so out of the loop! Been ages since I was anywhere in Georgia that wasn't an airfield."

Most of Archie's ops focused on guns. While that and the drug trade intersected, DAG had Archie covering a group out West for the past year. Mateo's former gang – the one he was still with undercover – dealt in drugs and guns, but was East Coast only.

"Gonna check on your family?" Archie asked in his soothing Texas twang.

"Yeah." She smiled. "Awesome to get here on DAG's dime."

"Hey, next time you're home, I found a new bar that features ax-throwing." Archie's devilish grin was hard to resist. It was usually an invitation to crazy behavior that she had yet to regret. In fact, an escapade with him normally led to adventure.

"What?" Amy asked. "Should alcohol and throwing sharp objects be combined? That sounds too awesome to pass up."

Archie smirked before he radioed the small field in North Atlanta that they were approaching.

Having Archie and his plane, Darcelle, was a perk for DAG agents. When he wasn't available, they traveled commercial, but if he was free, he loved having the flight time. Amy was glad he'd been available today. It was so nice to chat with him again.

Archie brought the sleek plane in for a perfect landing, and then taxied to where the tower indicated. They ended up near a small parking lot. Amy looked around for the charity lawyer that was supposed to meet her.

"That him?" Archie squinted out of the plane's windshield.

"Doesn't look like a lawyer, but definitely a local. He's certainly wearing the right hat," Amy noted dryly. "I guess I was expecting an Armani suit."

The tall man was leaning against the side of the hanger, his sneaker-clad feet crossed. He looked like a walking advertisement for a University of Georgia alumni sale. Curls of light brown hair stuck out from under a red baseball cap emblazoned with the word "Dawgs." His faded red sweatshirt proudly proclaimed "Georgia Bulldogs." Even his beat-up sneakers were red and gray. Faded jeans hugged his legs, the knees white with wear. From what she could see of his face behind his mirrored sunglasses, he looked bored. The thick stubble on his cheeks and chin said possibly hung-over, too.

"Bet you $10 he played football in college," Archie snorted as he began to turn off the small plane.

Amy laughed. "Nah, too thin. I'll bet you $20 he played rugby. Probably a rich frat boy pretending to be a bubba."

"Does bubba mean the same in Georgia as it does in Texas?" Archie asked with a chuckle.

"Southern slang for a local male, usually from a small town. Not interested in knowing about anything that isn't sports, boobs, or beer," Amy explained.

"Same meaning." Archie smiled.

Amy tucked the files from Malachai that she'd been skimming into the oversized backpack that served as her briefcase, handbag, and suitcase. She and Archie discarded their headsets, now that the engine was off and they could speak normally.

"Keep us in the loop." Archie's worried eyes tugged at Amy's emotions. Friends who cared were priceless, and she was so lucky. "We can be here in less than an hour."

"I know." She raised her hand for a fist bump; Archie was not a toucher. "Thanks for the ride. I'll let you know who won the bet."

She waited until Archie came around to open her door after securing a non-slip mat on the wing. She hoped this was the charity's lawyer, but he didn't look like a Hugh Bainbridge IV.

The man in question didn't move from his position. With the sunglasses, she couldn't be sure if he was awake. If he was really that hung-over, she would commandeer his keys. She wanted to make it to the car rental place as soon as possible, and Bubba Dawg needed to get with the program, or get out of her way. She should have time to catch Claire at soccer practice if they hurried.

At least his casual attire made her feel less self-conscious about her own clothing. Her wool peacoat covered her faded jeans and an untucked flannel shirt. Even with the hole near the hem, she looked more presentable than he did. She had dress slacks, a skirt, and some blouses rolled up in her bag. She and Del had shipped all of her undercover clothing, disguises, and equipment ahead to the hotel.

In truth, she'd dressed down on purpose, expecting

to meet a stiff lawyer in an expensive suit. While some agents preferred to lull others into accepting them, Amy rather enjoyed keeping people off-balance. Yet here he was, looking even more casual than she did. Was he playing the same game? The notion pissed her off. She squared her shoulders at the idea of being played. *Let him try.*

With one last wave to Archie, she slung her backpack over one shoulder and strode forward. Heat from the pavement seeped through the thick soles of her boots, sharply contrasting with the cool air.

As she moved closer, the man straightened from his slouch, and she realized he was much larger than she'd thought. Tall and lanky. She stopped a foot from him and peered over the rims of her sunglasses.

"Are you waiting on a prospective freshman, or are you Mr. Bainbridge?"

The giant cocked his head, and two woolly eyebrows rose in confusion above his dark lenses. Amy sighed and gestured to his outfit.

"Are you a UG rep or Hugh Bainbridge?" Her tone was snappy, but if this wasn't her ride, then she needed to find a cab quickly. She chafed to get going.

The man looked down at his sweatshirt and laughed. Amy was still staring in shock at the cute grin that transformed his face when he removed his sunglasses. *Ugh.* Of course, he was attractive. Laugh lines radiated out from the corners of his sparkling hazel eyes. Jesus, there was even a dimple sitting above the almost beard on his left cheek. Good thing she didn't find dimples appealing. Nor boyish charm.

"I'm sorry." He extended his other hand. "I came straight from a hunting trip. I am indeed Hugh Bainbridge, and you must be Amy Stuart."

Hunting. Of course. Southern bubbas loved killing defenseless animals. Good. That made him even less attractive. And while he didn't appear to be hungover, there was still hope she could win the bet. He towered over her. Maybe he'd played basketball instead. Either way, he radiated good health, so definitely some sort of jock.

She grasped the outstretched hand and gave it a fast, firm squeeze, all in the name of being a professional. His hand was large, like the rest of him, and she wasn't able to make him visibly wince in pain. Unfortunate. It usually helped to let contacts know who was boss.

She nodded toward the airport's minuscule parking lot. "Where's your car? I'm eager to get started."

Hugh made a move to take her backpack, but Amy tightened her grip on it and walked past him. Sometimes, she appreciated gentlemanly gestures. But today was about showing her power.

It was draining to start every op like this, but she'd learned long ago that most men – especially large men, and particularly Southern men – did not respect slight, blond females very much. Sometimes, she even used it to her advantage – widening her blue eyes, smiling coyly. It lulled most men into thinking she was harmless. Bainbridge wasn't a mark, though; he was a client, and he needed to feel he was in expert hands with DAG. She should be a bit more social, but it was difficult to rein in her desire to get going now that her endgame, and her niece, were in reach.

There were three vehicles in the lot. An old truck, a late-model sedan, and a newer SUV. Amy headed for the SUV, until she heard the creak of the door behind her. She turned, shocked to see him standing by the open passenger side door of the ancient red truck. Well, damn. It was looking like Archie may win the bet. She climbed in, settling her bag between her feet.

After closing her door, Hugh hopped into the driver's seat, buckled his seat belt, and had the truck in gear in record time for someone so large. Despite the size of the truck cab, his hand on the floor gearshift came within inches of her leg. By the time he turned out of the parking lot to hit the highway, Amy noticed the odor.

At first, it wasn't unpleasant. Wood smoke; the smell that lingered after a bonfire. It brought back fond memories of summer camp. Underneath was the scent of male perspiration. Normally, Amy appreciated that smell. It reminded her of the gym or being on an op with her teammates.

The tinge of smoke faded as the odor of stale, sweaty socks filled the truck. Amy craned her neck to look back into the well behind the seat, expecting to see a pile of old socks, stiff from use. Perhaps a couple of worn-out shoes Bainbridge used for jogging through mud.

An open duffel bag filled the space, overflowing with camo-print clothing. Worn waterproof boots had tumbled to the side. A dark stain splashed across the toe of one boot, and it shocked Amy that she hadn't smelled the dried blood earlier. That odor was also familiar to her. The stench of blood overpowered even the sock smell. Unable to breathe normally, she coughed to clear her throat.

She had to give the man credit. He realized what the problem was with one glance.

"Oh, shit!" he cursed, and signaled as he pulled the truck off to the highway shoulder.

He hopped out and quickly threw the offending articles into the truck bed. The duffel landed with a metallic thunk. Its absence made the air cleaner, but Amy still rolled down her window. Damn the cold, but it was better than the stench.

"I'm so sorry." Hugh grimaced as he pulled back onto the road. "I've been holed up in a cabin with my uncle and cousins for a week. Annual hunting trip. I'd planned to be back in time to shower and change, but a semi slid across I-285."

She waved away his explanation; she didn't need it. Unless it concerned the mystery, she didn't care what he did in his spare time. At least his voice didn't grate on her nerves. His Southern accent was light, but he still lost points for using the term "holed up."

While she'd enjoyed her time on the force here, she'd never gotten used to the slang and slow way of speaking. Audrey had loved it – one reason she'd attended college here. Amy had to admit, her sister had been the perfect stereotypical Southern homemaker, before . . .

Amy pushed that thought away to stay focused on the business at hand. This first, then she could turn her attention to Claire. Right now, she needed everything she could find on how this matter tied into The Duke.

"What can you tell me about the situation?" Amy

half turned in her seat to face him.

"Not much more than what I gave Mr. Pierce." He shook his head. "I've been out of the loop. We're scheduled to meet with Roderick, a representative from the board, and the president tonight at seven o'clock for an update."

Roderick was the shipping supervisor who'd found the tainted shipment. He'd first notified the head of the charity, who then alerted the board. They had elected to hire DAG rather than report it to the police. With DAG, the public would never know such a thing had occurred. Even a whiff of bad press could endanger the charity's standing and its future donations. Contacting DAG had been a smart move.

"Fine," she bit off.

She swallowed her frustration down to join the tsunami of emotions and old coffee in her stomach. The delay was frustrating, until she realized that the late meeting time would give her the opportunity to see Claire and meet with Papa G. She relaxed, but continued to watch Hugh out of the corner of her eye.

He drove too quickly and competently for her to order him to hurry. Despite her laser gaze, he looked unaffected, which didn't help her mood. It wasn't fair to take her frustration out on him, she knew. She'd make sure she was in a better humor for their next meeting. Right now, though, it wouldn't hurt their working relationship for him to be a little uneasy around her. After all, she was here to crack a drug case.

While she was staring, she noticed his beard grew unevenly on this side of his face. It resembled a mountain range with peaks and valleys. That imperfection made her feel better, petty as she felt right now.

AMY STUART WAS not anything like Hugh had expected. If he were truthful, she looked like a young soccer mom on her way to a yoga class. Her coat hid the muscles he'd expected, and she had the face of an *ingénue*, not a hardened ex-cop. Her wide blue eyes came closest to revealing her true self – they were shadowed with pain and annoyance.

He felt off-balance himself. He should have had plenty of time to show up here looking respectable, yet that traffic accident had screwed up that plan. He must look as bad as he smelled, he guessed from her reaction. Not a good way to start.

The annual family trip always used to include him, his dad, his uncle, and two male cousins close to his age. The others would go off hunting while Hugh and his cousin, Matt, hung out at the sprawling vacation house by the lake. They would play cards or shoot hoops with an old basketball until the others returned. If they'd been successful, everyone would pitch in to help dress the deer. They spent the evenings re-watching college football games.

Bless his family. They'd tried to continue the tradition this year, but it just wasn't the same without his dad. The trip had turned into more of a tribute than a vacation, even though Alexander Hugh Bainbridge III had died over a year ago.

Hugh had spent most of the time worrying about the discovery of drugs at the charity and his mother. While she seemed to do well adjusting to living alone for the first time in her life, he was uneasy at being hours away if she had an emergency. It relieved him to be coming home. He only wished he'd made a better impression on this cute, yet prickly, agent.

The best he could do under these odd circumstances was to play the gracious host and hope to change her perception of him at the meeting tonight.

"Are you warm enough? Should I turn up the heat?" he asked, noticing she hadn't loosened her coat.

Weather was fickle in Georgia, meaning a spring day could offer a trip to the pool or a chance for snow sledding. Despite the sun moving in and out from behind the clouds, it was chilly. The week ahead was rumored to be cloudy, more cold and gray days. It meant no working outside at his house, but it was just as well. His absence meant extra workload when he returned to his office.

"I'm fine," she replied.

Hugh searched vainly for another topic of conversation, and he felt relieved when she spoke again.

"How long have you worked for Joshua's Vision?" Amy asked as they joined the masses on the interstate.

"Oh, I'm only volunteer help," he explained. "Mostly, I deal with contracts and grants. Some tax questions. I also help pack shoes once a month, alongside my mother."

"That's nice of you." Amy didn't sound impressed.

"Makes my Mom happy. How about you? How long have you been a corporate spy?" He shrugged with a smile.

"A few years," she hedged.

"I understand you lived here once? And you were a cop?" Hugh kept tugging on strings, hoping to get her talking. He wanted her to know that he wasn't simply a yokel hunter idiot who never bathed. Why it mattered so much, he didn't know. His skin was plenty thick, thanks to the past few years.

"Feels like eons ago," she answered candidly. "I was in narcotics. Peter thought that that connection would help."

He exited the interstate and merged onto a freeway, which was even more crowded. Two turns later, he pulled into the lot of a car rental agency.

Before he could even turn off the ignition, Amy hopped out with her bag. "Thanks for the ride. See you at seven at the warehouse."

Then she was gone.

As SOON AS she left the rental car lot, she activated the pre-loaded address in her phone's GPS. She should get some water – her throat was dry with excitement and despair, common emotions when it came to her niece.

Fortunately, she found she was only ten miles away from the practice field. *Excellent!* Luck was on her side, and traffic was sparse on the back roads. She found a parking space in the packed lot and piled her hair under a generic black baseball hat. Oversize sunglasses completed her disguise. There was an actual game today, not merely practice, so it was likely Chris would attend. Yes, she would give the vile man that much – he was an involved dad.

Most of the spectators had seats on the two sets of metal bleachers, but there was a cluster standing under a large oak tree, seeking shade from the periodic sunlight. Amy joined this group and was relieved to hear from the conversation that these parents belonged to the other team. In order to keep them from chatting her up, she pulled out her phone and pretended to be engrossed in something she was reading.

However, everything inside her focused on Claire. The girl had cut her hair again, she noticed with shock and some envy. The past year, Claire's hair had slowly gone from mid-back length to the now adorable bob that hit her shoulders when she didn't pull it back with a hair tie. *Bravo*, Amy thought, wishing she had the guts to do that.

White-hot fire suddenly burned her throat. It wasn't fair that Audrey wasn't here. She belonged with these other stylish young mothers, gossiping about TV shows, sipping on lattes. It had been Audrey's dream life. Was Amy furious at their abductor, herself, or her sister? All of them, to be honest. Focusing on her own culpability was best. She could never, should never, fault Audrey for being fragile.

The game was almost over, but she was able to watch Claire score a goal. Mindful that she was among parents for the opposing team, Amy cheered inwardly. Since neither Chris nor Audrey had been athletes, this was one area where she felt a bond with Claire. If only she could talk to her.

Once Claire had settled on soccer, Amy had learned all she could about the sport. She religiously followed the

USA women's team, even to point of getting Del hooked. If they both were free, they would gather to watch the matches, often the loudest fans in the bar. One day, she believed, one day she would share all that with her niece.

It was a physical ache inside the center of her chest. She couldn't imagine what it was like for a parent to be separated from a child. This was painful enough, but she rarely complained to anyone. It wouldn't be proper penance if it didn't hurt. She knew, deep down, that she deserved the agony. It was her fault Audrey had died.

The game ended, and the teams rushed off the field to waiting family. It was then that she spied Chris. He looked the same – average and immaculate. So different from Hugh Bainbridge, she noted. This comparison made her like the bubba lawyer more, not that he fit the bubba part now that she'd met him. Chris's stylish barn coat and tan slacks were too neat, his leather shoes spotless. Hugh may be too far over in the messy category, but Amy preferred that to pristine Chris.

She stood up on her toes to get a good luck at the woman who was with him. Yes, it was the same tall brunette from her last visit. Laura Tetlow. One picture had allowed Malachai to identify her. There was nothing strange or alarming in the file he'd amassed for Amy, more's the pity. No messy divorces, no links to organized crime, not even a parking ticket.

She wondered if things had changed between Laura and Claire since her last discreet visit. She saw her answer as Claire stalked past the couple without any acknowl-edgment. Her father's mouth thinned in disapproval, and the date's face fell. Amy felt torn. Part of her wanted to high-five the girl, and the other part wanted to hug her. *Poor kid.*

Amy pivoted on her heel and hurried back to the rented sedan, her stomach roiling with fury. Damn, she needed to eat, even though food was the last thing she wanted. She wanted to be there for her niece. To listen to her unload about her dad's new girlfriend.

However, that was impossible. Right now, she needed to find a meal, her hotel, and to prepare for the two meetings she had tonight.

SHE WAS GRATEFUL for DAG's attention to detail when she found that her hotel was close to the warehouse. Normally, she stayed in a furnished apartment for ops, but a hotel suited her cover better this time. Plus, Peter and Del thought she could wrap this up within a couple of weeks. It wasn't as if she used a kitchen, anyway. As long as the room had a mini fridge, a coffee maker, and a microwave, she was happy.

Her room was typical – a queen-sized bed, desk, chair, and chest with a massive TV. The box from DAG containing disguises and surveillance equipment had been waiting on her arrival.

First, she set up her laptop to charge, and then she unpacked her things. Since this was a meeting only with people in the know, she wouldn't need her undercover guise tonight. She did, however, change into more suitable clothes. Grey slacks topped by a black turtleneck with matching low-heeled boots.

She applied makeup with care – it seemed to help

people take her more seriously, which was quite a crock of shit, in her opinion. She supposed it made her look older and more urbane. She exchanged the messy knot of hair for a sleek French braid and added demure silver earrings. *There!* She approved the image in the mirror as one of cool professionalism.

She had arranged to meet Papa G between the hotel and the offices of the charity. It would be foolish to stage the meet at one of his stash houses or in her hotel. As a major dealer, he was always under some sort of surveillance. Sure, since he assisted in keeping the more violent gangs out, the local and federal authorities rarely popped him for anything other than information. Amy's concern was that The Duke might catch them together. She didn't want to give away her reason for being in town or mess up the truce between the two dealers.

She walked into Bob's Bargains and stopped to grab a basket at the entry. The store was in an economically-challenged area, and it showed. The shelving looked like it was original to the store when it had opened thirty years ago. Amy strolled down an aisle and added a pair of socks and a box of allergy medicine to her basket. The meds had surely expired, but this was just for show. The next aisle led back to the restrooms. She heeded the posted sign that said to leave all unpurchased products outside. Instead of entering the ladies' room, she twirled on her heel and slipped through the door on the opposite wall marked Employees Only.

"Welcome back, Ms. Stuart."

Papa G's voice fitted his body – strong and deep. He rose from where he had been propped on the corner of a desk and extended his hand. Despite the colder temperature, he wore loose terry shorts that hit mid-calf. As far as she knew, he wore shorts year-round. She supposed the heavy Atlanta Falcons sweatshirt was enough to keep him warm. Graying tufts of hair circled his bald pate, and his beard had turned white in her absence.

"Thanks for meeting me." She returned the firm handshake that swallowed her hand.

Knowing that he would allot her only a few minutes, she launched into why she was here. They had proof that the drugs hidden in the shoes were The Duke's unique mixture.

"Doesn't he already have a pipeline to LA? Why go to all this trouble for such a small amount?" she asked.

"Unless something is about to happen with his normal courier, I have no clue. Doesn't sound like anything he would mess with." Papa G shook his head. "I'll see if there's any news on the street." He crossed his arms over his chest and frowned down at her. "No messing with him, you hear?"

Amy gritted her teeth, knowing he was right, but chafing just the same. "I can't take him on directly. Not if I want to keep my family safe," she acknowledged.

"He didn't give the call to have you taken, and he didn't approve of what happened. You know that."

She nodded, still keeping her jaw stiff. That didn't absolve him, not in the slightest, but her beef came from the fact that he was still hiding the man who had carried out the atrocities. That was who she blamed. "I still want Ajax, not The Duke."

"I understand. I'll be in touch if I hear gossip." Papa

G nodded and squeezed her shoulder. "Stay safe."

"You, too. Thanks again." Amy smiled and watched as he disappeared through another door in the back of the long office. She would wait a few minutes, then leave the way she came in, purchase her items, and drive off to the next meeting.

WHILE THE WAREHOUSE was close, the principal offices were farther east. *Thank God for GPS*, Amy thought. The city had changed so much in the few years since she'd moved; she would be lost without help. The representatives from Joshua's Vision weren't meeting Amy at the warehouse in order to avoid arousing suspicion, in case anyone was watching. They would meet there tomorrow, to welcome Amy in the guise of her cover.

The charity itself took up the second floor of a small office building that was older, yet well kept. They'd painted the brick veneer a light brown, and then sandblasted the wall in certain areas so the red bricks showed through. The look was artsy, especially combined with the red millwork around the windows. It would have been at home on a college campus.

Even this late in the day, most of the lights were on inside, and a dozen cars sat in the side parking lot. She pulled in between two vehicles. One was an older maroon van with a sticker on the bumper that proclaimed the driver was the proud parent of an honor student at Madison Elementary School. The other was a sleek, black, mid-sized SUV that evidently belonged to the man leaning against the side – Hugh Bainbridge IV.

He had backed into the space, a maneuver that

screamed "dick move." However, it was also how most investigators, including her, usually parked; strategically, she could zoom out with no wasted time backing up. It shocked Amy to see not a UGA tag on his SUV, but one that depicted a dragon, twisting and spitting fire. More arrested development, or a streak of quirkiness? With this guy, she could not yet tell.

He was full of surprises, was he not? Gone was the beat-up truck and the college dropout attire. He waited while she parked and exited her car, clutching her leather case with her files and laptop.

He still wore jeans, except these were dark, without holes, and hugged his hips and thighs. Damn, she had a weakness for strong thighs. His black all-weather jacket covered a green plaid button-up. He had shaved, too. Without a hat, his hair was a riot of sun-streaked brown curls. They weren't tight like Kit's, and Amy thought his hair might lay flat if cut shorter.

There was no breeze, but damned if his curls didn't look windblown. *Rakish*. Yes, that was an apt word for how he looked. Damn – it was too bad he was a good ole boy, or she might have been talked into a quick fling. He was certainly hot enough, now that he was cleaned up.

Once again, she moved personal stuff to the back of her mind and advanced with a polite smile. Her steps faltered when he blasted her with a full-watt smile, which appeared to be genuine, since it matched the warmth in his eyes. She needed to be on her toes tonight.

"All settled in at the hotel?" he asked, and gestured toward the door.

"Yes, thank you," she replied, and allowed him to

hold open the door for her.

A shorter, older man was waiting for them inside the plain foyer. Hugh introduced him as Roderick Mentz, the warehouse manager who had uncovered the tainted shipment. Roderick wore work clothes and a Dolphins ball cap. On his left wrist were several braids of colored string that looked to have been fashioned by a child. They were faded and frayed, but he seemed in no hurry to cut them off.

"Well done," she said as she shook his calloused hand.

Roderick blushed. "We do important work here, Ms. Stuart."

"Everyone else should be in the conference room." Hugh pushed the elevator button.

Amy had read all of the background on Joshua's Vision and knew they had started it in memory of a boy who'd lost his legs in a car accident. He'd wanted to donate his shoes to children in need. Once word of his selflessness got around his school and community, everyone wanted to help. When his parents couldn't find a charity that specialized in donated shoes in Georgia, they created Joshua's Vision. Now in its ninth year, the non-profit shipped out thousands of shoes all around the world. They accepted both new and used children's shoes from individuals and footwear companies. What they couldn't donate, they recycled.

The warehouse, which she would be seeing the next day, was where the shoes were sorted into sizes. They weeded out the pairs that were too worn, and then separated them by type. It wouldn't be useful to send sandals to an area that was icy most of the year. Before they were ready to ship out, Roderick was tasked with doing spot inspections, mainly to make sure the boxes were full. They shelved incomplete boxes to wait for the next order.

"What made me take a closer look were the soles on the shoes from Sporticus," Roderick explained as they entered the door to the second floor. "They're usually bright red – it's their signature look. These soles were more orange. I pulled them out and noticed the glue was still tacky around the heel."

"That's where the drugs were hidden," Amy guessed.

"Bingo! The inside of the sole had been cut out." He smiled, but then turned very serious. "I went straight to Mr. Hallister, the director. It makes me furious that someone would want to harm what we do here!"

He seemed quite put out, but Amy couldn't cross him off the suspect list yet. Until she had more information, everyone was a possible trafficker.

Amy had been briefed on what happened next. Roderick had set the box aside, and the charity had called DAG. Peter ordered them to ship that box to DC and replace it with an untainted box, even down to the counterfeit shoes.

Once on the correct floor, she was surprised not to see a reception area. Perhaps they actually were a sparse organization that put all their money into the shoes. They passed a couple of doors labeled Accounting, Marketing, and Development, before arriving at the end of the hall. On their left was a closed door marked President, and on the right was the conference room.

It almost looked like the one at DAG, Amy noticed, and she smiled. Except that DAG didn't leave their plans and ideas hanging up. Things like that were always destroyed. These plain walls held all manner of whiteboards, sheets of paper, and posters – all marked with proposals for growth. The room felt vibrant from the colored markers used on the notes scrawled in the margins. This was a collaborative space where ideas were welcomed, she felt.

Two people rose from their seats at the oblong table: a man, presumably Mr. Hallister, and an older woman who must be the board member. As they piled their coats on the chair by the door, Amy had a moment to study them. Hallister was an older man with thinning salt and pepper hair. Lines of tiredness creased his face. His suit was off-the-rack, unlike everything the board member wore. She looked to be in her sixties, but well-preserved. Her snowy hair complimented the edgy haircut and her perfect makeup. Her dress surely cost more than Amy's laptop, but she admired its bold colors. Diamond jewelry screamed big bucks, specifically the giant rock on her ring finger. Yet the woman had a kind, welcoming face.

Hugh made the introductions. "Amado, this is Amy Stuart from DAG. Amy, this is Amado Hallister."

They shook hands, and Amy wondered if the president's sweaty palm came from worry or guilt. Could be either, but she filed the note away for now. So much could be derived from body language. Once she was back at the hotel, she would type up everything she'd gleaned from the people at this meeting, along with her impressions.

Law enforcement had given her much insight into behavior, but working with DAG had been a master class with Peter's and Daniel's CIA skills. She'd learned how to not only spot tics and tells, but also bring them forth from people. It required finesse. Interrogations and interviews were very different, and the agent had an important part to play in the direction the meeting took.

Here, she would scrutinize the participants more than trying to trip them up. While it wasn't unheard of for the actual perp to hire an investigator, it was rare. At this point, she couldn't rule anyone out, even the hot lawyer, who was gesturing to the older woman.

"Amy, this is Candace Bainbridge, the board VP."

Amy raised her eyebrows at him before returning the woman's firm handshake.

"Yes, Hugh is my son." Candace chuckled. "Did he not explain that?"

"Um, no." Amy threw Hugh a curious look as she dug in her bag for a notebook and pen.

"Joshua's Vision has been my baby for years, and Hugh has been gracious enough to provide pro bono legal help whenever we need it." The woman smiled and patted her son's arm with pride.

Amy briefly wondered why Hugh hadn't mentioned his mother. *Hmm…interesting.* But she couldn't dwell on that now, because Mr. Hallister was asking what clues DAG had found on the tainted box.

Everyone sat, and Amy flipped to her most recent notes. "Did Peter tell you that the drugs were from a local dealer? The Duke and his gang have been a plague here in Atlanta for about ten years. The oddity is that it's such a small amount."

"Maybe a trial shipment?" Roderick asked.

"Could be," she conceded. That had been her first thought. Was Roderick guessing, or did he know? She filed that note away mentally. "There were no usable prints, other than the workers here. We really didn't expect to find any, since The Duke is crafty and knows better than to leave DNA," she added. "We replaced the box, and it ships out tomorrow. That batch should arrive at its destination in five days. That gives me plenty of time to investigate and rig the warehouse before someone on the other end realizes the switch."

"Rig?" Candace asked, her brow creased.

"I'll set up motion sensor cameras. If I haven't uncovered the culprit by then, it will snag whoever comes to check on the error."

"Or if they come back to try again," Roderick muttered with a scowl.

Amy nodded and continued, "My cover will be a reviewer from the website, Superior Generosity."

She passed out a printed sheet with a photo. Hugh chuckled, but the others looked lost. The photo was a head shot of a plain, older woman. One had to look quite closely to recognize Amy's eyes behind the wire-rimmed glasses.

"Mimi Joseph's LinkedIn bio. Anyone looking online will find a trail of pictures and info for the last twenty years," she said proudly. "We have the best cyber hacker in the business."

"This looks nothing like you." Amado Hallister waved the sheet weakly in his hand.

"It will." She smiled. "You'll see tomorrow when you welcome me at the warehouse."

"How will you set up the cameras with all the workers there?" Roderick asked.

"I'll sneak back in after hours to install it. It may take an hour or so with the testing. I'll need keys and an access code."

"I can help with that," Hugh offered, and before she could say no, he added, "They've known me to go in after hours to do paperwork."

"Hugh has a desk there since we're cramped for space here," his mother explained.

"Plus, I have experience with that type of equipment," he said with another brilliant smile.

Amy wanted to call him out on this, but that could be done later. She was certain he'd seen something similar before. Most law firms had several investigators on retainer. Which reminded her, she hadn't yet inquired what type of law he practiced, now that she knew he wasn't with the charity full time. She deliberately hadn't read the background files on any of the major players yet. She wanted to leave her first impressions unmarred, unclouded. Everyone started out as a suspect. Later, she could fill in the blanks.

"The board has decided that Hugh will be our point man," Amado explained. "He knows the charity, its legal responsibilities, and the warehouse."

"Makes sense," Amy agreed, and squashed a small shiver of delight. What? She had no time for bubbas, no matter how rakish they looked. *What a lousy time for hormones to kick in*, she thought. It was good that she had no issues fighting off lust when necessary.

"How deep into our files will you need to go for your cover job?" Amado asked, concern lines furrowing his brow. "I know our contract is confidential, but will you need to mess up our data?"

"No." She shook her head. "That part is only for show."

She wished there was a way for her to wipe the expressions of apprehension from their faces, but she knew that nothing short of a successful mission would do that. She didn't take it personally. It was a common sight during preliminary meetings. Peter and Del handled the big cases, and the agents dealt with the smaller ones. The charity had taken a chance not calling in the police or the DEA. It was natural they were uneasy.

She felt she had presented a knowledgeable, professional front. The trust would not fully come until she actually began the job and showed the client that she and DAG were capable and ruthless.

"We should have a resolution within a couple of weeks," she finished on an upbeat note, after all the questions had been answered.

Roderick left first, eager to get to one of his kid's dance recitals.

As Amy packed up her things, she caught Hugh's mother ruffle his hair out of the corner of her eye. For a moment, she imagined what his curls must feel like, and she tightened her fist. What was it with this guy?

"I know." Hugh playfully rolled his eyes and hugged the older woman. "I have court next week and will get a haircut before then."

No! Amy wanted to cry. She liked the curls, but admitted they were the opposite of lawyerly.

"He rarely looks so wild." Candace smiled across at Amy as she allowed Hugh to help her with her coat. "He took time off to have surgery, and then went on that trip with his cousins."

"He looks fine," Amy commented, and then wanted to punch herself for sounding so lame.

What surgery? she wondered. No one offered an explanation, and by then, they were all moving toward the door. Amado set the alarm as they left the offices. He also locked the front door and escorted Candace to her vehicle, a solid, expensive silver sedan.

Ever the gentleman, Hugh walked Amy to her rental. She stowed her bag and turned to thank him. Not that she needed the escort, but it was polite. She guessed he would catch hell from his mother if he didn't.

"We could meet tomorrow night," he suggested. "You can debrief me, and then we'll set up the cameras."

"Sounds good." She nodded.

"I'll come by the hotel at seven, then?"

She nodded again. That would give her time to change out of her disguise and eat her small dinner.

"See you then." Hugh smiled and climbed into the dark SUV. Only then did Amy take a breath.

Why hadn't she declined? She was more than capable of handling the cameras alone. He has a gracious smile and spectacular thighs, her libido answered. *I do not need this*, she silently answered back. A throb in her lower abdomen responded. OK, it had been a long spell since she'd last hooked up with someone. She was overdue, and Hugh did ring all of her libido bells.

Maybe, she thought. But before anything happened, she had to eliminate him as a suspect. No way would she screw a trafficker. By the time she cleared him, if he was innocent, her fascination might fade. Now, it was just a game of wait and see.

DAMN! HUGH LEANED his head back and started the truck. That meeting had been surprisingly hot . . . sexy, even. Amy Stuart had been in total command. Maybe it was that, despite the fact she looked like an innocent college debutante with those big blue eyes, she could probably kill him with her pinky finger. And to him, that was even sexier, damn it!

Hugh liked confident women. His last girlfriend had been the youngest woman on the state legislature. She had lit not only his libido, but also his brain. Sadly, it had fallen apart after his father died and he'd walked away from politics. He still felt a stab of guilt, even after a year. The breakup had been cordial. In fact, Leigh was now engaged to someone much more suitable than Hugh. She had been one more facet of how he'd tried to please his father, rather than lead the life he wanted.

Not that his life was peachy at the moment. While his office had begun to build up a client list, he was still unsure of what he really wanted to do with his life. For so long, the choices had not been his to make. His father's ideas and career path had felt suitable, at first. Yet Hugh couldn't seem to wash off a layer of slime after becoming fully immersed in local politics. Pricey dinner parties one night, and helping a homeless defendant the next. He'd started making plans on the side, waiting for the right time to approach his father. Of course, his father wouldn't hate him or disown him, but it would be a crushing disappointment. Before Hugh could make the leap, his father had died instantly of a heart attack.

Now, Hugh could move into the life he'd wanted, albeit with massive amounts of doubt and guilt. At least he was able to keep up with his duties for the charity. It gave him time to spend with his mother, and now it had led to him meeting a fascinating woman.

He badly wanted to stroke Amy's cheek. Was it as soft as it looked? He thought he detected some interest in her, but it would have to be temporary. She was only here for a few weeks, at the most. He snorted at the pang of disappointment he felt. Was he really not wanting a brief affair?

Must be fatigue, he guessed. A brief liaison might be just the ticket. He had little time outside growing his business and fixing his house. He didn't need a serious, long term relationship now. His new future should come before his sex drive.

Might still work, though, he thought. She seemed interesting and utterly luscious, if only he could break past the prickly exterior.

Chapter Three

T HE WAREHOUSE WAS a typical brown two-story box with high-barred windows. It had some landscaping in the form of a neat sidewalk and holly bushes that hugged the sides of the building. There was no name on the front door, only a number. Strategically placed spotlights illuminated the small parking lot to the side, back, and the front walk.

The industrial area was nicer and newer than Amy had expected. Along with warehouses, there were smaller buildings that housed companies that specialized in drafting, engineering, and accounting. She had expected a more depressed area with some abandoned buildings and broken pavement.

She walked into the foyer and immediately saw why the alarm system had been so easily breached. The keypad was right inside the glass door. Anyone with binoculars could see when an employee typed in the code. She would need to let Hugh know to have this moved before the op was over.

She pushed a button on the wall under a large sign

that stated to ring for service. Judging by his expression, Amy could have knocked Roderick over with a feather when he answered the door. His gaping mouth and wide eyes showed his shock. Her lips tightened in displeasure. That was why she'd shown them the picture – so no one would make a scene!

He saw her foul glance and quickly recovered. "Please come in, Ms. Joseph." He gestured for her to come inside. "We have a desk ready for you. We hope you will enjoy being here."

She smiled, glad that he accidentally stumbled over his words. It looked appropriate, since her cover was someone who could make or break the charity.

"Call me Mimi, please."

He showed her to a small cubicle off the main warehouse floor. It was quieter, and Amy thought that maybe the space opposite her belonged to Hugh. No reason exactly, purely instinct. The other two cubicles were much neater, like hers. This desk had folders all over it. Not that she thought of him as messy. He had remarked that he wasn't here very often. On the other hand, the disorganized desktop matched the rakish curls.

Roderick booted up the desktop and gave her a piece of paper with all the log-ins and passwords she would need. She was glad to see that when she settled into the chair, she had a superb view of the main floor through high glass partitions.

Roderick gave her a moment to get her bearings, saying he would be back with coffee, and then they could tour the facility. Mr. Hallister and Mrs. Bainbridge would stop by later to answer any questions she might have.

Amy logged into the primary system and plugged in a thumb drive so that she could easily grab anything that seemed important. As she had promised Amado, she was mainly going through anything related to shipping, the alarm system, and staffing. Any red flags or oddities, she would send to Malachai for a thorough inspection. She had no need to barge through all of their information.

She patted her wig and snuck a peek in the compact mirror she pulled out of a small handbag. Mimi was in her 40s. Gold wire-rimmed glasses hid the age lines she didn't have. She wouldn't be interacting that much with the staff, so no need to go as far as wrinkle prosthetics. She did, however, have padding that added roundness to the face below the cheekbones. The wig was a brown bob, with a few gray hairs that frizzed out.

She was attired in a muted dress and blazer, under which was a padded bodysuit. Luckily, it was cool in the warehouse. She hated wearing the padding when it was hot. It gave her the shape of someone the correct age, though. Low, stocky heels completed the outfit. She looked totally unassuming and forgettable.

Roderick was back with a steaming cup of coffee, into which he had added her requested one packet of sweetener. She didn't grab her notebook. This needed to appear to be only a first look around, meeting the staff. Later, she could explore all she wanted on her own, and no one would think anything amiss if she were constantly making notes.

She spent the morning diving deeper into the shipping and receiving staff. Malachai had provided a basic overview of everyone. Now it was her turn to look for gaps or warning signs in their backgrounds. After that came scanning for ties to anyone remotely linked to The Duke. While she doubted that that avenue would turn anything up, she wasn't one to cut corners. It amazed her how many criminals screwed up the most basic matters. She'd learned long ago to never assume you were smarter or denser than your opponent. "Start with inept and work your way up," was Peter's motto.

After a quick lunch at a nearby diner, Amy walked the floor, taking notes. Her objective was mainly scoping out the location of the box they had switched out and planning where to install the camera system. She noted which employees seemed nervous around her and which ones ignored her. Either reaction could be a sign of guilt. It relieved her to see that all of DAG's background research seemed to put Roderick in the clear. The charity relied on him, and her instinct was that he was clean.

The same held true for Amado Hallister. While she had yet to delve into the files on the Bainbridges, Malachai had deemed them innocent, as far as he could tell. Why was she hesitating on learning all about Hugh? For some reason, it felt like spying. That was ridiculous, considering her profession. She just wanted to hold off for a day or two, at least. That way she could compare what he might reveal with the hard data. She would need to get him into a chatty mood tonight.

Yes! That was why she'd agreed to his help. Not because she thought he was hot, but because it could give her more time to study him. *Bullshit*, her brain whispered. Amy shrugged with a wry smile. Either way, tonight might lead to something; whether intel or connection, she'd be satisfied.

The day passed perfectly. She was so immersed in work that she didn't dwell on Claire. Since she was making actual headway on her personal vendetta, some stress left her shoulders. Occasionally, her thoughts wandered to Hugh. Hard not to, when his name would appear on hiring memos and other documents. His office provided thorough background checks on all potential staff and volunteers.

She was packing up for the day when she received a text from the man himself.

> **Hugh:** *"Could we possibly meet at 9pm? I have an unexpected late client."*
>
> **Amy texted back:** *"Of course. Should I come to your office?"*
>
> **Hugh:** *"That would be helpful. Thanks."*

He texted her the address, which she immediately stored in her GPS. Instead of being annoyed, relief consumed her. This gave her time to ditch the disguise and see the end of Claire's soccer practice before the meet.

BECAUSE OF A traffic issue, Amy was later than usual getting to Claire's soccer practice. She knew she should leave exactly when it ended, but she couldn't. She watched the team huddle and didn't move until the girls ran to the field house. Chris usually waited in his car for Claire, but she hadn't spotted the gray luxury SUV yet. She slipped through the trees and bent to unlock her car.

"What the hell are you doing here?"

"Chris, please! Don't make a scene!"

Both voices came from behind her, and Amy sagged in defeat. *Busted.* How had she missed Chris and his girlfriend? How unusual for her. She pulled off the ball cap, disgusted with herself, and shook her hair back off her shoulders.

She turned to see Laura – the girlfriend – pulling on Chris' arm. His face was blotchy red, and his jaw was clenched. He didn't speak again, only stared at Amy with fury. He took two deep breaths and then shocked her by turning on his heel and marching away. Surprisingly, the girlfriend didn't follow him. She actually stepped closer.

"I'm sorry." Laura sighed and held out her hand. "I'm Laura Tetlow."

Still in a daze, Amy shook her hand automatically. Of course, Amy already knew her name and other details – from her graduating the Savannah School of Design, to owning a clothing boutique in high-end Buckhead. She was in her late twenties, widowed and childless. At least she didn't favor Audrey. Laura's dark hair and eyes matched her tanned skin. Malachai's report of course didn't delve into DNA, but Amy guessed there was some Hispanic or Mediterranean heritage somewhere. The end result was lovely. The only commonality with Audrey was her petite stature.

"I was hoping to meet you at some point," Laura said, her heeled boots bringing her almost to Amy's height.

Now Amy truly was in shock. Why? To crucify her like Chris did? She took a suspicious step back, narrowing her eyes.

"It's not fair," Laura explained in a rush, frightened at Amy's change of spirit. The gloved hands she held up perfectly matched her gray wool coat.

"Oh?" Amy's poker face masked her confusion. That was the last thing she'd expected Laura to say.

"To keep you and Claire apart, I mean." Laura's hands fluttered.

Oh? Curiouser and curiouser. Amy decided to hear her out, even though she figured it would probably be utter bullshit. She had some time to spare. It would be worth it, if only to imagine how angry it might make Chris.

"We've been talking," Laura explained. "I think Claire needs you in her life. Chris and I . . . our relationship is becoming serious. Of course, Claire has issues with this. It's perfectly normal, and I understand. I think it would help if she had someone to talk to about it."

Laura tried to smile but her lips trembled with uncertainty. "Plus, I can't imagine how awful it has been for you, to be ostracized from her. She truly is a lovely girl."

Amy wanted equally to hit and hug this woman. She honestly didn't know what to say, which was an uncommon occurrence for her. Bullshit was a language she knew very well, and she used it often in her job. She decided to say nothing. It would keep Laura off-balance. She had no clue if the woman was worth trusting yet.

"Let me work on Chris some more," Laura offered. "He knows that some blame sits with him. I think he's close to agreeing. Can I get your number?"

The cell number Amy gave her was a temporary one

Del had hooked up specifically for this op. It rang through to her phone but was untraceable. She normally didn't give it out, but she was in shock. *Chris claimed part of the blame? Since when?*

Was this some sort of trap? Laura didn't exude that vibe, but Amy didn't trust anything to do with Chris. The man had made the last three years hell for her. It was too much to hope for, so she squashed the ray of sunshine that had hit her soul. Better to wait and see.

She had to know more. Right now, she would give up a kidney if it meant they could even discuss visitation.

AMY CONTINUED PONDERING the strange encounter with Laura as she grabbed a quick dinner and headed for Hugh's office. In deference to her greasy yet tasty lunch, she selected a salad and coffee protein smoothie.

Was it a trick? At this point in her dealings with Chris, she had no clue. She refused to get excited, though. Until she had solid proof, she wouldn't get her hopes up. Thanks to her work, she still had a busy night ahead that would keep her mind from wandering. A busy night with a hunky, bubba attorney.

She snorted at the dichotomy. She couldn't deny that he was interesting, despite the Southern frat boy side of him. After tonight, she should have enough insight to finally read his background files. Since he donated his work for the charity, she assumed he either worked for a big firm or was wealthy enough for his own shingle. She could imagine the ritzy building housing his office. The room probably had dark walls and plush, leather furniture.

Her GPS chirped, "You have arrived at your destination."

Surely, this couldn't be right. She double-checked the address to make sure. Instead of a sleek tower, she saw a strip mall that had seen better days. That was being generous, she amended with a closer look.

Of the eight storefronts, three of them were empty. What remained was a hair salon dubbed Cutz & Curlz, an Oriental grocery, a check-cashing business that promised low rates, a thrift store, and one that was blank but for the suite number.

Amy checked the GPS yet again. The address was correct. The suite number matched the space with no business on the door or front window.

"Grr," she growled through clenched teeth.

She didn't have time for this shit. Was it a prank, a joke? Would she walk in and find him laughing? She snatched up her bag and locked the car after she slammed the door. She was going to rip him a new one for wasting her time like this!

A gauzy curtain covered the front window. She could see only vague shapes inside. Frosted glass covered the front door. She jerked the handle and heard a bell tinkle above her head.

"Hello. May I help you?" a woman's voice called from her right.

Amy took a moment to appreciate the warm air after the chill of outside. She turned to see an older woman sitting behind a desk, her gaze openly curious. She wore a floral headband from which short graying braids spilled out. She removed her chunky red reading glasses and raised her eyebrows.

Amy cleared her throat and stepped closer. "I'm looking for Hugh. Hugh Bainbridge."

Instead of the confusion she expected, the woman only nodded. "You must be Ms. Stuart. Go on back." She nodded to a dim hallway at the end of the room.

"OK," Amy breathed.

This was a very elaborate joke. The room that held the woman behind the desk was carpeted in older brown shag. The wood-paneled walls held a few framed landscapes from unique artists that appeared to be from the neighboring thrift store. A couple of mismatched chairs sat in front of the window, possibly bought at the same place. A vintage couch upholstered in a hideous brown plaid sagged along the opposite wall between two floor lamps.

Amy marched down the hallway, passing an open closet that contained supplies and an ancient copy machine. Opposite that was a small kitchen from which floated the aroma of coffee left on too long. Beyond that, two other rooms faced each other, their doors ajar. Even without a light, one was clearly a restroom, while the other appeared empty. At the end of the hall, she knocked on the cracked door.

"Hey, Amy!" Hugh's voice called. "Come on in."

The office also had walls of cheap paneling, which would have been horrific if not for the row of high, narrow windows on one wall. Sunshine probably made the room less oppressive, but at night, it was gloomy. In contrast to the outer room, these walls were bare, although she could see some empty frames leaning against a tall file cabinet. That cabinet was one of three, all lined up opposite the desk. *Wow.* Who kept that many paper files anymore?

Next to them sat a wooden bookcase painted white, filled with what Amy assumed were law books since they were large and bound in cloth or leather. OK, that was impressive. There had to be at least fifty books there. She wasn't used to anyone who didn't do their research online. The books weren't just for show, either. They appeared well-used, including the one that lay open on top of one file cabinet.

Hugh's domain included two other mismatched chairs and a massive wooden desk. Overall, it looked straight out of the 1970s, except for the shiny new desktop computer. The rest of the desk looked like organized chaos. There were several wire baskets filled with files, as well as random leather-bound books strewn about.

She finally looked at Hugh to see him grinning ruefully. "Not what you expected?"

Upon seeing the office, she'd discarded the idea that this had been a prank. He actually worked *here*? She had been sure he was a trust-fund baby. His mother was certainly comfortably wealthy. What was with the good ole boy persona that he'd greeted her with at the airfield? What a mystery. One Amy looked forward to picking apart.

"This is your law practice?" she asked, and sat down in one of the chairs.

Hugh rubbed his eyes with a thumb and forefinger. "Uh, yeah. It's a long story."

"I bet," she agreed, and he chuckled.

"Give me one second to finish up, and we can go. You brought all the equipment?"

She nodded. "In my car."

Hugh typed some more, and then turned off the computer. When he stood up, she saw he was dressed all in black, like she was. Perfect for a nighttime op. While she wore a long sleeve tactical shirt, he had donned a waffle-weave Henley. And, yes, she glanced to see if his ass looked good in the black denim. It did, indeed.

He grabbed his coat off a hook behind the door and gestured for her to precede him into the front room. She was getting used to his automatic gentlemanly ways. He probably didn't even realize he behaved that way. Another thing she missed about living in the South.

"Amy," he announced as they entered the reception area, "this is Neddra. She calls herself my assistant, but this is really her world, and I just work here. She keeps me straight and beats me when I don't eat well. Neddra, this is Amy."

They all laughed, and the woman stood up to shake Amy's hand. Neddra didn't ask questions, so Amy assumed Hugh had either filled her in or made up a story to explain her presence.

"Welcome, Amy." The woman smiled, and up close, Amy noticed a small ring bisecting her lower lip. *Quite daring for someone her age*, she thought. Neddra's firm handshake was another point in her favor.

"*Meow!*" They all turned to see a brown-striped cat walk into the room from the hallway. The feline blinked at them sleepily and sauntered over to rub against

Neddra's legs.

"And this is Nancy." Hugh leaned down to pet the cat.

"One day I came to work, and she was waiting outside," Neddra explained with a smile. "I opened the door, she came in, and *voilà* – we had an office cat!" She and Amy shared a chuckle.

"We need to get going," Hugh announced. "Be safe going home."

"I'll lock up as soon as my son gets here." Neddra nodded and went back to her desk.

"I can drive us," Hugh offered.

"I can follow you," Amy countered. There was no need for him to drive all the way back here to drop her off.

"Fair enough," he agreed, and walked her to the rented sedan before getting in his SUV.

Even though she was dying to ask questions about his long story, she knew that she would get more information from him if she acted disinterested. She'd worked with suspects and worked with men. If he wasn't talkative, there was always DAG's research file to enlighten her.

The radio station that had been her favorite before now played only current country tunes, so Amy switched on a national news station to pass the time during the drive. Too bad the rental didn't have Bluetooth, or she could have listened to her current audiobook. It was a mystery set during the Prohibition and, so far, very engrossing. She'd have to hit a gym soon and catch up using her headphones while she worked out.

They both parked in back, and Hugh walked around to the front entrance. A few moments later, he unlocked the back door for her, and they brought what they needed inside.

"After this is over, you need to relocate the alarm pad," she informed him, and explained why.

"Aw, shit." Hugh shook his head. "I should have seen that."

He was admitting he fucked up? *Wow*. This man continually surprised her.

They turned on as few lights as possible. Once in the primary area, no one could possibly see what they were doing without using a ladder to reach the tall windows. Hugh watched in fascination as Amy unpacked the equipment from the foam-lined hard case.

"Wow," he breathed, looking over the assortment on the table. "These make my stuff look a hundred years old."

"You don't have an investigator?" she asked, surprised, and started booting up her laptop. "I thought that was standard for law firms."

Most law offices either had private investigators on staff or on retainer. They normally handled surveillance, witness interviews, anonymous data gathering, asset searches, depositions, background checks, etc. She knew many former cops who had transitioned into these jobs. Before finding DAG, she'd considered taking that path, as well.

"Nah," he answered. "Just me, but I haven't yet had any cases that required much surveillance. I enjoy battling wits with witnesses, and Neddra helps with record searches. If the practice keeps growing, I'll need to hire someone."

Amy desperately wanted to ask what types of cases he took on, but made herself wait. They needed to be in and out as quickly as possible so as not to arouse suspicion. Clearly, his clients were not corporations or the wealthy elite, as she had first assumed. Yet he must make enough off of billing to be able to donate his time to the charity.

HUGH WATCHED AS she typed on her keyboard. Quick and unemotional, so focused. What a mystery Amy Stuart was, he thought. He wondered why she hadn't asked him questions about his practice. He'd dropped enough hints. Despite her poker face, he could tell his digs puzzled her. Hell, everyone who'd been there had been aghast. It looked like a sketchy last resort for lowlifes.

Her tight t-shirt had a slightly scooped neck, and Hugh had trouble keeping his eyes off a mole that sat on the edge of her delicate collarbone. Could be because it was a contrast to the actual woman, who was far from delicate, except in her features. High cheekbones and a sharp chin, combined with her fair coloring, reminded him of an elf or fairy. That was it! Tinkerbell without bangs. The similarity ended there, since she was taller than average. He had a hunch she wouldn't appreciate the comparison and vowed to keep it to himself.

"My mom didn't recognize you today at the warehouse," he said with a smile.

"That was the point," Amy quipped, and flashed a

quick grin. "But she recovered very well."

"She's had practice," Hugh admitted. "She and my Dad were constantly rubbing elbows with powerful people, most of whom were pretty distasteful."

"Your father was in politics?"

"He wished." Hugh shook his head. "The closest he got was being part of the group of business owners who influenced policy with money."

Amy made a face but didn't speak, mesmerized by something on her laptop screen. Hugh didn't mind. It gave him a moment to study her. Christ, she was pretty to look at, even more so now that he knew the tough competence underneath. He wondered what her hair looked like down. Every time he had seen her, it was up in a messy knot or braided. *Why have long hair, then?* he wondered; but women and their hair preferences had always confused the hell out of him.

"OK." Amy looked up. "These cameras have a battery life of five days if we run them only after hours. If nothing happens by then, we'll have to come and change them out."

Hugh nodded, and she continued, "They also have a wide range, so one in each corner should cover the entire main floor here."

Hugh set up the ladder in the first corner, marveling at the tiny size of the cameras. DAG truly had the latest equipment, considering their fee was pretty reasonable. He held the ladder steady while Amy climbed up and attached the first camera with the small portable power drill she'd unpacked.

They repeated the process in silence and went back

to sit at Mimi's desk with the laptop. Amy took a small black box out of the desk drawer and unfolded three antennas.

"This is a modem router that will run the cameras. It secretly piggy-backs the Wi-Fi here," she explained, and placed the box on her desk behind a tall file sorter.

"Damn it!" she swore after typing on her laptop. "I'm sorry. Somehow, the cameras missed the latest update. I need to run the download. Should only take fifteen minutes or so."

"I'm in no hurry." Hugh sat back in the chair he'd pulled over.

Amy frowned, annoyed by this small screw-up. She typed and then pushed away from the desk as the process began. Hugh stretched out his legs, grimacing as he straightened the right one. *The surgery*, she remembered.

He must have read her mind. "I was on the swim team for my first three years in college, then blew out my knee playing touch football. I put off the surgery until my doctor put his foot down. Waiting any longer would have made the recovery worse."

"Oh, I'm sorry you lost your spot on the team." She grimaced. That would have crushed her college-aged self.

"Don't be." He shrugged. "I wasn't the best, only good enough to make the team."

"Do you miss it?" she asked, hoping to fill the quiet.

Hugh smiled. "My first answer was *fuck no!* All the practice, details, earaches. Although, I still swim at the gym to stay in shape." He held up a finger. "But I miss competing. Maybe that's why I like the investigative and oral argument parts of my job."

He turned his sharp eyes to her in the dim light. "Why do you like your job? I think there's more to it than spying safely from a distance or playing dress-up."

She shifted, suddenly exposed by his astute question. Had he guessed, or was it just a stab in the dark?

"What makes you think that?" She knew her tone was nonchalant, yet his eyes twinkled as if she'd revealed the answer by mistake.

He shrugged again and kept the mild smile on his mouth. "You don't seem the sort to stay inside the lines."

Irritation, and something else, curled her toes. Whatever the "something else" was, it made her feel on display. Normally, she avoided such situations. Yet Hugh had leaned forward, awaiting her response with an interest that didn't feel invasive. *Ha! He couldn't handle the real Amy*, she thought. Time to set him straight.

"I see. You have me pegged as an adrenaline junkie?" She leaned her head back to stretch and felt her bun slide sideways. The time it took to re-twist her hair and apply the elastic gave her an excuse to stop talking for a moment.

"Not exactly." He tilted his head, continuing to appraise her. "I think you like action."

Amy felt a bolt of electricity between her legs. When had the subject shifted to sex? Probably when Hugh's eyes darkened with innuendo during his last sentence. If so, he was correct. She was not the sort of woman who lay passively in the missionary position. Was he intimating he preferred an engaged partner? She was grateful she'd worn a sports bra. Hopefully, it would disguise her suddenly hard nipples.

Whoa, she cautioned herself. *Pull back. You're on the clock right now. Focus!*

"I like most aspects of my job, even sitting in a van doing surveillance for hours. DAG was my dream job," she responded. It wasn't a lie. She could do whatever it took to catch a perp. Like anyone, there were aspects of her job she loved, and some she disliked.

DAG had been a godsend at a time when she needed to physically work on her anger and guilt surrounding Audrey and how she'd failed her. The same actions that had hastened her departure as a cop – using excessive force while trying to catch The Duke – had been acceptable behavior at DAG. The team's usual combatants were hired security forces, not innocents. Amy rarely felt sad about inflicting sprains and bruises on people who were getting paid to fight.

She breathed a sigh of relief when Hugh fell silent, not asking any follow-up questions about her job. Hopefully, she'd also signaled that hot and heavy was off the menu, for the moment. This was professional time. The reprieve allowed her to realize she'd used the past tense regarding DAG. *Was her dream job.* Why? She couldn't blame it on her recent assignments or Mick's fuckery.

Her team was in the midst of transitions. Del had already moved off most active assignments and into management. Mateo was fast becoming Malachai's protégé, even though he was still undercover most of the year. Only she, Archie, Whittaker, and Mick still enjoyed active postings. So, why was she thinking of pulling back on it? Perhaps it was age. Her body didn't move quite as fast as it used to.

Nah, she brushed the disturbing thoughts away. Her head wasn't on right because of Claire and the new wrinkle with Chris and Laura. Plus, she was in the midst of righting a three-year-old mistake. Of course, she wasn't thinking clearly about her future. Now was not the time for big decisions.

"So, you were a cop here in Atlanta?" Hugh broke into her musings.

Good, she thought as he moved the conversation away from the present and all its problems. Although delving into her past was equally a minefield, if the conversation took a wrong turn. When had she lost control of this? She should be leading *him* into revealing answers. *Get back in the game, Stuart!*

Amy nodded. "Narcotics. I moved here to be closer to my sister. I wasn't cut out to be a small-town cop."

"So, why leave? Was it an offer from DAG?"

The question was innocuous and expected. A lie came easily to Amy's lips, and it shocked her when instead she told the truth. At least, part of the truth.

"My sister died."

Go for the throat, she decided. Lay out something deep, and he was sure to reciprocate. Hugh jumped in surprise and fell over himself apologizing. She waved it away.

"So, now it's your turn to confess a deep, dark secret," she quipped, hoping to lighten the mood and get him back to where she wanted him. All under the guise of getting to know him. She felt a small stab of guilt. He seemed like a good guy, but this was her job.

"My father died last year, and I'm currently defying his dying wishes and legacy."

She turned to him, her mouth open and eyes wide. She hadn't expected that! From the look of surprise on his face, neither had he. Her ploy had worked better than expected, and she responded without thinking. "Defying in what way? By being a lawyer, or your unconventional office?"

Yikes! She should have phrased that better, she realized, as a black cloud came over his face. He shook it off quickly, but not before it became plain she'd misspoken. She cringed and placed her palm over her sternum. She truly hadn't meant to sound flippant. *Damn.* She usually had better control of her mouth.

"I'm sorry," she began, but he waved the apology away as unnecessary.

"For the last three generations, each Hugh Bainbridge has become something great. Hugh the First grew up on a farm. He worked his way up to become president of a ship building yard. My grandfather went into lumber and founded a successful pulpwood company. My dad started with a small car dealership and expanded to become the largest dealer in Georgia. Every generation has been challenged to create some sort of industry leadership." Hugh sighed. "But what my Dad never achieved was a spot in politics. He ran and lost a few times."

Amy recalled what he'd said about his mother earlier. Hugh would have also been part of that schmoozing, back-slapping world growing up. To Amy, that sort of life made her shudder in revulsion. To be constantly "on," watched, and picked apart. *Ugh! No way.*

"So, that was my job. To be the influential politician." Hugh smiled ruefully. "Luckily, I enjoyed studying law. We argued over specialty, of course. He wanted me to go into corporate law, but my Mom and I convinced him that joining the DA's office would look better with voters."

"You were with the DA here?" That surprised her. "Hard to believe our paths didn't cross before then."

"I'm sure we know a lot of the same people," he noted.

He fell silent, lost in his own thoughts. Her fact-finding mission had taken a turn towards fascinating. Hugh IV was not a total bubba, as she'd first thought. She had all the respect in the world for the Fulton County District Attorney's office. She yearned for more information, and not just for case background. What was this rich boy doing housing his office in such a neighborhood?

"Why leave?" she asked, since he'd lobbed the same question at her. Fair was fair.

"I actually didn't until after Dad passed. Heart attack." He swallowed and looked away. "I hated politics. Honestly, I hated all the parties, underhanded deals, all of it. But I loved my job, until I realized some of the people we helped send to prison shouldn't be there. It was merely their bad luck. Some court-appointed attorneys are awful. They want to plead out rather than help their clients."

Hugh held up both hands and laughed. "I know you're thinking, I'm a schmuck! But my Mom has always been involved in non-profits, and I saw another side through her. My dad would have been horrified if I'd said I want to help those people." The last two words he added air quotes to and explained further, "The people who have less. Not just racial disadvantages, but the schools-to-prison pipeline is a real thing. It exists."

"Oh, I know!" Amy agreed with a vengeance. That had been her issue with her old job. It had caused her pain the many times they'd arrested the user to get to the dealer. It had been unfair, but that was the system. Either work within it, or get nothing accomplished. She was floored by his reasoning and by the fact that he put his beliefs into action.

"So, you're a real-life Atticus Finch," she teased.

Hugh snorted and shook his head. "Probably more like Matlock. Atticus Finch is the top fictional lawyer for most people, but I do like Jack McCoy from *Law and Order*. He had flaws, but was a fierce fighter for all sorts of clients."

He smiled, basking in the glow of her compliment, and leaned forward, his elbows on his thighs. "I'd taken a leave of absence to help my mom through the funeral and downsizing when a friend introduced me to Neddra. They'd grown up together. She'd come to him looking for someone to help her son. The cops stopped him for a broken taillight, and then arrested him for intoxication. Neddra swore he didn't drink. Turns out, she was right." Hugh grinned. "Her son has a metabolic disorder that has dire consequences when combined with alcohol consumption. Most kids in his position would have no way to fight back."

Amy grimaced. "Fuck dishonest cops. I'm sorry that happened, but I'm not surprised."

"The day I had that case thrown out was a game-changer. I finally felt like a real lawyer."

His smile was radiant, and Amy was helpless against it. She had a similar story from her days as a cop. And from her work with DAG. Even though she had many terrible stories, the peak ones kept her going.

"Turns out, Neddra is part of a group of women in her community who fight for social justice. She kept at me to take on more cases." He chuckled. "I left the DA's office. I told myself and my mom that I was taking a break to do this while I processed my dad's death."

"I'm glad she approved," Amy said.

Hugh waved his hand. "Ah, my mom would approve anything as long as I was happy. I'm very lucky to be her son. She gave only a token protest when I quit politics. Seems she'd had her fill, too."

"So, how did Neddra end up as your assistant?" Amy asked. "Gave you no choice?"

Hugh chuckled again, and the sound charmed her. "Close! She convinced me to set up an office and let her help. She's taking classes to become a legal assistant. She's free to use the office and equipment for her community activism."

"So, this is permanent?" Her eyebrows raised in surprise.

"Nah. I don't know." Hugh sighed, shrugged, and looked away. "I've yet to make a decision on it. I'm flying by the seat of my pants. Feels good to be doing something to make a difference. Seeing what Neddra and her friends are accomplishing energizes me. There are situations that cannot be helped by only throwing money at it."

You know what you want, she thought. He was certainly different from most people she'd met who had grown up with money. Instead of showing it off, he seemed almost guilty about it. No doubt what his father had wanted for him still hung over his head. She couldn't imagine going against so many generations of tradition. At least he had his mom on his side.

She was thankful that both her parents supported her job choices, although they had no idea how dangerous her work with DAG really was. She'd grown up working-class. Despite the fact that neither of her parents had attended college, her father had become a construction foreman, and her mother worked as an executive assistant at a swanky advertising company. They'd made sure both their kids worked hard to make the grades necessary to attend college. Neither parent had demurred when she chose law enforcement as her profession.

She was blessed, she realized. After Audrey's death, they could have begged her to quit the force. They didn't, although it relieved them when she left for more corporate investigative work. She let them believe she was with the public side of DAG. To worry them more would be cruel. Losing one child was bad enough. They deserved to rest easier as they neared retirement.

Just then, her laptop pinged, alerting them that the download was complete and the cameras were operational. She was actually disappointed. She wanted more time to talk to Hugh. The last fifteen minutes had flown by.

While the update was successful, Amy noticed another error when she looked at the camera readings on the screen.

"Damn it!" she swore, and looked at Hugh. "Can you climb up to that camera by the loading dock? Move it left until I say stop."

"Sure."

He hopped up and retrieved the ladder without asking annoying questions. They tested a few angles before Amy announced it was perfect. Did she also sneak glances at his ass in the tight black jeans? Of course, she did. She wasn't dead.

Hugh put the ladder away while Amy started packing up. He was back by the time she stowed her laptop.

"Hey, thanks for helping with this," Amy said. "Turns out, I needed an extra set of hands. Let me know if I can ever return the favor."

"Actually, there is something you can help me with Friday night."

Immediately after speaking, Hugh grimaced. Was he regretting asking her? Did he think she couldn't handle it, or was it too minor? She was intrigued and had to know.

"Sure," she jumped in, figuring she could always cancel later if needed.

Hugh still looked pained, but forged ahead. "I have to meet an informant at the rural redneck bar."

"Ooh, I love dressing for that kind of undercover," she quipped, perking up with excitement. "Much more fun than being Mimi!"

"Good." He smiled a little. "But what I need help

with isn't the informant."

She waited patiently as he inhaled. "I . . . uh. This bar is always loud and crowded, and I need help to stay grounded. It's work, so using alcohol is out of the question."

His gaze was fixed somewhere over her left shoulder. Why did he look so embarrassed? His cheeks were actually red, and he refused to meet her eyes. Amy wasn't sure exactly what was happening or what he meant yet. She tugged on his sleeve and motioned to the chairs.

"I'm happy to help, but could you explain a bit more?"

Hugh thudded down to a seated position and kept his eyes on his clasped hands in his lap. "Too much noise, movement, lights – I get overwhelmed and can't focus. One doctor said I have a mild form of autism; another proclaimed part of my brain is too sensitive to stimuli and it overloads. I have no idea."

"Oh, OK." Amy shrugged.

He looked across at her with suspicion. Loud places, big parties made her skin crawl, so she could see how it would affect someone susceptible. She was opening her mouth to tell him it wasn't that odd when he continued.

"In college, I drank like a fish to get through the frat parties. It worked, but I was terrified of becoming an alcoholic. Once I hurt my knee, it became harder to recover from the hangovers. Luckily, the class load of my last year kept me from participating too much with the frat. I left the first law firm that hired me." His smile was rueful. "It was an open cube farm, and I couldn't concentrate, even with headphones. Too many people always walking by."

"Wait. How did you manage all the parties? I mean, as a rising politician, didn't you have to attend all sorts of fundraisers?"

"Bingo!" Hugh, now more relaxed, leaned back and snapped his fingers with a bitter smile. "I couldn't do it. I saw a doctor, and we tried some different drugs, but either they didn't help or, worse, gave me mud for brains. On one hand, it was a blessing that Dad died before I could tell him I couldn't hack it. On the other hand, it's hard not to feel guilty. I don't think he would've gotten over the disappointment."

"I'm sorry," Amy whispered, and laid a hand on his arm. "But that's bullshit. I mean, he might have been pissed, but he would've gotten over it."

Hugh reached over and squeezed her hand. His warm palm was slightly rough; a working hand, not pampered. She liked that.

"Thanks." He then changed the subject. "I can pick you up at nine tomorrow?"

"Sure." She smiled, eager for anything to pass the time. Working a job beat the hell out of waiting around for the cameras to go off. Now that she knew part of the story behind this hunky attorney, she looked forward to finding out more. Despite his age, there were already smile lines around his eyes and mouth. That was always a positive sign when looking for temporary companionship. He had been easy to talk to, even if she herself had revealed little.

They walked outside after resetting the alarm and, on the way back to the parking lot, Hugh said, "This bar is pretty nasty. If a fight breaks out, I can still jump in so you aren't hurt, despite my knee."

"Ah! You don't think I can fight?" While Hugh, observably embarrassed, sputtered a reply, she waved her hand. "Come here."

She didn't check to see if he was following. After she found a cushioned grassy spot between the parking lot and the building, she turned around to see that he was right behind her. The streetlights illuminated the hesitation in his expression. Yeah, he was going to regret questioning her abilities. Welcomed anticipation zinged along her nerves.

She rolled her eyes, but inside she was gleeful. "Come at me. Give me your best shot. I promise to steer clear of your bad knee."

When Hugh gave a disbelieving laugh, Amy charged. At first, all his moves were defensive. He either deftly moved aside or carefully pushed her away.

"Stop! I don't want to hurt you!" he bellowed, dodging her punches and kicks.

"I'm going for your balls unless you stop me," she announced, her voice calm and certain.

"Fuck," Hugh swore under his breath, and tried to grab her but somehow ended up on the ground.

"Goddamn!" he swore again and lunged for her leg.

Amy let him rise and wanted to laugh in glee when he began to actually fight back. Wow, he was good. Especially for such a big man. But her edge came from being a small woman. The larger the guy, the harder he would fall. They traded blows until a train horn shrilled in the distance, making Hugh turn his head, losing concentration. That was all Amy needed. She tripped him, and soon had his arm in a hold that would hurt if he tried to move.

Straddling his back, she felt as well as heard his laughter. "Goddamn! I think I'm in love!"

Well, that was unexpected. Amy scrambled off him in surprise, her moves clumsy with haste. Why wasn't he defensive or angry? Surely, Hugh meant the remark as cute or condescending. Of course, that was it.

Still chuckling, Hugh maneuvered himself off the ground, dusting off grass and dirt. When he turned to her, she saw nothing on his face but good cheer and admiration. He wasn't patronizing her? Not being a smart ass? *Really?*

"OK, I'm sorry for being a dick." He held out his hand. "You are more than capable."

She shook his hand but quickly jerked hers away. Right now, sexual awareness zinged through her veins. That had been *hot*. They were both disheveled and breathing heavily. His curls stood out on one side, and there was brown dirt on his elbow. Anyone looking on would think the two of them had been making out. She looked away, hoping he hadn't noticed how turned on she was.

Who *was* this guy? For that matter, who was *she* tonight? Throwing out personal tidbits to someone she'd just met was not her style, even if it was a ruse to get information. She normally made shit up on an op. Was she that starved for conversation, or was he that easy to talk to?

Either way, it solidified her decision to make some

changes when this op was over. She needed to get out, find more people to hang with. Contact her teammates, except Mick, when she was free, and invite them out more.

Actually, she should thank Mick. The idea made her gag, but he was the reason she'd been working lone ops. If not for that, she might not have realized how solitary her life had become since moving to DC.

Face it, she scolded herself, *not everyone will judge you harshly, no matter how guilty you feel.* If she was the badass that she considered herself, moving back into the real world would not destroy her. Tonight, could be a baby step. It wouldn't hurt to have another friend in Atlanta, especially one tuned into the criminal world.

The more she considered it, the better the plan seemed. Since she wouldn't be staying here, any awkwardness would fade with time, anyway. But that begged the question – did she want a new friend, or a new fling? Most guys couldn't handle both. While he was easy to talk to and seemed to like what he'd learned about her so far, she couldn't deny her attraction to him physically.

OK, she mentally shrugged; that was an understatement. She wanted to climb him like a monkey on a tree. Sparring with him had been highly erotic, especially when he'd conceded without being a crybaby. He had wicked reflexes, and she'd felt the toned muscles when she had him pinned.

Best choice was to wait and see, she decided. If he made a move, then fling would win. If not, perhaps it could lead to a friendship. The ball was in his court.

Chapter Four

TEDIUM RULED THE next few days. The expected call from Laura didn't happen, and there weren't any more soccer practices Amy could crash this week. She put in time at the warehouse, but nothing panned out. The cameras only showed an empty warehouse at night. The charity and its staff were squeaky clean.

That included the charismatic attorney. His background folder included additional information, and Amy had read the file with eagerness. He'd been a rising star at the DA's office and in political circles. He'd also failed to mention that he'd been doing pro bono work for Joshua's Vision for years, and not just a few times. The only blight she saw was a drunk and disorderly citation from campus cops. He seemed to view his refusal to toe the family line as a weakness. When he'd thrown that tidbit out, his shoulders had hunched, and his eyes shadowed. However, she failed to see why. All he did was try to make his dad proud. When it became clear it wasn't working for him, he made a fresh path. His father's death was untimely, adding an extra layer of guilt.

Amy threw the folder down with a huff. Jeez, was there nothing distasteful about this man? There was still a chance he had an awful temper, or maybe he hated dogs – anything to make him less appealing. Perhaps she could uncover more Friday night. Hugh's op was the only bright spot on her horizon. This was the part about her job she disliked – the forced waiting. She wished she were more like Archie – laid back and laconic. She was built for action.

And, perhaps, avoidance? Ella, the psychiatrist that she'd been Skyping, had asked her that during her last session. Amy knew herself well enough to admit it. If she let herself be still, she thought too much. This mission … this could be her chance to clear all her baggage out. She could leverage The Duke into finally giving up his toady Ajax, as well as possibly reconnect with Claire. This was her chance, and she wouldn't throw away her shot. Afterwards, she could tackle reflections into her past. Now, she needed to remain sharp and alert.

If it hadn't been for some last-minute research Del had asked for, the past few days would've been endless. It seemed to be eons until the workweek was over. She left the warehouse at the stroke of five and raced to the hotel. She'd carefully planned her outfit and was practically vibrating with anticipation when she heard his knock.

She opened her door, and they stared at each other, her in shock and him in amusement.

"Wow," Hugh spoke.

Amy, however, was rendered mute by the way he looked. He should look ridiculous, but all she could think was, *yummy*. His Georgia Bulldogs t-shirt had to be two sizes too small, the way it hugged his chest muscles. He'd covered it with an opened denim shirt, and he held a beat-up ball cap in his hand. It was the jeans that made her mouth go dry. They were old – worn at the knees and frayed at the cuffs. And tight. Dear God, they were tight. The material hugged his thighs and cupped his sex. She wished he would turn around so she could see how fine his ass looked. *No. Bad idea.* She forced her gaze to his feet. Scuffed work boots completed the good-ole-boy look.

"Wow," he repeated with a grin. "That's a lot of makeup."

What? He should be drooling over her, too! Amy tossed back her curled, teased hair and raised her eyebrows. Of course, she had piled on the makeup. It was a big part of the costume. No self-respecting Southern girl goes to a bar on a date, *au naturel*. Why wasn't he ogling her? When she'd picked out the outfit, she'd imagined him agog.

Why was she so disappointed? She wanted him to be horny? Well, yeah, she realized. She was, so why shouldn't he be? Damn it!

The cheap, black fuck-me heels were new. While she owned a couple of pairs, they were all back in DC. The leggings were hers and specially made. They appeared to be black denim that hugged every curve she had. The secret was the built-in pistol pocket that resided below the back waistband. The over-sized red plaid shirt that hung open covered it up. Under that, she had cut up a Lynyrd Skynyrd t-shirt. The bottom three inches of her belly were exposed, and the top was cut low enough to glimpse a bit of the lace on her push-up bra. Was something wrong with the man?

"Um, well, OK." Hugh clapped his hands together and moved to collect her coat. "Let's go."

Amy controlled her smile as he fumbled with his keys and avoided her gaze. Color rode high on his cheeks. Ahh. He *had* noticed!

Instead of his SUV, he'd brought the old pickup he'd used the day she arrived. The bench seat made a rusty springing noise when he climbed in. His mass filled up the cab, and Amy pressed her thighs together. Jumping him was out. For now.

"What specifically can I do to help you?" she asked, striving for professionalism.

Hugh frowned, but then shrugged. "I won't flip out, I promise."

"I wasn't thinking that!" she objected.

He held up a hand. "Sorry. I didn't mean to offend you. I ... get defensive. We shouldn't be here long, but if I feel wiggy, I need something to focus on."

"Should I talk to you, or pinch you?" she asked, hoping to tease him back to a good mood. She hadn't meant to start the evening off in a bad way.

His bright smile lit up the space. "Neither. I think I'll focus on your cleavage."

Amy almost protested, but why? That was the reason she'd worn this uncomfortable bra, after all. She *wanted* him to look. Later, she wanted him to do more than look. Her breasts felt heavy and sensitive simply thinking about contact with his hands, his mouth. The same hands that were only an inch away from her knees. She clenched her thighs again.

"OK," she said, and he straightened in shock at her agreement. "It'll work with our cover of a date night."

THEY LEFT THE city behind and drove until the streetlights were few and far between. Hugh finally steered the old truck down a worn gravel road that ended in a clearing. Similar trucks and older cars were parked without rhyme or reason on an area scattered with grass and mud. The bar was well lit on the outside. It could have been a barn at some point in its lifetime – the roof was tall enough. Along the way, someone had added doors, a wooden deck, and a couple of windows.

Various neon beer signs hung on the exterior, and loud country music drifted out as patrons came and went. Hugh opened her door, and she slid carefully down to the ground. She held onto his arm as she teetered to the porch. Damn! She should have taken the heels off and braved the mud in her bare feet. But with her luck, there would be broken glass hidden within the bits of gravel and chunks of rocks. She could actually run in heels on flat surfaces; it was part of her job training.

They entered the bar and were assaulted by loud music and the smell of old sweat and beer. It surprised her to see the patrons actually obeying the "no smoking indoors" law of the state. That must've been why they'd built a deck on the far side.

Hugh nodded to her, and they assumed their personas. He grabbed her hand and led the way by the bar into the next area. His palm was damp, and she resolved to watch him closely. For now, he seemed calm and in control.

She wanted to smile at how well he fit in with his rolling walk and rounded shoulders. She exaggerated her steps, making her bottom wiggle under the tail of her shirt. She and Del had named it the Stripper Walk, and she tossed back her hair for good measure. The song blasting from multiple speakers sounded familiar to her, even though she wasn't a fan of the style. Within a couple more lines, it came to her, and she laughed. It was an old Kiss rock song, redone as a two-step.

The music became muted in the far section of the bar. There was a space to throw darts and two pool tables surrounded by booths whose vinyl seats had seen better days. Luckily, one was empty, and Hugh pushed her in and crowded the seat after her. She threw him a black look that he completely missed. OK, he was the one with an informant here, but she hated being pinned on an op. At least they were both facing the rest of the bar.

He kept his gaze on the people and not her until a waitress approached for their order. Only then did he lean towards her and ask, "Beer or liquor?"

"Beer," she answered.

He gave the waitress their order and turned back to Amy. His gaze was restless, but she was also keeping a careful watch of the other people in the bar. Trouble could come fast and from nowhere. Letting your guard down was bad and could be lethal. Her initial glance around showed nothing suspicious.

The next second her gaze passed by him again, she noticed perspiration on his upper lip. It wasn't that warm inside the bar. Looking at his neck, she couldn't tell whether or not his pulse was high – the lighting was too dim.

"Hey," she said, and grabbed his wrist. She wanted to get his attention, but she also wanted to discreetly check his pulse rate.

He looked at her, eyebrows raised. Was he stressed? She honestly couldn't tell. His heart rate was higher, but not too high. She lowered her gaze to her own chest, hoping he would catch the hint. No such luck. She then pressed her upper arms against the sides of her bra, causing her cleavage to pop out even more. She wanted to giggle when his eyes dropped and his mouth fell open. *There!* She had his attention.

His gaze roamed over every inch of her exposed flesh. She could almost feel heat on her skin. *Wow.* He was ogling her, and it was hot as hell. His tongue licked his upper lip, and the unconscious gesture caused a throb between her legs.

Their erotic bubble burst when a slender, older man plopped down in the other seat of the booth. Hugh squeezed Amy's knee under the table. That was the signal; this was his confidential informant. He moved out of the booth, allowing her to slip free. The plan was for her to visit the ladies' room while they chatted. The CI was very suspicious and afraid to be heard by anyone other than Hugh.

Amy understood. It was standard procedure. Moreover, it would give her the opportunity to splash some cold water on her face. She was horrified that she'd dropped her surveillance, for even a second. She hadn't even seen the informant's approach. This man was proving to be too distracting tonight.

By the time she came back, Hugh was sitting alone, sipping on the beer that had arrived while she was away. There was a group of about five bubbas clustered around one of the pool tables near their booth. They were loud and undeniably drunk, arguing over some sort of bet they'd made on the game. She tried to slip past them, but the group suddenly shifted.

"Hey!" Amy chastised the group as the tallest one bumped into her.

She picked up her beer and tried to slide into the booth opposite Hugh. But the tall man decided he was offended by her one word. He loomed over her, menace oozing from his sneer and every pore of his body. "Sit your ass down, babe."

"Excuse me?" Amy sat her beer bottle back on the table and placed her hands on her hips. Her response was automatic. She shouldn't be trying to start a fight. *Bad move*, she thought.

Tall Asswipe nodded toward Hugh. "Sit down. I don't think your man wants to fight me tonight."

All eyes swung to Hugh as he laughed. He kept his seat and held up his hands. "She doesn't need me to fight for her. You're on your own, pal."

Warmth spread through Amy, and she couldn't stop her smile. Hugh smiled back, winked, and toasted her with his bottle. He wasn't angry? The news from his CI must have been good, then.

Amy saw a couple of the guys take a step backwards. *Excellent.* She'd been told this particular smile looked bloodthirsty and bat-shit crazy. Unfortunately, Tall Dude was too inebriated to see its nuance. He laughed, along with the only man who hadn't wandered off.

Distaste filled her mouth when she saw that the shorter, rounder man was wearing a Proud Boys t-shirt. *Nazis. Fucking redneck Nazis.* His bloodshot eyes were fixed on her cleavage. *Eww.* He was almost drooling, too.

Hugh must've noticed the fury in her eyes, for he was suddenly by her side. "Let's go before you hurt someone, and we get arrested."

Good call, she acknowledged silently, and allowed him to lead her through the maze of patrons and out the door. There was no need to let Nazis ruin such a promising night. Now that the business part was over, they could start on the personal aspect. She couldn't wait, wanting to sprint to the truck, dragging Hugh along. Where had this incredible state of horniness come from? She couldn't recall the last time she'd been this keyed up over a guy.

"Wait just a minute!" The tall redneck and his round friend followed them out into the parking lot.

Hugh turned around first, his voice even and firm. "Hey man, we don't want any trouble."

While he held their attention, Amy scoured the surrounding ground. Finding what she was looking for, she held it behind her and finally turned.

The tall one was leaning against the wall as the faux-Nazi advanced. She stepped to the side of Hugh and calculated the distance. The man needed to advance about a foot. *Come on! Come closer!*

Hugh held up his hands. "Seriously, dude. Go back

inside. We're leaving."

The man halted and laughed. "Your bitch and me are going for a ride."

The second he turned his revolting, horny stare to her, Amy let loose. Her form wasn't perfect, but her aim was still good. Her speed was off, but it was hard to manage her usual 60 miles per hour with an object that wasn't an actual softball. The rock was about the size of a tangerine orange, and it hit the neo-Nazi right in the crotch.

Either the speed or the weight was efficient, because all the man uttered was a croak before falling to his knees. His drunken friend looked on, confused. He blinked at them before it occurred to him that he wasn't safe. Panic had him fumbling for the door. Pulling it open so hard it smacked him in the face, he fell inside.

"We need to scram." Hugh laughed and tossed her the keys.

Amy didn't stop to ask why she was suddenly the driver; she sprinted to the truck as fast as she could in heels and started it before moving the seat forward. Hugh flung himself inside. "Punch it!"

Within moments, they were flying down the street and onto the highway.

Hugh couldn't stop laughing. "Ms. Stuart, you are a bundle of surprises!"

Amy grinned, feeling his approval wash over her like warm bath. "I played softball all my life," she explained. "But I didn't start pitching until joining a rec league a few years ago."

"Damn!" he exclaimed, still chuckling.

"Before that, I was a catcher." She grinned and couldn't help herself. "That's where my fine ass comes from. Years of squats."

Even though he was still laughing, the look he gave her was scorching, full of heat. Amy felt it everywhere, but especially between her legs. She squeezed her thighs together as best she could while driving and turned onto the interstate.

"Why did you toss me the keys?" she finally remembered to ask.

"Common sense," he scoffed with a grin. "With my bum knee, you're much faster than I am. You were inside, with the truck in drive, before I even opened the door."

That made sense. But Amy was still stoked from his faith in her. Most men would've wanted to fight for a lady's virtue and all that nonsense. They would've wanted to screech out of the lot, flinging gravel from the tires. They would've been butt-hurt if their date had saved the day.

But not Mr. Hugh Bainbridge IV. Masculinity covered him like a cloak, yet he'd shown no qualms about letting her do her thing. In fact, he'd watched, amused and confident that she didn't need help. Of course, she had no doubt that he would've stepped in, if needed; he was too much of a gentleman. Their tussle outside the warehouse had proven he could hold his own in a fight.

Once they were off the gravel road and on the two-lane, Amy switched from defensive maneuvers to traveling a mile over the speed limit. No one had followed them. She relaxed back into the vinyl seat and confessed.

"I have to admit," she said, "I was aiming for his leg. My aim was slightly off."

"Oh, well, you suck, then." Hugh giggled. The sound was charming. He was clearly enjoying this.

"I know you can't divulge specifics, but was your CI useful?"

"He was!" Hugh beamed.

As she neared her hotel, she had to admit, she was searching for a way to get him inside. Shouldn't be too hard based on how he'd been looking at her all evening. Maybe he read her mind, because his hand landed on her thigh above her knee and squeezed. She was torn between wanting him to leave his hand there and needing it to move higher.

"I hate we didn't stay longer." Hugh's voice sounded regretful.

"What?" She laughed, confused. "Why?"

"Yeah. I didn't get to ogle your breasts for very long." His sigh was dramatic.

She burst out laughing, and he joined in. Yes – he was definitely coming inside with her. She couldn't wait to climb that muscular body. "The night is still young."

She parked by the back entrance to the hotel since it wasn't as well-lit as the front. She secured her gun in the pocket of the coat she'd left in the truck. Ever the gentleman, Hugh came around to help her out. This time, she waited. She slid off the seat and stepped closer as he closed the door with a thunk.

They looked at each other. The air was so full of yearning, it was hard for Amy to breathe. Maybe she should just grab him?

"I'm dying to kiss you." Hugh finally broke the silence.

Amy felt his gruff voice down to her toes. She placed her coat carefully on the truck hood in order to have two hands free. He dipped his head, and she did the one thing she'd been impatient to do. Her hand pushed the cap off his head, and then her fingers were tangling in his curls. That contact made their kisses even hotter.

The first kiss was tentative, his lips barely touching hers. She felt a puff of air as he moaned, and the next kiss was deep, hungry, glorious. She still wasn't sure how fast or how far he would go. He seemed like such a good guy. Nothing like the sort she was usually attracted to. *Whatever.* She wasn't afraid to initiate moves.

He certainly did not kiss like a good guy, her body screamed. Jeez, all her systems felt dominated, overcome in the best way possible. Reality faded, and all that existed was desire and pleasure. His hair was silky and long enough to hold onto. She combed her fingers through one side and moved to the longer curls in the back.

She wiggled closer, and his hands grasped her ass, pulling her up, rubbing her against an impressive erection. *Oh, God, yes!* Leggings were so much better than jeans. The material was thin and flexible, and she could feel the heat coming off his thighs.

The wild but thorough kisses continued as he slipped his hands under the waistband of her leggings. Good thing she'd removed the gun, she managed to think before his fingers tightened on her bare cheeks. He growled, making their lips vibrate, as he discovered her thong. Such an animalistic sound for such a nice guy!

"Love this." He moved her again, a slow swipe up and down his crotch. Was he referring to her underwear, the friction, or to her ass? She wasn't sure, but it didn't matter. It was all amazing.

She hated to break the contact, but she wanted to get her hand on him. He'd probably be shocked if she unzipped him in public. She was about to find out.

As if he'd read her mind, he lowered her until she was again standing. One hand gripped her nape as he kissed his way down her throat. Before she could make her move, his other hand followed the side of her thong around to the front and dipped between her thighs. Amy parted her legs on instinct and dug her nails into his shoulders the moment he made contact.

After stroking once, leaving them both shuddering, he asked, "Too forward?"

"Fuck, no," she gasped, her voice as winded as his.

"Good." He drew the word out near her ear and pushed a finger inside.

All assumptions about him taking it slow and being cautious fled. *Yes!* This was what she needed. It was even better when he bent his finger, stroking in and out, searching for that perfect spot. A nice guy who knew how to find a g-spot? Had she won the sex lottery? She widened her stance, teetering on her heels.

"You feel amazing." His voice was growly again, and he nipped her earlobe. "Sleek and soft and wet."

Amy twisted against him. "I know what would feel better."

She found his erection pushing against his jeans and squeezed. He groaned, throwing his head back, but still bent over so he could continue pushing her to orgasm. She should stop, pull him inside, and devour him. Doing this in public was risky and taboo. But she was too close to call a halt.

Suddenly, tinny classical music filled the air. Hugh broke away, cursing, removing his hand from inside her pants with a regretful groan. He dug his phone out of his back pocket and looked at the screen.

"Shit, shit, it's my mother," he gasped, and answered the call with a somewhat normal voice. Amy could hear only his side of the conversation.

"Wait, what? Are you OK?" His questions were short and sharp, his body on alert. "Where are you? On my way," he ended, and returned the phone to his pants pocket.

"Mom had a fall," he explained while he opened the door to the truck. "May have broken something. She's at Northside emergency room."

"Go! Let me know how she is," Amy said, and stepped away from the truck.

"I'm so sorry." He bent down and quickly kissed her again. "I wouldn't've answered if it'd been anyone else."

She had to smile. He looked so regretful. "I would do the same for my mom. Go, and don't forget to send me an update."

He smiled back, relieved but still visibly worried. "Will do."

He jumped in the truck and left. Amy blushed as she realized her leggings were down around her hips, and she quickly pulled them back up. *Oh, well.* She hoped his mother would be all right. She also wondered how soon they could pick up where they'd left off. Her heart was racing, and she could feel the sweat on her lower back. Nice Guy Lawyer had some mad make-out skills. She was eager to see what else he had.

As she turned for the entrance, she noticed his ball cap still lying on the pavement. She scooped it up, intending to return it. Despite the cool evening, the canvas was still warm. She pulled it over her teased hair with a smirk. Until she saw him again, it was a friendly reminder that she'd finally gotten her hands in those luscious curls.

THE TEXT CAME through two hours later. Too keyed up to sleep, she'd scrolled through the TV channels, landing on an action movie. She'd seen it before, but the stunts were just killer. She hoped the familiarity would help her wind down.

> **Hugh:** *"X-rays back. Finally. No broken bones, but she sprained her wrist."*
>
> **Amy:** *"That's good news!"*
>
> **Hugh:** *"It is. I'll drive her home as soon as she's discharged. I owe you a rain-check."*

Amy flushed, delighted. She knew he didn't mean dinner. What a gentlemanly way to point out he owed her an orgasm. It was sweet, really. Such a contrast to the boldness with which he'd touched her. She was beginning to like this guy.

Amy: *"You do. But take care of your mom. She'll need help at home."*

Hugh: *"Thanks for understanding. We'll talk soon. Good night."*

Amy: *"Good night, and be careful."*

SATURDAY DAWNED WITH no plans. She hoped Hugh might call and schedule the dinner/orgasm he'd promised her, but it was a long shot. She knew he would have his hands full with his mother. She checked her work email, then her personal email, and lastly, her favorite news website. There was nothing new or urgent, so she switched off the laptop.

Damn it, she swore five minutes later. She could have poked around a new athletic wear website she'd heard about recently. That would have wasted at least twenty minutes. She paced the short distance from the mini kitchen to the sofa, too antsy to sit down and watch TV.

There was no way she could hang around the hotel room all day without going mad. She picked up the room phone and dialed the front desk.

"Please tell me there's a gym nearby that offers temporary memberships," she begged.

"There's a Get Fit franchise two blocks away that offers special rates to our guests." The clerk's accent held only a hint of the South.

Luck was with her! She'd used Get Fit locations on many of her jobs, so their machines were familiar to her. Since it was the weekend, the facility was busier than she preferred, but beggars have to make do, she supposed. She managed a significant run on a treadmill, followed by weight machines to work her shoulders and legs. She desperately wanted a go at the kickboxing dummies, but she decided to save that for tomorrow. No need to overdo a workout and wake up stiff and sore the next morning.

After stretching, she returned to the hotel, showered, and nuked a frozen protein bowl. Still no news from Hugh or a call from Chris' girlfriend, so she was bored enough to go shopping.

Normally, she wasn't a fan of the activity, but she wanted something that would wow Hugh when they met for "dinner." This potential hookup was not something she'd planned on, and the clothing she'd brought was either casual or business wear. She did, however, have plenty of suitable lingerie. Amy loved lace, ribbons, and matching sets, as long as her clothing covered it. It was a shame Hugh hadn't made it very far last night. She had dressed to impress.

Lenox Mall had been Audrey's favorite, so Amy headed into town. Of course, it had drastically changed, but she found some shops that held promise. She was in a fitting room when her cell buzzed. Her breath caught in anticipation. Had Hugh's mother made a vast improvement? If so, she could be ready within an hour.

She lit the screen and saw the name Tetlow with an Atlanta area code. This wasn't Hugh, but her heart still raced. Finally, it was Laura calling. Amy answered with what she hoped was a carefree voice that disguised her eagerness.

"Amy Stuart."

"Hello, Amy. This is Laura. We met at the soccer

grounds?"

"Yes, I remember." Amy rolled her eyes. As if she hadn't been waiting on pins and needles for this call!

"Can we meet? The three of us? I was hoping tomorrow afternoon?" The woman's voice was quiet with a tinge of anxiety. Did she truly think Amy would say no? How absurd! Then again, all she knew about Amy was what Chris had shared with her. In that case, Laura probably saw her as a fire-breathing demon from hell. Normally, that suited Amy just fine, but she wanted this woman on her side.

"Yes, I would appreciate that very much, Laura," she answered immediately, fearing Laura might suddenly change her mind. She wanted to ask if Chris was willing to behave in public, but she assumed Laura would insist upon it. She had millions of other questions about what the couple might have discussed, but now wasn't the time.

Laura named a coffee shop in a bookstore – one Amy knew was close to where Chris lived. She agreed to meet at four o'clock. It shouldn't be too much of a hassle to drive into the city at that time on a Sunday. The call ended, Laura sounding relieved.

Not as relieved as Amy. She sank down on the padded chair, her knees wobbly. She didn't want to get her hopes up. She needed to go to the meet armed with resolve. She also should prepare to make concessions, she realized with a sick pang in her stomach. If she wanted contact with Claire, Chris was sure to demand something big in return. Begging on her knees? Maybe. Truth was, she would do it gladly, but he didn't know that.

In fact, she could think of nothing she would object to if it meant seeing Claire. The idea of actually talking to her again formed a big lump in her throat. It had been too long. Yes, she would gladly beg.

HUGH CALLED LATER that evening. Amy had been attempting to watch a horror movie, but the premise was too absurd. A demon that only preyed upon serial killers was unusual, but hardly frightening. Well, unless you were a serial killer. She now regretted not choosing the sci-fi epic showing on the other channel.

"Hey, you!" she answered. "How's your mother?"

Hugh launched into a frustrated vent. "She refuses to rest and won't let me help! Even small things, like loading the dishwasher. I wish the doctor had given her stronger painkillers! At least then she would get some rest."

Amy smiled, assuming his mother was equally frustrated with how her son was babying her. He continued venting, his tone sharp and raised. Finally, he seemed to run out of steam and swore. "Fuck. I'm sorry. It wasn't fair to unload on you like that. Hope I haven't ruined your day."

"Nonsense," she insisted. "I can see myself having the same issues if it'd been one of my parents. They're both independent and hardheaded. I'm glad you called. I hope venting helped."

The minor temper tantrum made him more human. She bet his eyes sparked green and yellow fire when he was riled up. Was he a man who gestured when he raged? With his long arms and expressive hands, she'd bet that was a sight to see. *Wow.* Just imagining it made her tingle.

"Hearing your voice helped. I was hoping you were free for dinner tomorrow night?" he asked, his tone now low and sexy.

"Yes," she answered immediately, her heart leaping, and then backtracked. "Is seven too late?"

Surely, three hours would be enough time for Chris to berate and curse at her. She wasn't ready to tell Hugh about her family baggage yet, even though he'd been open about his own issues. She might never be ready. It was a scar only few people were invited to see.

"I'll be there at seven." He lowered his voice even more, to nearly a growl. "I'm looking forward to it."

His suggestive tone had her pressing her thighs together again, remembering how he'd touched her. Sunday was looking like a busy day for her. She could suffer through the meeting with Chris, and the date with Hugh would be her reward.

THE COFFEE SHOP was as busy as she'd expected it to be at four o'clock the next afternoon. As she'd hoped, the others were already there, seated around a table in the back. Chris was dressed in what he considered casual attire: khakis and a golf shirt. His sandy hair was thinning on top, she noticed from this angle, and refused to be sorry for feeling smug.

Not wanting to dwell on him, she studied the woman as she approached. Trim black jeans, trendy heels, and a jade sweater – Laura looked like the epitome of a boutique owner. Dark hair fell in a straight curtain almost to her shoulders. Amy idly wondered how she would act if she knew all her background information was in a file on her laptop.

While she'd toyed with the idea of dressing as sloppily as she had the day at soccer practice, Amy chose another way. She'd kept her boots but added black leggings and a red tunic. Power colors. She'd left her hair down and added some makeup. Not for Chris, but because she had a feeling the success of this meeting hinged on Laura's influence over him. She needed to look like a worthy adversary.

Amy sat, grateful for the cup of coffee that had been ordered for her. She needed the caffeine kick, as well as something to keep her hands occupied. She normally added sweetener, but the bitterness of the black coffee suited her mood. She braced for a confrontation, but she was surprised by Laura's opening statement.

"Chris knows I think withholding Claire has been unfair," Laura spoke baldly, ignoring the black look from her boyfriend. "I understand his grief, but it isn't right."

Chris stayed silent, his mouth in a thin line. Amy covered her shock by taking a sip of the warm coffee. This was not what she'd expected. Unsure of how to react, she kept her mouth shut and waited. Finally, Chris broke the silence with a sigh.

"I'm still angry." He flicked a sharp look at Amy. "But I've come to accept I had a role in what happened to Audrey."

Chris visibly deflated. He sagged back into his seat, shoulders slumped, and shook his head. Amy froze as his words echoed in her brain. Had she heard correctly?

How many bombshells were they planning on dropping today?

She and Laura watched in silence as Chris rubbed both hands over his face. The other woman's expression was full of sympathy, and she reached over for Chris' hand. He looked at Amy, taking a deep breath.

"No," he said. "I've put all the blame on you for too long." His wry smile held a touch of humor. "Thank Laura for making me see the truth. I need to own up to my part."

Amy moved to the edge of her seat. That one sentence made her head spin. What on earth could he be about to confess? Probably utter bullshit, but she was so desperate for atonement, she needed to hear it. Chris held on to Laura's hand. Amy clasped her own hands together in her lap, squeezing in anticipation.

"Our dream was to work hard, raise Claire, and then retire early to somewhere on the coast."

Amy nodded. This was nothing new – everyone in the family knew about this plan, even before they'd gotten married. Her sister had yearned to live by the ocean one day. Knowing what the future held had been a must-have for Audrey. Luckily, Chris was the type to plan out everything in his life, so they'd been a suitable match.

"That involved me working late nights, weekends, anything I could do to make partner." Chris glanced once at her, but otherwise kept his eyes on a spot to his right. "After Claire was born, it made financial sense for Audrey to quit work. Not that she argued; it was her preference."

Except the realities of being a stay-at-home mom to a baby weren't easy for her, Amy mentally supplied the next sentence. Audrey had been easily overwhelmed and sensitive. A baby's constant needs and crying had been harsh. Soon, she'd become an emotional wreck. Their mother had stayed until they enrolled Claire in part-time day care. This seemed to work until Claire entered kindergarten.

"Once school started, Audrey had too much time on her hands. I thought that her despondency would be temporary. Once she adjusted to the change, she would be fine – like when Claire was a baby. I was thrilled when she spoke of spending more volunteer time at the Literacy Center."

Chris heaved a heavy sigh and glanced across at her. "I didn't want to see anything amiss. I was working so hard, so close to making our dream a reality. I *needed* her to pull her weight. Claire was happy and healthy. Audrey was always a bit off-balance, so it was easier to ignore the signs that something more was wrong."

Years of hatred welled up, but Amy had to admit, "I'm sorry I wasn't around enough. I was focused on my career, too. I agree, she didn't seem that bad off. Well, at least until … that day."

Chris waved her off. "I was her husband. I should have looked into it. You never saw what I did until it was too late. I promise I didn't know about the drugs until after the attack." His eyes pleaded with her for understanding. "And it was wrong of me to keep the secret. She was horrified of the family knowing. Never wanted Claire to find out."

Everything faded into the background as she digested his confession. It was a knockout punch to her gut, and for a long moment, she sat speechless. This wasn't possible. Her sister hadn't been a drug user until after the abduction. That single event had caused her downward slide. If what he said was the truth …

"What?" Amy snapped, then lowered her voice. "She was on something before the abduction?"

"I swore to her I'd never tell." Chris gritted his teeth. "She was ashamed, and I know she'd stopped. I know it!"

Amy shook her head, well aware that she wasn't hiding her look of disgust. But not towards her sister; this was squarely focused on Chris. What else had he been holding back? Did he not realize that that had been a crucial piece of what Audrey had been going through? If Amy had known, she would've stayed glued to her.

"Things were fine for a few months. After the incident, though, she fell back into the habit. Remember the inpatient center for trauma victims she went to for two weeks? She was also there to detox," he admitted. "Despite everything you and I did to keep her going to therapy, it never took. I'm not sure when she started using again. Must have been in small amounts, because she didn't act any differently. I wouldn't have guessed if I hadn't found the stash later."

"Maybe she didn't. Maybe she kept the drugs just in case," Laura breathed. "You can't be certain."

Yet, looking back, Amy had known. It'd been little things – one day Audrey laughed all day, but other days, she cried uncontrollably. Until they'd found the baggie of pills and had them tested, she would've sworn her sister never used. Why would Chris keep such a secret only because he told his wife he would?

A pang of guilt hit. She knew what her reaction would've been. Addiction was a disease, but she would've still judged. Their parents would've panicked, making it worse. Trying to help. They might have insisted Claire stay with them. That would've brought Audrey's ending closer. At least Chris had stood by his wife. She believed him when he said he'd had no clue that she was self-medicating. She snorted silently. Even she, a narcotics cop, hadn't seen it.

She mentally willed her face and posture to relax. The cloak of fake nonchalance was her best disguise. Showing no emotion threw people off-balance. The fact that she hadn't done this before annoyed her. To let Chris see this many of her genuine emotions could be detrimental to this negotiation.

Chris shrugged his shoulders and leaned forward with his elbows on the table. He'd aged considerably since the conversation began. His skin wore a gray tinge. He looked Amy in the eye with a sad smile.

"I'm sorry I pushed all my guilt on you. It's past time I owned up to my part. I should have said something. I swear, I swear to God, I watched every move she made that last year, and she seemed fine."

"Audrey's mental health was her own," Laura pointed out. Her voice was soft. "She didn't have the strength to deal with this. Not her fault. But the blame for that lies nowhere. It was just the way she was built. Everyone around her did what they could to make life easier, but in the end, it was her life to control."

Amy wanted to rage at the woman for describing Audrey that way, but she knew it was the truth. Where Amy could take dozens of hits and keep fighting, an unkind word would cut her sister to the bone. If she could have donated some of her resilience to her, Amy would have in an instant. Even if it meant a long, painful transplant procedure. Her heart equally ached with loss and burned with pain.

God, she missed her! Even though they'd had little in common as adults, they'd always had regular lunch dates. Amy was at their house at least once a week to either babysit her niece or stay for dinner. In three years, that hole in her had grown smaller, but never healed. When would it get easier?

It would have been better if Chris hadn't heaped all the guilt at her feet. The driving force of her anger reared its nasty head to remind her. The desire to punch him was so strong, she gripped the wood of her seat. Yet she had no doubt, none of this showed on her face.

Remember Claire, she cautioned herself. She needed to pull her head out of her sorrow and focus on right now. This could be a breakthrough, as long as she kept her anger in check and watched her mouth. No sacrifice was too great, even sucking up to Chris. He was the one apologizing. She should use that. The three of them sat in silence, sipping lukewarm coffee, until Amy spoke.

"Thank you." Amy looked at Chris with as much sincerity as she could manage. "I'm sure this was difficult for you." She then added, totally truthfully, "You know, I will carry the guilt about the attack the rest of my life."

He smiled without humor. "What good will that do,

Amy?"

She shrugged. Her therapist asked her that question regularly, and she still hadn't found a good answer. She blew out the rest of her anger, saving it for later. Damn, it would be easier if Chris were his normal snotty self. She wasn't ready to absolve him, any more than she was ready to forgive herself.

She looked down at her mug and saw Laura squeeze Chris' hand out of the corner of her eye. She looked up when he cleared his throat.

"I'm sorry that I made you miss knowing Claire for so long," he ground out. "I was afraid for her. They never caught the guy behind it. It was easier to put the blame on you."

As difficult as it was for him to say, Amy gave him points for maintaining eye contact with her. Jesus, why did she want to cry now? *Damn him for this.* In just one moment, he'd made her feel grateful, relieved, furious, and sad. Amy took a breath and went with relieved as her predominant emotion. Anything to stay calm and in control of this crazy situation.

"We hoped you might help us." Laura and Chris shared a look that Amy couldn't read. "Our relationship has become … serious," Laura said. "Claire is understandably hesitant about accepting me." She stopped and fluttered her hands, the chunky emerald ring on her right hand catching the light. "If there's any way you could help with the transition, we'd be grateful."

Ahh! Now they were at the reason for the meeting. Chris's turnaround was already suspect, but now it made sense. Laura was smart to have asked her, rather than

Chris. Of course, Amy would agree to any strings he attached, but he didn't need to know that.

"In no way do I want to replace Audrey," Laura rushed to explain. "But I do hope Claire can accept me."

"I don't know you," Amy said, bluntly. Laura's face fell, and Chris started to stand.

Her instincts screamed abort, and she held up a hand to stop him. He sat back down, distrust plain on his face. She needed to backtrack. Think about Claire, not Audrey. She'd sworn that she would do whatever it took. Well, here was her task. Put up, or shut up.

"But maybe we could do some things together," she offered, trying not to panic. "You, Claire, and I. The three of us. Girl things?"

She would gladly endure spa days, shopping, the ballet, whatever it took to spend time with Claire. While she wasn't sure about Laura yet, this would be a good way to monitor her. To make doubly certain she was sincere. Her relationship with Chris had surely reached a point that suggested long term. No one got that close to her niece without her approval.

Laura's face wreathed in a grateful smile, and Amy relaxed. "That sounds wonderful!"

"How do we go about re-introducing them?" Laura directed her question to Chris.

The tender, loving smile the couple exchanged was almost repulsive to Amy. It had nothing to do with her sister. It was so kissy-kissy, over the top, heart eyes. It was obvious that they had deep feelings for each other, and Amy felt like a voyeur who'd been forced to eat a bag of sugar.

"Look. You, my parents, everyone has told her that I'm still in law enforcement and have been working undercover. That lie can still work. I'll never tell her otherwise," Amy offered, her heart swelling with hope.

"Does your new job involve any danger to her?" Chris frowned. "What about the head of the drug gang you went after?"

"I doubt he even remembers who I am. I've had no contact with him since I left. All my intel says Ajax hasn't returned." Amy was blunt. "I haven't felt at risk since I joined DAG. But if that changed, my company would provide protection. I would die before I brought harm to her."

Except for the home address leak, she thought. Even then, she'd not felt unsafe. She'd been on her guard, and after Kit's abduction, they'd all been relocated. Malachai had had the breach repaired within hours. There was no need to inform Chris of all this, though. She believed in DAG and would protect Claire with her life. That's all he needed to know. She remained frozen while the couple whispered back and forth.

Could this really be happening? She took another swig of coffee and wanted to whoop when Laura and Chris finally consented. She brushed clammy hands along her leggings as they discussed a suitable date and time. Maybe it was truly going to happen. No more hiding behind trees or lurking on the corner.

"You would probably prefer some time alone with Claire. What about Friday afternoon for a few hours?" Laura asked, and looked at Chris. "It's a half day at school, and you've already taken it off from work to be home."

"I can make that work," Amy replied over the knot in her throat.

They agreed on a time, and then the couple left. Amy sat in silence and finished her cold coffee. *Damn.* Hope and caffeine left her feeling dizzy. The crazy thing was, she badly wanted to share this news with Hugh. That realization knocked her upside the head.

If she did, however, she would need to share the entire story. Tonight's date was about getting laid, not carving out her heart. Another out-of-character impulse. She shrugged, blaming it on the emotional upheavals of the last week. At least she had enough sense to use her better judgment. As long as she did that, weird impulses be damned.

Leaving a tip on the table, she walked out and dialed Del on her phone. Yes, better to share the good news with her friend, then her parents, and not some guy she barely knew, no matter how much she enjoyed talking to him.

Chapter Five

*U*GH! A**MY** CHIDED herself as she looked indecisively in the mirror. *You asked him about the restaurant's dress code! You shouldn't be overdressed or look like you want to get laid!*

Well, but she did want to get laid. She simply didn't want to appear desperate. It was a fine line, and she wished Del were free so she could get a second opinion. Amy paid no mind to fashion, selecting her wardrobe based on what was comfortable. Maybe she should have asked Laura's opinion. She had to laugh at that. True, the woman was an expert, but Amy couldn't see herself going that far.

Of course, she wore her nice shoes – matte black with a skinny heel that was barely short of fuck-me-pumps height. The straight black skirt ended right above her knees – also very proper. She couldn't decide between a pink angora boat-necked sweater that begged to be touched, or a deep blue silky blouse that showed off the cleavage in the push-up bra Hugh had admired last night. She'd found both during yesterday's shopping trip.

She let her hair air dry, so it retained some curl on the ends. Basic makeup, especially after the way he'd cringed at her redneck look. Outside of her disguises, Amy owned two pairs of earrings: some pearl studs and small silver hoops. Her only other jewelry was the wide silver band she wore on the second finger of her right hand. She'd given her last one away to Kit, Mick's former girlfriend. Her hand had felt naked afterwards, so she'd bought a replacement.

Lord, she hoped Kit was OK. Leaving everything behind to go into witness protection wasn't a life she'd wish for anyone. Yet, it'd been a solution that allowed Kit to stay alive.

With the same fervency, she hoped Mick died a painful death. Of course, the best solution for Kit would have been to remain with the man she loved and let DAG protect her. Bastard Mick had taken away that option.

Was it too much to hope that his knife wound became infected? She was so grateful that she didn't have to work with him anymore.

A knock on the door broke into her dark thoughts, and she glanced at the clock by the bed. Shit – she'd lost track of time! She decided on the spot that she'd wear the pink fuzzy sweater tonight.

She opened the door and scrutinized Hugh as he simultaneously looked her over.

"Wow," he said with an appreciative smile.

Before she could turn to grab her coat, he reached out to rub the fabric of her sleeve between his thumb and forefinger. Yep, it'd worked! For some reason, men were suckers for angora.

"Very soft," he said. "You look amazing."

"So do you."

That was an understatement. With his curls, the suit should have looked ridiculous. It was black, with a faint charcoal plaid pattern. Topping off his plain white dress shirt was a gray tie with thin blue stripes. However, as she closed her door, she noticed a faint pattern in the tie's background.

"Wait a minute." She lifted the tie for a better look and laughed. "Is that Thor's hammer?"

His face lit up when she recognized the hidden logo. "Yep! I have court ties, but this is one of my fun ties."

"So, you're certain we'll have fun tonight?" she flirted.

"I intend to make certain of it." His voice lowered suggestively, and he gallantly offered her his arm. She took it with a smile, and they were off.

The restaurant was perfect. Snazzy, but not pretentious. They sat at a small table by a window that overlooked a slate fountain. Muted lighting and candles set the tone, and soft music muffled the chatter. Hugh checked with her about the wine selection, which she appreciated. He also didn't order a bottle, only two glasses, after he explained to the waiter that he was driving.

Damn! Nice guys had never been so appealing to her, until now. Beats the hell out of that one time she'd had to call a cab when her date was too blasted to even take her home. Surely, there had to be something unappealing to this guy! She shouldn't push it, considering how much she wanted to sleep with him. Yet her inner detective and cynic always came out, given time.

"So, I don't understand why your office is in a strip mall," she started.

She mentally pinched herself. She should have phrased that better. How could she be so delicate and precise when speaking on the job, and yet so blunt in person? *Oh, well,* she mentally shrugged. He could take her the way she was, or leave her. Pretending to be a nice human was exhausting.

Hugh smiled, not seeming to mind the question. "Well, that's where my clients are. They wouldn't feel comfortable coming to a swanky office, and getting downtown is costly for some. Plus, they feel better about my low fees once they're there."

"That makes sense." Amy nodded. "Um. Exactly how low are your fees?"

"Well, most won't accept free help, so I have to charge them something." He shrugged.

"But how are you going to make a living?" she asked. "You pay for space, investigators, Neddra, cat food."

Hugh sighed. "Dad left me some money, and I have savings. I'm frugal. The rent on the space is low, and luckily, Nancy loves dry food. The biggest expense is Neddra's salary, but she's worth it. Like I said, right now I'm trying to decide what comes next for me." He sat back with a rueful smile. "I suppose you think I'm a schmuck, huh? Trying to stop the deluge by plugging my thumb in the dam? Wasting my money?"

"Not at all." Amy leaned forward and touched his

hand on the table. Her chest filled with warmth. "That was the toughest part of being a cop. For every win, there were a dozen losses. With DAG, I see more wins."

She declined to specify how. Thanks to their under-the-table governmental ties, DAG didn't always operate by the rule of law. They gathered information by hacking into computer systems, infiltrating businesses, and sometimes by breaking in and stealing what they needed. Whatever it took to bring down the guilty. Amy felt no remorse. The intel they'd acquired from Thompson Enterprises, for instance, had stopped a bioweapon from being released. One of her last ops revealed the target was funding a sex traffic ring. She was proud of her work, even if it crossed some lines sometimes.

Hugh inclined his head and lifted his glass in a toast. "Exactly where I'm at, too. Here's to justice."

She clinked her glass with his and sent a mental thank you to whoever in The Duke's crew had engineered the shoe job. She'd met a sexy guy, and after all these years, she might finally be seeing some closure in Audrey's case.

Their food arrived, and Amy changed the subject to something more mundane and less dark. For the next half hour, they debated on which superheroes were the best. Hugh argued for Spider-Man, while Amy picked Wonder Woman.

"She left her home, her family, to fight for a country she didn't belong to!" she pointed out, gesturing with her fork.

"But Spider-Man juggles his duties with being a teenager. Can you imagine how hard that is?" Hugh countered, holding up a finger to make his point.

Amy had to bite her lip. That was the very finger that had been inside her. She was grateful that she'd worn the sweater now. The higher neckline hid the flush she could feel spreading on her chest. She swallowed hard and forced her mind off these carnal images.

While they disagreed on heroes, they both picked Lex Luthor as their favorite villain. Amy turned down dessert and coffee. The spirited discussion had cranked up her lust. If the heat in his eyes was any indication, the same was true for Hugh. She squeezed her thighs together as he paid the bill, grateful that her hotel wasn't too far away. She was so far gone, even the way he helped her with her coat was sexy.

The drive to the hotel passed in a blur, and soon they were back at her door. Hugh leaned against the door frame as she took out her key card. It was difficult to swipe correctly when he started nibbling her ear.

"I need to confess, I had a thing for Tinkerbell," he said lightly.

She chuckled. "You perv. Are you about to ask me to wear a costume?"

"Nah." He chuckled and kissed his way across her cheek. "You remind me of her. Feisty, blonde, able to kick Peter's ass."

The compliment made her want to swoon, even though her knees were already like gelatin.

"Might be better if we do it inside rather than out in the open." Her gaze flicked down the hallway.

As quickly as she could, she finished unlocking the door, holding it open for him to follow her. She'd left a lamp on by the TV, making it easy to drop her keys and handbag on the table. Nearby was a chair padded in emerald suede, onto which they shed their coats.

At that point, Hugh took over, capturing her face between his palms for a sweet, short kiss. A kiss that took her breath away immediately followed it. His tongue licked inside her mouth with a thoroughness that had her grasping for him, lest she fall down. His hands were still tangled in her hair, so she clung to his back, feeling the muscles move underneath his shirt.

He pulled back, his eyes glazed, his lips slack and wet from her mouth.

"Damn," he panted, "I could kiss you for hours."

"If that is your only plan, I might have to kick you," she joked.

Hugh's sexy demeanor crumbled as he dropped his head to temper the giggle that burst out. Amy smiled. Damn, she loved that silly giggle, which always came out at the oddest times.

When he raised his head, the stern sex-god was back in control. She gasped as both his hands squeezed her ass and brought her body flush against his. His erection pushed against her abdomen. Even though she stood on her toes, she couldn't make the contact she needed. He was so tall.

"Does this feel like I want to tease?" he growled.

Groaning in frustration, she broke his hold and wrapped her arms around his shoulders, raising herself those few needed inches. He ground her against him as he kissed his way down her neck.

"Oh, yes!" she moaned.

He felt hot, hard, and delicious against her. It would be even better if she could wrap her legs around his waist, but the damned straight skirt wouldn't allow that. Hugh teased her with short kisses, and she retaliated by lightly biting, then sucking at his throat.

"Oh, fuck, Amy," he groaned, and she assumed that meant he liked it.

She loosened her hold around his neck, and he gently lowered her to her feet. Her hand went quickly to his crotch and squeezed as much as she could through the fabric. His hips bucked toward her involuntarily.

BY NOW HE was panting, and he looked down to watch her hand grasping at him. How sexy was that? Not as sexy as the look on her face, he realized when he looked up. She was biting her lip. The lips that were swollen from his kisses. She was also watching her hand, mesmerized. It was so freaking hot, his cock jumped in reaction.

Not sure how to undo her black skirt of sin, he started pulling it up her legs until the hem straddled her thighs. Just high enough for his hand to slip between her legs and up. At the first touch of his hand on her bare skin, she widened her stance, easy now without the skirt hampering her movements.

So sexy, his brain whispered for the millionth time that night. She wanted him to touch her as much as he wanted her hand on him. He vaguely felt her fumbling to undo his belt, but that took a backseat as his fingers brushed against damp silk. *Hell, yes!*

His first two fingers found the elastic band around

her leg and slid inside. His knees went week at how hot and slick she was. Yet he couldn't fully touch her this way, so he pulled out and slid his entire hand inside the waistband of her panties. *Yes!*

WHEN HIS FINGERS parted her, Amy abandoned her work on the button of his pants and held on. She spread her legs wider, and Hugh wrapped an arm around her back to help her stand.

"So sweet. Amazing," he murmured between kisses. "I want to be here."

At that, he slid a finger inside, and Amy cried out his name. She could almost feel him there, too.

"Bed," she choked out.

She pulled him towards the bed by his tie and quickly shed her skirt and sweater. Blond hair fell back onto her shoulders, touching the straps of the lace bra.

Amy gasped as Hugh actually growled before stalking towards her, his eyes hot. Was she ever glad she'd packed this bra. It was uncomfortable, but that didn't matter now. The push-up cups were nude, covered with red lace. The cut was low and barely covered her nipples. That made it easier for High to slide his fingers under the straps and pull the bra until it settled around her waist.

Before she could take a breath, his mouth was on her, sucking one nipple in deep and flicking it with his tongue. Amy arched her back and grabbed handfuls of his hair to stay anchored. His arm around her waist kept her steady as he moved to the other breast, lavishing attention on it.

He didn't seem to mind that she wasn't very endowed, judging by his enthusiasm. Amy writhed against him as he altered his mouth between her two breasts. One arm remained banded behind her back, and the other squeezed her ass. She ran her fingers through his hair, loving the way his curls felt. As marvelous as this was, she'd been in a state of high arousal for two days.

"Hugh." She pulled his head back. "I need you to touch me."

His eyes darkened with lust. He raised a hand and rubbed a nipple with his thumb.

"Where, baby? Here?" he asked, his voice hoarse, but his eyes twinkled with mischief.

"Asshole," she groaned, and they both chuckled.

She pulled his hand, sliding it under the matching lace underwear, not letting go until it was wedged between her thighs. He flexed his fingers, and they both groaned. She pulled her panties down to her knees to give him more room. After that, she held onto his shoulders, gripping the fabric of his shirt in order to stay balanced.

HUGH'S FINGERS SLIPPED through her wet folds, and he watched her hips pump against his hand. *Fuck*, it was so sexy. He managed to get two fingers inside her, but he needed more room. She couldn't widen her stance because of the clothing around her ankles.

Speaking of clothing, Amy was trying to pull his shirt off. He yanked off the tie he'd loosened earlier and fought with the buttons on his cuffs and the first few from the collar. Then it was easy to jerk it over his head.

Her hands started on his pants, but he pushed them away and knelt down to pull her panties the rest of the way off. Damn it, she was coming first.

How could he resist? Once her clothes were off, she resumed a normal stance, and the room between her thighs was too luscious to ignore. He licked into her. Her cry was sexy as hell, so he gripped her hips and moved to continue. Her hands were in his hair as she cried, "Wait!"

For some reason, she pulled his head back. Confused, he blinked up at her.

"I'm not really into that. Besides, I need you inside me. Now, Hugh," she panted.

He grew impossibly harder. How could he refuse *that*? He nodded, rose, and fumbled through his pocket for a condom. He got rid of the rest of his clothing, while Amy pulled the covers back on the bed. He was standing by the bed, opening the wrapper, when he felt her grip him. He pumped into her hand, helpless. Her grasp was perfect. She flashed him a wicked look and sucked him into her mouth.

His yelp might have been unmanly, but he was so surprised and turned on, his toes curled against the carpeted floor. That she enjoyed giving, but not receiving, was a question he would puzzle over later. There was no way he could form coherent thoughts now. He was too primed.

"Oh, fuck. Your mouth is perfect!" he gasped.

She pulled off and beamed. He huffed out a chuckle and finally had the condom ready. He needed to gather his wits in order to give this hot-as-hell woman a night to remember.

He joined her on the bed and with no other foreplay, was on top of her and then inside. It must have been exactly what she wanted, judging by her delighted moans and the way her hips moved.

OH, GOD, YES! Amy wanted to cry out, but could only make incoherent sounds. He felt so big inside of her. She wished the lights were brighter so she could see his face, his chest, more clearly. He braced above her, so she could move her hands between them. Oh, *yes!* He wasn't too hairy, and good grief, the muscles! He was lean, so she hadn't expected him to be so toned.

She wrapped her legs around his waist and urged him to go faster. She was so close – no wonder, after being in a state of arousal for days.

HE OBEYED HER silent command and ended up pounding into her. He paused, afraid it was too much, but she dug her heels into his ass. She repeated his name with a groan.

"Hugh, don't stop!" she gasped.

He roared her name in a way that helped send her over the edge. He didn't let up as she wailed and writhed under him. He faintly uttered a string of curse words and her name before he stiffened and started shaking.

She came down first, loosening her legs, but continued to stroke his sweaty back as he lay atop her. He turned his face toward her on the pillow and pressed a kiss above her ear. She hugged him, loving the sound of his labored breathing. She lay still, enjoying all the tingles that still sparked along her limbs.

Hugh raised himself with a groan and looked down at her. His expression was soft, satisfied, and probably matched hers.

"Wow," he whispered, and she nodded with a laugh.

"Be right back," he said, stopping to cover her up before he left.

Amy floated, not moving until he returned and pulled her against his chest.

"I should go soon," he mumbled as she played with the wiry hair in the center of his chest. "We both have work tomorrow."

"Mmm," she murmured. "Five more minutes, McCoy."

"Five more minutes, Tink," he agreed, hoping his body would cooperate and not head straight for sleep.

He felt utterly boneless, yet he mentally congratulated himself on lasting as long as he had. *Damn*, but he'd wanted to come during the first few minutes. It felt like all their previous interactions had been simply foreplay. All he wanted to do was drift off to sleep with this sexy woman in his arms, but if she'd wanted him to stay, she would've asked.

With a groan, he lumbered to his feet, searching the floor for his briefs. He pulled them on and then turned his pants right side out. Amy was lying on her side, watching him with a small smile. If she expected him to be shy or modest, she was in for a surprise.

Once he had his slacks and shirt on, he sat down on the bed to slip on his loafers. He felt the mattress shift, and then she was pressed to his back, one hand in his hair. He turned to see her face and was gratified to see that she wasn't shy, either. She was sitting up, no sheet to preserve modesty. He lost focus for a moment, her breasts swaying as she finished fluffing his hair.

"I hope you still find me attractive after Tuesday," he joked.

She looked at him, puzzled and a bit sleepy. He was helpless to not kiss her. God, she was sweet.

"I have a haircut scheduled," he answered her look. "This wild mop is not professional lawyer hair."

"Are we talking buzz-cut or trim?" She frowned, eyeing him with apprehension.

"Trim," he said, and was relieved to see her smile.

"OK."

No sooner was the word out than she yawned. Which made him yawn. They shared a chuckle, then she threw on a t-shirt and followed him to the door. The shirt ended mid-thigh, displaying her delectable legs. Remembering them wrapped around his waist, it shocked him when he began to harden again. *That was quick.* He wanted to laugh. He thought he was too old for that, but Amy Stuart was hot enough to defy biology, it seemed. Yet another reason to like this woman.

"Talk to you tomorrow?" he asked, his heart in his throat as he feared she might want a one-and-done.

"Yes." She smiled, and he waited outside the door until he heard her re-lock it.

MONDAY FLEW BY, thanks to a water leak at the warehouse which required all hands-on deck to shift shoe boxes away from the staff restroom. Amy was thankful. It kept her too busy to moon over last night's phenomenal sex with Hugh. By the time the plumber arrived and they'd helped clean up, it was quitting time.

Once in the sedate sedan, Amy checked her reflection in the visor mirror. *Eww!* She looked ghastly. The heavy makeup had melted on her face, and she could feel that her hair was a sweaty mess under the wig. Earlier in the day, she'd arranged to meet Hugh after work, but she needed more than a quick change from her undercover get-up. She texted him, begging for thirty more minutes, and rushed to her hotel.

Everything was on schedule until she finished her shower and heard her phone pinging. After reading the text, she threw it on the bed and called upon every curse word she'd ever learned. Once she calmed down, she called Hugh to break the bad news.

"Archie needs my help," she rushed on, "I swear I'm not brushing you off."

"Amy, it's OK. I believe you." His voice was warm and light. "Is it something you can take care of in town, or do you need to leave?"

"Oh, no, I can do it over the phone. He has to break into a building I'm familiar with," she explained matter-of-factly.

"I have no clue if that's real or not, but I don't care," Hugh laughed. "You made me smile."

"Thanks. Maybe tomorrow night?" Amy crossed her fingers that he would say yes.

"I'm totally free after 6."

They said goodbye, and she pursed her lips to erase the stupid grin she was wearing. That had actually been the truth, and she'd trusted no one that quickly before.

There had to be some limit to his acceptance of her and her weird job. She was certain it would come up soon. It always did.

EIGHT DAYS LATER, and nothing had triggered the cameras. No one at the warehouse behaved out of the ordinary. The fake shipment had arrived at its intended destination, a community center in LA, the day before. At this point, the best thing would be to let Mimi finish up and leave, Amy reasoned. Maybe her presence here during the day was spooking their culprit. She would give her recommendation to Del and Peter this evening, she decided as she packed up her laptop.

She hoped they would be available when she returned to the hotel to ditch her disguise. She had plans with Hugh later. Her entire body burned hot for a moment, just thinking about it. Any free time they'd found in the past week, they had spent together. That included two days ago when Hugh had only an hour early in the morning. That had been a delicious quickie up against the wall. She'd met him at the door of her hotel room wearing only a towel, and he hadn't even taken off his coat or tie. He'd left her feeling wicked, silly, and thoroughly fucked.

She chuckled and moved that thought to the back burner for now. Who knew such a nice guy would be hell-on-wheels in bed?

Roderick and three other workers were waiting for her in the foyer. It wasn't in her cover story to make friends with the staff, but they'd all passed DAG's background checks and seemed like good people. The smuggler had to be outside the company, and she wished he would make his move. She hated suspecting these people who were surely innocent, based on her hunches and DAG's intel.

Roderick set the alarm, and they moved outside. Amy waited with him as he locked up, and then they followed the others to the back parking lot. As soon as they rounded the corner, Amy hit the remote start on her key fob. The temperature had dropped during the afternoon, and luckily, the car's heating system worked quickly.

There was no warning, only a click, and then a huge fireball blew her backward. Pain radiated through her skull as her head made contact with the sidewalk. Stunned, it took a moment for her instincts to kick in.

Another explosion boomed. The fireball that was her rental car had spread to Roderick's van in the next parking space. The other cars were further away, but the fire could still move quickly.

Her training took over. Amy rose to her feet as fast as the straight skirt of her guise would allow and began searching for the others. Roderick was pulling up to his knees nearby. He looked to be moving under his own steam. She quickly found the other three by the sounds of their panicked cries through the smoke. The younger man had staggered to his feet. The older woman was curled into a ball on the grass, screaming. The younger woman lay still on the pavement.

"Check on her!" Amy shouted to the man, and pointed to the woman in the fetal position. "If she's OK, get her to the front of the building!"

She raced over to the prone woman, first checking for a pulse. There it was! Nice and strong. Amy saw no outward signs of trauma, so she hoped the blast had only knocked her out. It was dangerous to move her, but the fire was so hot, she could feel the skin on her hands tightening. The victim was slight, and if not for her disguise, Amy might have been able to carry her with no help. She could drag her, she decided. She moved into position and was joined by Roderick, who appeared unhurt.

"Grab her feet," Amy ordered, and together they moved her to the grassy patch on the front of the building, joining the others.

"Where are you hurt?" Amy asked the older woman, who had gone back to her defensive position. All she heard was a string of Spanish which she couldn't decipher.

"She's bruised, but OK," the younger man explained. "Very frightened. I think her hair saved her," he added, indicating the thick bun the woman wore on the back of her head.

"You're OK?" Amy asked him, and he nodded, holding up his arm. His falling slide on the concrete had scraped through the layers of his light jacket and cotton shirt. The revealed flesh looked raw and bloody.

She could hear sirens approaching. *Shit.* She needed to call this in to DAG. Before she could pull her phone from her pocket, Roderick was shoving his ball cap into her hand. She looked at him, confused.

"Your wig is crooked," he explained, and she wanted to hug him.

She straightened it and pulled on the cap, hoping it covered any of her natural hair that had escaped. As the first firetruck pulled in, she moved away and dialed DAG's emergency number. They all took turns being on-call, but most of the time it was Malachai who pulled that duty – he was at the office more than anyone, often working well into the night. She was in luck when the man himself answered the line.

She wasted no time. "My car exploded after I hit the auto start. Two blasted cars, four injured witnesses, one unconscious. Cops will be here any second now. I'm fine," she added as an afterthought.

All she heard for a moment was the flurry of Malachai's fingers at his keyboard. "I'm sending info to your phone. Mimi had issues with an old boyfriend who was stalking her. The detective's name and number are there. Give this info to the police. I loaded a case file to the national database too."

Damn, Malachai was fucking brilliant, she thought for the hundredth time since meeting him. That story would solve everything. The local cops wouldn't look further after speaking to the detective, who she assumed would also be Malachai.

"Will do," she said. "You need to get someone on my brother-in-law and niece. Make sure they're protected. Just in case."

"On it now." His calm voice eased her panic.

"Thanks, Malachai. I'll call when I'm done." She ended the call after his promise to see to her family first eased the iron cage of worry around her lungs.

She put her phone away and adjusted the cap. The

band had been pressing on what was now a big knot on her head. Maybe her wig had helped her, too, just like the woman's bun. She allowed herself a small chuckle and re-joined the others as the police and an ambulance pulled into the lot.

"I called Amado," Roderick yelled over the noise.

She nodded and groaned. Shit, it would filter down to Hugh. He would most likely panic, rush in, and try to take over. She didn't need that right now. Everything was under control. She sent off a quick text: "Don't panic. Help is here. I'm OK. Talk later."

By the time the paramedics raced over, the younger woman had regained consciousness. After quick examinations of everyone but Amy – who swore she was unhurt – it looked as though no one was critically injured. Amy agreed with Roderick that they should check everyone out at the closest hospital. The women could have concussions, and the man needed his wound cleaned and dressed.

"The company will cover it," Roderick insisted when the young man wanted to refuse due to lack of insurance.

"My company will cover your van," Amy quietly told him, and he waved it away.

"I never imagined something like this would happen." He dazedly watched as the firefighters brought the blaze under control.

Me either, she thought. This was unusually violent for a drug gang. Either she had blown her cover, or the gang suspected Mimi. Or perhaps they only wanted a newcomer out of the way. She knew DAG would somehow get the arson inspector to rush the investigation. She prayed something connected it to this case and not her personally. Any reconciliation with Claire would go up in smoke if The Duke came after her. No way would she ever endanger her niece.

She spent the next fifteen minutes with a Detective Phillips. He had the bulk of an ex-football player and the nose of a former boxer. She played the part of a shocked and terrified victim. He seemed to buy her story, taking down the bogus info she provided. He was sympathetic enough to worry about her safety at the hotel.

"I will pack up and move," she assured him in a quivering voice. "Right away."

He was asking if she needed an escort there when Hugh's SUV skidded into the parking lot. He parked sideways and scrambled out, leaving the headlights on.

"There's my ride," she smiled and sighed. So much for no extra drama.

The detective waited until Hugh approached. She tried to signal him to be calm. He wasn't having an affair with Mimi, and she needed him to play his part appropriately to make this cover believable.

"Are you hurt?" he asked urgently, grasping her shoulder.

"I'm *fine*, Mr. Bainbridge. This is Detective Phillips," she introduced.

Hugh finally caught on and stepped away from her. The cop asked him for background on the charity, and Hugh responded in terse sentences. He was understandably rattled, but she was in work mode. They could deal with emotional stuff later.

Finally, the cop closed his notebook and went to join

his partner, who was interviewing the others. After making sure they weren't being watched, Hugh turned to her. She expected an embrace (which would look odd) or a slew of worried comments (which would piss her off), but instead he asked, "How can I help?"

He was still breathing heavily, flexing his fingers. She wondered if it was over concern for her or due to all the bright lights and commotion around them. Either way, that was certainly a calm question for such a situation.

She was too surprised to respond. It must have been obvious, for his mouth quirked. "This is your rodeo, not mine." He tilted his head closer and quietly added, "I'll fuss over you later, in private."

Lord, she had to smile. She looked around. The fire was out, the firefighters poking through the remains. The cops were finishing up, and the ambulances had taken everyone but Roderick away.

"We need to get him a rental," Amy said as he joined them. "Let me find my bags, and then you're going to the ER, right?"

Roderick nodded at her pointed look and sighed. "Yes, ma'am."

The two men helped her find her laptop and handbag and then piled into the SUV. She returned the cap to Roderick and pulled off the wig as he filled Hugh in.

"She was fucking amazing, man!" he proclaimed.

From the back seat, Amy snorted and blushed a bit.

"It messed my head up, and it felt like I was in slow motion. I couldn't think straight. By the time I could walk, she'd already checked everyone out and only needed help moving Angela to safety."

Hugh turned slightly to throw her a smile. "That's a professional at work, Roderick. I agree, she's amazing."

Now she was really blushing. She lowered her head to free up the band holding her hair. The ringing in her ears was fading. Hugh took the hint and changed the subject.

"Amado will start a workman's comp claim so that our insurance will cover all this. He's contacting the hospital with all the information," Hugh told them. "He called me right before Amy's text arrived. You should give everyone the day off tomorrow," Hugh suggested to Roderick. "Yourself, too. The arson investigator will still need the area."

"Good idea." Roderick's voice softened as pain overrode his adrenaline.

"That's essentially what the perps want," Amy pointed out now that she'd had a chance to think. "This could be good news. The camera system works in daylight, too. All I have to do is reset the timing. Oh, and DAG will replace Roderick's van," she added, lightly probing the knot on her head.

"What a way to make sure the warehouse is empty!" Roderick exclaimed as they pulled up to the closest car rental agency.

Lucky for them, this was Atlanta, and they were open late. The men went inside. Hugh insisted on putting the rental on his credit card for now. After moving to the front seat, Amy took the opportunity to investigate her injury in more detail. *Shit!* The tissue she used came back bloody. Not too much, though. She could feel the crustiness of dried blood in her hair. It certainly hurt like a bitch. But it wasn't her first concussion, and she knew the symptoms. She had meds at the hotel she would wash down with something caffeinated as soon as Hugh dropped her off. She could then pack, relocate, and check in with Malachai. She should go in and get herself a replacement vehicle, but it would be easier to let DAG handle that. She could take a cab later, and they could deliver the new car tomorrow. She should also let Malachai find her a new hotel. The fewer details she had to handle tonight, the better.

She looked up Papa G in her phone and hit call. All she got was an electronic message to leave a voicemail. "When did The Duke start using car bombs?" she said. "Was my cover blown?" Lord, she hoped she sounded blasé or pissed, rather than concerned.

Hugh rejoined her, and soon they headed to her hotel. While he'd been fairly laid back and calm so far, his hands were tight on the steering wheel. Was he gritting his teeth? It was hard to tell in the dim lighting.

"I think you should stay at my house tonight," he said, and shot her a sharp look when she started to argue. "I can keep an eye on you. I know you were hurt and refused help. You need rest, and I can keep an ear out for the camera alarm. Tomorrow, I'll help you get another car."

Well, that all made practical sense, and she was in too much pain to argue. The knock on her skull must be worse than she thought. Normally, she would have pitched a fit at the mere insinuation that she couldn't take care of herself. It wasn't worth his anger, she lied to herself, liking the feeling of warmth his concern gave her.

He followed her up to her room and watched as she downed her pills with old coffee heated in the microwave. She needed the caffeine jolt to make it through the next couple of hours. She shed her disguise in the bathroom and replaced it with jeans and a sweatshirt.

When she came back out, Hugh was packing up her food and fridge items into a plastic bag he'd nabbed from the closet. She gathered her clothes and disguise pieces, stuffing them and the box she'd saved from DAG's delivery into her backpack. Soon they were back in the SUV, headed to Hugh's. About halfway there, the pills kicked in, and she leaned back with a sigh, careful to keep her head turned so the knot wasn't in contact with the headrest.

Hugh made a pit stop to grab takeout at an Asian restaurant after he heard Amy's stomach rumble. He brought back a huge paper sack that smelled divine.

"Hey, I'm hungry, too." He grinned in response to her raised eyebrows.

They headed south to an area on the outskirts of the city. The street was off the main drag for the suburban town, but still within the city limits. The homes were spaced farther apart here, but one could still see her neighbors. Most of the houses were standard brick, built between the 1950s and '70s. Every third or fourth home was a "shirtwaist" style house, dating back to the 1900s.

She wasn't surprised to see that Hugh had bought one of those. Whatever landscaping there had been in the front yard had been cleared away. The area around the wide covered porch was empty dirt, awaiting new plantings. The large tree was probably maple, but Amy couldn't discern its bare branches in the dark.

The porch was clean and empty, and the screen over the front door was new. Hugh parked on the side behind his old truck, triggering a floodlight that illuminated the path to the door. He insisted she carry only the food and her laptop bag, while he brought the heavier items. Inside was a small foyer that ended in a set of stairs. To the right was a shadowy living area, and beyond that was the kitchen, judging by what she could see by a light over the sink. She walked through, setting the food on the kitchen counter, and looked around the space that was larger than she'd expected.

The cabinets, counters, and appliances were all spotless, so she assumed the restoration of this room was complete. Had he completed any of the work? A small maple dining set was in the far corner. It looked like the door opened up onto a sun porch, but she couldn't tell for certain in the dark. The room smelled glorious. Fresh cut wood mingled with the aroma from the takeout.

She texted DAG that she was ready to debrief, but then Hugh started opening the food, and the enticing smells made her stomach growl again. She added a second text asking for ten extra minutes. Her phone buzzed with a reply, and she huffed when she read it.

"Everything OK?" Hugh asked as he brought dishes and cutlery to the small table.

"Yeah." She sighed. "Malachai wants a video call. To make sure I'm OK."

"Good." Hugh nodded. "I'll look at that knot as soon as we finish."

"I can take care of it." She frowned.

"Amy." Hugh leaned forward. "It's on the back of your head. I can check it out, make sure it's clean. Be practical."

Amy gritted her teeth, realizing he was right and she should accept the help. She was just used to looking after herself. It felt wussy to not insist upon being independent, but in reality, it was weak not to accept aid. If her head felt better, she might have agonized over how this man tied her up in knots by being logical.

They ate in silence, each too hungry to make small talk. Amy turned down wine in favor of water. Hugh had both. He insisted upon cleaning up when they finished so that she could make her call.

"There's a lap desk behind the recliner," he offered, gesturing to the next room where he'd turned on a light.

Amy found it, but sat on the sofa instead. The big brown leather chair was unmistakably his domain, and it felt too personal to use it. Thank heavens DAG had the latest technology and equipment, she thought when the computer booted up and connected in record time. It surprised her to see not only Malachai but also Del when the screen filled.

Amy gave them a moment to look her over. "I have a bump on my head. My ass took most of the impact, honestly. Maybe a mild concussion."

Del suppressed a smile, and Amy knew she wanted to make a crack about her full bottom. It was a long-standing joke between them. She hoped Del would see it as more proof that she was fine.

"There should already be security at Chris's house," Del assured her. "They'll never know they're being protected."

Amy breathed a sigh of relief. She wanted Claire out of danger, but she didn't want Chris to renege on his offer.

"Your detective is one of the good ones." Malachai scratched his gray bearded chin. "He called as soon as he was back at the station."

"Malachai already has a bug in the arson database. It'll tell us whenever the police input info from the investigation," Del added. "Luckily, since your pretend stalker made this multistate, it will be given priority."

"Hopefully, they'll try to enter the warehouse soon. Even expedited, the results will take days," Malachai explained.

"This car bomb – it's more radical than we expected," Del said. "Peter and I think you need reinforcements." She held up a hand when Amy frowned. "We don't know if your cover has been compromised, or if the gang members are overly suspicious. Either way, this was an attempt on your life."

Amy nodded, more to placate her friend than from actual agreement. She thought someone meant to just scare Mimi off. It was public knowledge that that brand of car had a remote starter, and it was fucking cold here. She changed the subject.

"I changed the camera timing from my phone already. The warehouse staff is taking tomorrow off."

"Excellent." Malachai smiled at Amy. "I arranged a new hotel and car for you. The car will be delivered tomorrow."

Again, Amy felt a blush creep up her face. *Damn it.*

She hated having such pale skin.

"I'm going to stay here tonight. At Hugh's."

This time, Del had to cover her mouth to hide her smile. Thankfully, Malachai kept a poker face. Amy glanced behind her, relieved to see Hugh was still in the kitchen and couldn't see. All she could safely do was glare at Del.

"Good idea." Del cleared her throat. "He can monitor that head injury. Plus, I bet you're exhausted."

Amy sank into the cushions, relieved that her friend understood, and also realizing that the adrenaline and caffeine had worn off. Exhaustion consumed her, and every inch of her ached. *Must be time for more meds.*

"Check in tomorrow," Del ordered with a stern face. "Let everyone know Mimi went back to St. Louis. There's no need to have you back at the warehouse until the cameras go off."

"Will do." Amy signed off, happy that she wouldn't have to deal with the uncomfortable disguise any longer.

Hugh must have been keeping an ear out for silence, for he entered the room a minute later, carrying a first aid kit. Amy chuckled – it was massive! It was at least the size of a briefcase. The red nylon unzipped to reveal several fold-out sections.

Hugh shrugged at her look. "Hey. When you do your own home improvements, it's best to be prepared for anything."

That answered her question about the kitchen. He rose another notch in her estimation. After all, she already knew he was talented with his hands. He opened a small gel pack and cracked it between his hands to activate it. He sat it aside and moved behind her. His fingers slid gently through her hair, parting it around the injured area. She held it out of the way for him as he selected an antibiotic wipe.

"There isn't much bleeding," he explained as he dabbed the area.

Amy held her breath at the sharp sting. No way was she going to gasp or complain.

"It's a good-sized knot."

Hugh next opened a packet of salve. Some of it would rub off in her hair, but at least the abrasions would be covered for a bit.

"Where else are you hurt?" he asked.

No way was she telling him her ass hurt. She might punch him if he made a crude remark. She shook her head and helped pack up the kit, placing the now cold ice pack against the knot.

"You might feel better if you took a bath," he offered.

She raised her eyebrows at him. Yes, she would feel better, but that might not be his real motivation.

Hugh held up his hands. "Amy! I don't take advantage of injured women. I know we haven't known each other long, so I'll ignore the implied mark on my character."

His slight smile told her he was teasing. *Good.* She liked him and didn't really feel like kicking his ass tonight.

"Have a glass of wine and take a long bath," he ordered. "Look, I'd feel better if we slept in the same room, in case you woke up ill, but I can also set you up in the spare room."

Something in the center of Amy's chest went warm and squishy. That happened far too often around him. Exactly what she needed. She told herself it was because she was tired and injured, otherwise she would be immune to his niceness.

"That's … practical," she conceded.

God, his smile radiated beauty. *Ugh!* She really was off to be thinking like this!

She hurried out of the room, heading for the kitchen and the wine. OK, she was running. And one small glass wouldn't interfere with the headache meds. Hugh had beaten her to her luggage; she came out to find him halfway up the stairs. She huffed in annoyance, but conceded that it would be difficult to haul all that and the wineglass. She handed over her phone and charger so he could monitor the camera alarms until tomorrow.

He left her alone after sitting her things on the old chest at the foot of the bed. She took the opportunity to look around while the tub was filling. This room was definitely not finished. There wasn't a head or foot board, only a mattress and box spring on a frame, covered with a homey quilt. The massive dresser looked newer and expensive. The wooden floor needed refinishing, and the one rug matched nothing.

She wondered what the room would look like when completed. Would he paint over the cream walls? It was a pity the house was in a state of upheaval, for one could tell so much about a person from their living space. The bathroom also hadn't been updated, but she wanted to swoon at the sight of the immense bathtub.

Amy snorted and slid into the claw-foot tub. What her apartment shouted to people was that she was never there. Maybe when this was over, she'd actually decorate. It could be that Chris might trust her enough one day to let Claire visit. Yes, she would definitely need to spruce up before then. What a lovely incentive.

By the time the water cooled and her glass was empty, Amy was a human noodle. Drying off was a chore, as was looking through her hastily packed bag for her sleep shirt. She should let Hugh know she was turning in, but she was too weary to go downstairs. She crawled under the quilt and slept.

HUGH TURNED OFF the stereo when he heard the bathtub drain. He listened to make sure Amy didn't slip or fall. He knew she didn't want him fussing over her, but he desperately wanted to go linger outside the bedroom to make sure she was OK. He put aside the magazine he'd been trying unsuccessfully to read and was grateful he'd bought this old, creaky house.

The noisy floorboards tracked her movement back into the bedroom and groaned louder as her weight settled into the bed. He took a deep breath and relaxed. *She was safe.* He would give her enough time to fall asleep before going up himself.

God, he was exhausted, too. Not that he would admit it to her. He must have done a good job of hiding his concern, because she hadn't frozen him out.

He rubbed the back of his neck to ease the tension. Her text had arrived right before the call from Amado. He'd been at a fundraiser and couldn't leave, so he had to call Hugh to investigate. It was a miracle that Hugh hadn't wrecked or gotten a ticket, the way he'd sped to the warehouse. Yes, he had not doubted her text; it had merely been a gut reaction on his part.

He sighed and rose to shut down the house for the night. Score one more for Dumbass Hugh, always falling for the wrong woman. There was nothing wrong with Amy herself – she was practically perfect. She was strong, independent, and amazingly competent at her job; smart, funny … the only negative was how close she kept personal details. He knew very little about her authentic life. Considering they'd known each other for only a few weeks, that didn't concern him for now.

But she would be leaving in a month or less. With her job, even trying something long distance would be impossible unless his expectations went down to zero. For now, things with her had pushed his life's concerns to the back burner. She was a mighty distraction, yet he didn't think he was using her as that.

He double-checked the locks and set the alarm before climbing the stairs. She'd left the bathroom light on and the bedroom door cracked. He stopped for a moment to check on her.

She seemed to be breathing fine. He carefully pulled a lock of hair off her cheek and again marveled at how utterly pretty she was. *Fuck.* He was so gone over this gal. He needed to step back; he knew it. When she learned his complete story, she might change. Based on his dating experiences over the past year, the odds were against him. Yet he couldn't stop hoping. Amy touched something deep inside him. If things went bad, it would be excruciatingly painful.

He closed his eyes, vowing to protect his heart as best he could. *Don't get your hopes too high*, he told himself. *Wait and see. Enjoy the present.*

Yeah, he knew it was bullshit. Time to see how tough he truly was.

Chapter Six

A CRASHING THROBBING in her head woke Amy. It was too intense to ignore, so she finally blinked open her eyes, only to have them stabbed by sunlight. As she carefully rolled over, she discovered more areas of pain. Still under the covers, she tried stretching and found her back ached, as did her butt. There were probably visible bruises there now. At least the rest of her body seemed in good shape. She'd had much worse mornings during her time with DAG. On a scale of being hit by a bicycle to being hit by a jet, this was maybe car level.

Still, her head throbbed like a timer waiting to go off. *Ugh! No bomb analogies*, she told herself.

Despite the sunlight, the room was blessedly cool and quiet. She needed to get up and take something for her headache, though.

Coffee. Yes, Hugh would definitely have a pot of strong coffee on – an addiction they both had in common. She groaned, and then frowned when she had to move like someone eighty years old, slowly, carefully, and hunched over. The icy floor reminded her to stop and pull on leggings and socks. The top stair creaked under her weight, and a moment later, Hugh walked into view at the bottom.

"OK?" he asked.

Not wanting to nod – that would hurt – she whispered, "Yeah."

He smiled and held up the steaming mugs he had in each hand. "Come and get it. I can make plain or cheesy eggs. Do you have a preference?"

"Either works," she whispered as she reached the bottom and gratefully accepted a mug.

"Haircut looks nice," she remarked. She'd noticed it last night, but the time to comment had not come up. This morning, it stuck up adorably. Even his bedhead was attractive.

"Only a trim. I can gel the curls down for court," he pointed out.

He looked luscious, and she wished she felt better. His morning stubble was sexy, and she approved of his clothing choices. The gray sweatpants hung low on his hips, and he'd left the blue flannel shirt unbuttoned. Over the past few days, she'd gotten many chances to ogle him, and she still wasn't tired of the view. Their first night had been spent in dim lighting, so the fraternity letters tattooed on his bicep had surprised her, as had the scars around his knee from the recent surgery. His second tattoo was the most entrancing. It was low on one hip, easily hidden by underwear or swim trunks. It looked like ripped flesh exposing fish scales. The colors were faded, which made sense when he explained that he'd gotten it done illegally back in high school.

"Might be noisy in the kitchen while I'm cooking," he warned. "Want to wait on the sun porch?"

"Thanks. I'll get my pills."

She loved this room at first glance, unfinished as it was. It held only an overstuffed green floral sofa and a standing lamp. The floor was hideous, covered with artificial turf, like the kind used on athletic fields. The wall of windows looked out onto the fenced-in backyard that held two large trees. There was a wooden shed with a couple of new sawhorses outside. The yard had been well-landscaped once, but now was a tangle of weeds and bushes.

She wondered what color Hugh planned on painting the room. Right now, it was a horrid brown. If it were up to her, she would pick something peaceful and not too bright for when the afternoon sun hit. She was grateful this morning was overcast, and she didn't have to hide inside. Before she sat down, she cracked open a window. Cool air and bird sounds floated in. Back here, cars were barely heard passing by out front. It was easy to believe she was far outside the city.

She snuggled into a corner of the sofa, pulled her legs up, and quietly enjoyed her coffee. She was only halfway through her cup when Hugh opened the door to announce breakfast was ready. Between the meds and the coffee, her head was feeling almost normal-sized. She felt well enough to moan when the enticing smell of bacon hit her nose as she entered the kitchen.

HUGH TWISTED HIS head and smiled when he saw she

hadn't cried out in pain. He was grateful his mother had sent him to cooking classes after college. She'd visited and had a fit at finding dozens of frozen meal boxes in his recycling. At the time, he'd protested, but a month later, he could not believe how much better he felt – physically and mentally. Cooking became a way for him to re-center himself. And eating well was vital now that his knee was improved enough to go back to the gym.

They sat across from each other at the small table, and Hugh tried not to stare. He knew she hadn't slept well – every time she would roll onto her back, the pain from her knot woke her up. He'd remained still, but ready to spring to help if she needed him. Such a trooper. She'd merely adjusted her position and gone back to sleep. This morning, she had circles under her eyes, but she was still lovely. Her hair was in her usual messy bun with tendrils curled around her face. What was he going to do when this job of hers was over?

"Why don't you stay here instead of a new hotel? You won't be in my way," he said over the rim of his mug. He wanted her here, in his house, under his care and in his bed.

"I need to be closer to the warehouse," she explained, then smiled. "I appreciate the offer."

He nodded. She was right. Their perp could come back at any time now. While no one would make an attempt today with investigators, tow trucks, and a clean-up crew outside, they would probably try again soon. Maybe that was why the bomb was set? To get the area clear?

Hugh didn't care about the why. Amy could have

been killed. When Amado had called, his insides had become a block of ice that hadn't thawed even after her text. He hadn't felt right until he'd slipped into bed beside her and pulled her close. If it weren't for the fact that she had experience with this sort of thing, he would have been incoherent. He trusted her, but that didn't mean he couldn't still worry.

He smiled in amusement as she packed away an enormous amount of food, blushing when she praised his cooking skills. He rose to refill their coffee when her phone chimed an alert.

"I have the new hotel info. The rental agency will deliver a car this afternoon. Two of my teammates will be here tonight," she explained.

Hugh raised his brows as his heart rate increased with worry. "You think the perp will come back soon?"

"The bomb could be a way to clear the staff," Amy pointed out, and he had to agree.

Hugh wanted to protest, to force his way in to help, but he knew that that would be the kiss of death with this woman. She was more than capable. The not knowing until after the fact was going to chew on his insides. All he could do was ask her to call if she was bored and after it was over.

"Are there many of you at DAG?" he asked, and then held up his hands. "Sorry if that's too intrusive."

"It's OK." She smiled. "It's a small team. We all have our specialties."

"Like what?" Hugh wanted to keep her talking. The morning had been mellow so far, and he was dying to know more about her. Plus, he didn't want to dwell on the danger.

AMY THOUGHT OF Del and smiled. "Team leader is a former Army medic. She always has a contingency plan, which has saved our asses many times. We also have a former fighter pilot who's our sharpshooter. His hobby is knife-throwing, so he may be the team's secret weapon." She switched to Mateo. "The new guy is a double agent in a drug gang. Unfortunately, they're up north and have no ties to the ones here. That would make this job easier. He's quiet, nerdy with computers, but I don't want to know how many people he's killed."

Even though Hugh tried to mask his look of horror, she saw it. "We strive for zero body counts, but it's not always possible. He joined a gang in his teens and didn't turn until recently. So, his body count was from before he joined. And no – he's not a danger to anyone on the team. He truly wants to be the good guy now."

She rushed on, hoping he wouldn't ask for details, especially about her past. "We have a former spy who can break into any building, and the nephew of one of the founders who's mouthy, but good with guns."

She paused, and Hugh grinned. "So, what's your specialty?"

"Unarmed combat." Her smile was proud and cocky. She wouldn't downplay her expertise.

Hugh laughed, and that warmth spread through her veins again. "I should have guessed that!"

All she wanted was to sit and bask in his approval. She felt like a dying plant that was suddenly watered. Which is why she stood up and announced she would be ready to leave in fifteen minutes.

AMY UNPACKED IN another hotel room. DAG had booked what the hotel deemed a suite: two bedrooms off a small kitchen, and a living room with a pullout sofa. One room had twin beds. Hugh had helped her move in before heading to his office. Bless him, he'd wanted to stay. No, he hadn't asked, but she could tell he was worried. What surprised her was how much she wanted him to hang around. He was accomplished in self-defense, and he had great instincts. This could be out of his depth, though. Plus, she couldn't concentrate. He already took up too much space in her head.

But that was a problem for another time. Now, she needed to go over all her notes while keeping an ear out for the camera tone or the arrival of her teammates. She had expected to miss them more than she had the past few months. But she'd been working so closely with Hugh, it had been a suitable substitute. Del hadn't let her know who to expect. At least, Amy was sure she and Peter knew better than to send Mick.

She didn't want to think about him, so she dove back into her notes. When she finally felt satisfied, she headed for a shower. When she emerged, she saw Papa G had returned her voicemail. It was short and to the point: "No way. We don't deal in bombs. That's military shit or something. If he knows you're here, he isn't saying so."

That made little sense, but Amy relayed this information to DAG, anyway. Her car had been the one targeted. The Duke must have found out, but wasn't letting anyone know. No matter; that much desperation signaled the endgame was close.

Normally, she dreaded the end to an op, but not this time. Now, she actually had something in her personal life to look forward to: her niece. Surely, the perp would show himself before Friday. She didn't want to make any changes to seeing Claire. If that went well, it could lead to more visits. She would put up with the addition of Laura. It wouldn't be hard to take a couple of weeks off after this op wrapped to keep her end of the bargain.

Plus, you could see more of Hugh, her libido whispered. A couple more weeks of him would be awesome. Especially if he cooked. She snorted to herself. The man ruled at feeding her stomach and her sex drive. That's all it was. She couldn't afford to think it was anything else.

She jumped. Where had that come from? She wanted nothing more, surely! She wasn't a deep relationship sort of woman. Hadn't been for years. Her last one ended after Audrey died, and its demise had been for the best. Hugh was a nice guy. That must be what was throwing her off; yes, he was someone she would have dated back then.

But not now. Surely, he understood this was only a fling? He seemed to be light and easy going, so she hadn't felt uneasy until now. *Ugh!* Maybe she needed to make it clear? That could prove embarrassing if they were already on the same page. She would ask Del for advice, she decided. She certainly didn't want to insult Hugh.

The front desk rang with the news that her rental car had arrived. She dashed out for a quick lunch and some groceries for later. She stuck to the basics – sandwich fixings, coffee, water, and energy drinks. That should please almost anyone. Anyone who was hopefully not Mick the bastard Harris.

She was making a pot of coffee when someone knocked on the door. She checked the peephole and wanted to cheer. Archie's distorted face filled the circle. She couldn't see anyone else, but having Archie here was a blessing. He fought even dirtier than she did.

Her smile fell a bit when she opened the door and saw Whittaker lounging on the opposite wall. *Oh, well.* Not that he'd ever failed to have her back, exactly; he just wasn't the fighter that other DAG agents were. However, she preferred him to Mick, and waved them inside. She hadn't yet moved her items into a bedroom. She'd hoped Del would have been sent, and they would share the room with the twin beds. Of course, now Whittaker was bitching about not having his own room. What a whiny boy he was.

Archie followed him, rolling his eyes at Amy, and they shared a smirk. If there wasn't an obvious reason to complain, Whittaker would find one. One reason Amy and Archie worked well together was that they usually looked for the positives, not the negatives. Doing surveillance out in the rain? At least it wasn't snow. Forced to complete paperwork at the office? Unlimited coffee, tea, and snacks. Amy wondered how long it would be until Whittaker developed cardiac issues from his manufactured unhappiness.

Once their bags were stowed, they gathered around the coffee table, and she filled them in on the specifics. Whittaker was quick with schematics, and soon found the best way for them to enter the warehouse when the cameras turned on.

"He won't rearm the alarm, so that leaves the front and back doors." He pointed to the plans. "And if this stack of boxes is still here, then one of us can hide behind it after slipping in. That way, he'll think he has to fight only two of us."

"Amy should be the first one in," Archie pointed out. "So far, she's their only suspect. That will give us another edge."

They continued to plan, laying out their equipment on the breakfast bar to be handy when they set out. Archie preferred to keep all his knives and a gun in a tactical vest. Amy wished that worked for her, but every style she tried on was too loose. She had the option of either tactical pants or her yoga leggings with hidden pockets. These allowed her to move in any way she needed. The concealed carry pouch was sewn into the back waistband, and a short, thin knife rode in a pocket along her thigh. Other micro-knives slipped into pockets in her boots, making it easy to travel light.

Whittaker was not as subtle. His weapon of choice was a Sig Sauer 9mm fitted with as many custom accessories as he could buy. His utility belt carried three other guns as backup. He wasn't as skilled as Archie with knives or Amy in hand-to-hand combat, but he was an excellent shot both up close and far away. Amy took them on a quick tour of the route to the warehouse, and they decided where to park so as not to give their presence away. One quick stop for the cheese she'd forgotten to buy, and they were back at the hotel.

As the night wore on, they napped in shifts. Around four in the morning, Amy figured this night was a bust. Once the warehouse opened, they could get some proper rest before doing this again after the staff clocked out. She checked the cameras again out of boredom, making sure the decoy shoe box was still in its spot. She wondered what Hugh had done that day, who he might have helped, what he'd made for dinner. She could imagine him asleep under the thick quilt. If this weren't a way to get The Duke, she would've wished she were there with him.

Would it matter to Chris and Claire once The Duke was brought down? Ajax was the one who had taken Amy and her sister. If the gang member behind the drugs at the warehouse wouldn't turn on The Duke, the drugs could still be linked to him. Whoever they caught at the warehouse would be taken in by DAG and questioned. They didn't have to play by the book. Peter and Daniel had years of interrogation experience from when they were CIA. Rumor was that Daniel was shit-your-pants scary, but Amy had never witnessed him in action.

She got up to grab some water and run through some stretching exercises. Soon, it would be time for Archie's shift. Almost as if she'd called out to him, the man emerged from her bedroom. He'd been working on his laptop while Whittaker slept in their room.

"So." He plopped on the sofa next to her. "Who won our bet?"

It took her a few moments to remember what the bet had been. Oh, yes! They'd bet whether Hugh had played football or rugby.

"Neither." She smiled. "He was on the swim team."

Archie made a big show of scrutinizing her profile until she blurted, "What?!"

"You're blushing." He grinned. "Damn it! Not fair! I've met no one interesting in my last three assignments!"

Now she could feel her face heating. Archie laughed. "Although, he doesn't seem your type."

He was referring to Hugh's bubba look the day she arrived. She wanted to correct her teammate, but that might show she was more into Hugh than she wanted anyone to know. So, she merely shrugged.

She started to share the news about Claire when the camera alarm went off, and the team flew into motion. Archie banged on the door to alert Whittaker as Amy stowed her gun and knife. Archie pulled on his vest, and Whittaker emerged with the Sig slung over his shoulder. *Good thing this room is near the back exit*, Amy thought with a chuckle. *Otherwise, he would scare the crap out of someone.*

She tapped a button on her laptop. "OK. The camera feed should be live on your phones."

She carried the laptop to her car, setting it on the passenger seat. The men drove their own rental. All she could see in the feed was one figure. She hooked up her headset as she drove, pulling on a black knit cap to cover her hair. When she parked, she was proud to see that only a few minutes had elapsed from the time the alarm had dinged. One last look showed the man had pulled the boxes down, searching them.

They split up – Amy heading for the front and the men going to the backdoor, armed with her keys. She made noise coming in, as planned, while the guys used the commotion to cover their entry. She re-locked the door and stomped into the main floor of the warehouse, wanting her presence known.

"He's hiding behind the packing desk," Archie's calm voice sounded in her ear.

Amy hoped the guy would surrender with little fuss. He was nothing more than a peon. For once, she didn't feel as much battle-lust. No, she wanted the big cheese himself. Now there was an ass she would gladly kick!

"DEA!" she loudly announced. "Come out with your hands up!"

"Don't be stupid!" Whittaker yelled from the other end of the room.

Even with only the emergency lighting on, they both saw when the man made a run for it. Even if they couldn't see him, they definitely heard him. He must have tripped, for the sound of his gun hitting the concrete floor was loud. They all advanced toward him, guns out.

Amy saw the weapon first and kicked it away with her boot.

"Jesus." Archie sighed with discontent under his breath as he held his gun on the cowering man.

The man was blubbering as Whittaker pulled him into a sitting position and slipped the nylon cuffs over his wrists. Amy bagged the man's gun and hit a set of lights.

Adrenaline still pumped through her system, hot and tingly. What a let-down – the man had practically surrendered when they walked in. Her disappointment must have been clear from her expression, for Archie caught her eye and made a face. She had to snort, knowing he'd also wanted a fight. Some ops were really this easy, especially dealing with white-collar crimes.

Despite the leather jacket and artfully ripped skinny jeans, their perp looked like he should be in high school. Who wears bright white designer sneakers to a break in? His straight brown hair stood up from his head in bleached tips and matched the sad excuse for a beard on the bottom half of his face. His eyes were filled with fury and fear.

Whittaker pulled a chair from one cubicle and helped Archie hoist him up.

"Talk," Amy ordered when she saw Archie activate the cameras to record.

The perp slouched as best he could with his hands cuffed behind him and stared over to his left. His bravado was tempered by his trembling lips. Amy huffed in annoyance and stepped forward to plant her boot on one of his spotless shoes. He opened his mouth to complain, but then she pressed her gun under his chin.

"Look. We're not DEA. Not the local cops." Her smile was evil. "We're private. You can talk to us, or we can turn you over to The Duke, who I'm sure will be happy to know we caught you with his drugs."

That got his attention. He swallowed hard, his Adam's apple bulging. She moved her gun away and motioned for him to get on with it. His shallow breathing was the only sound. They waited, and soon he broke.

"He hasn't missed it!" he protested, licking his lips.

"It was just a gram – enough to help my cousin in LA out of a bind!"

Ugh, she thought, *of course*. Their catch was a punk who thought he could pull one over on a drug lord. It begged the question, though: did The Duke really not know this much heroin was missing? The perp was right – it wasn't a vast amount. But then, was The Duke slipping? It was odd that there was no word out. Papa G would have let her know.

"Why here?" she asked. "Why involve a charity?"

The man shrugged. "My cousin works at the youth center where the shoes are being sent."

Behind the man, Archie grinned. Amy rolled her eyes at him, but she agreed that it was pretty ingenious of a plan. She was also relieved that no one from Joshua's Vision was involved. They continued to question him and found out her guess had been correct about how he'd obtained the alarm codes.

"What about the bomb in her car?" Archie kicked one chair leg and scowled.

Amy was still pissed about that herself. The warehouse workers had been hurt and frightened. They deserved none of that. She hated when shitheads involved innocent people in their machinations. Her missing blood-lust was back with a vengeance.

The perp gasped in surprise and looked at Archie fearfully. Archie's beard stubble gave him a menacing air, especially combined with his longer hair. He could be on the cover of a mercenary magazine right now. Whittaker's gun probably helped. It was currently aimed at the guy's crotch.

"B-b-b-bomb? I don't know nothing about a bomb!" His voice pitched high. "No way, man!"

Amy believed him. He was a minor player. He also didn't know he'd been pegged until tonight. *Fuck. What was going on, then?*

"Daniel can get more out of him," Archie proclaimed, and they hauled Frosted Tips outside.

It was quiet enough to hear the wind whistling through the trees that separated the buildings on this block. She was glad they hadn't used the parking lot, which now held black smears where her car had been.

They secured the perp in the back seat so that he couldn't make a run for it or do anything else foolish. Archie would drive to the hotel to grab their gear before heading back to DC. Amy shut the door, not wanting to watch the guy cry. Whittaker's gun gave the guy enough incentive to remain still and quiet.

What a fuck-up. Yet he was part of The Duke's organization, so there was still hope to be had. It all depended on what information he could divulge.

"I can follow you and help," she offered.

"Nah." Archie waved her off. "You finish here."

She nodded. She knew the drill. Archie would fly them all back immediately to DAG to start finding answers. Peter and Daniel were already prepping the interrogation.

"Almost forgot." Archie held up a finger, signaling her to wait, and opened the trunk. "Del sent this."

Amy accepted the box with a smile. *She hadn't forgotten!* Archie asked no questions and moved to slide behind the wheel of the rental.

"Thanks, guys!" She raised her voice to include Whittaker, on the other side of the car.

"No problem." He waved.

"Always a pleasure, darlin'!" Archie winked.

Amy made sure to lock herself back in the warehouse and turned on all the lights. She glanced at her watch. *Wow.* Already 5am. She needed to alert Hugh about what had happened and let Roderick know it was over. She activated her headset on her phone and dialed Hugh.

After three rings, Hugh answered. He sounded sleepy, except for the note of panic in his voice. "Amy? Are you OK?"

"I'm fine."

Hugh's fright made her insides warm. Normally, she would be pissed off at that question. She hated when her abilities were questioned. This was different because she knew he cared for her. The warmth extended to her cheeks as she allowed herself to enjoy it.

"Caught the solo perp, and he's now on the way to DC for questioning," she added.

His deep sigh sounded in her ear along with creaking from the bed as he moved. "Only one guy? Wow. What happens now?"

"I'm still here, finishing up."

"But you and your team are fine, right?" Hugh asked.

"Not a scratch," she answered, more warmth hitting her blood.

"I'll let Roderick know. And I'll alert Amado," he offered.

"Thanks," she said. "I'll have a preliminary report ready by tomorrow. The final report will happen after the guy spills his guts. But we're pretty sure it was only him and his cousin on the other end."

"I can come help you." She could hear Hugh moving around through the phone line.

"There's no need. I'm heading back to the hotel. I'm exhausted."

And she suddenly was. The adrenaline crash combined with over twenty-four hours of no sleep had suddenly caught up with her.

"OK." Hugh sounded so disappointed she had to smile. "Call me after you've slept, and I can bring some food over."

"Deal," she agreed without hesitation.

AMY MANAGED FIVE hours of sleep. A long shower helped her feel mostly human again. She took some over-the-counter meds for the slight headache that pounded her temples. The knot had shrunk considerably, and a scab now covered the abrasion.

She checked the contents of the box Del had sent via Archie. Inside were a couple of gifts for Claire that Amy had picked up over the years. Del had a key to her apartment, so it'd been easy for her to retrieve them. This allowed her to go to the meeting prepared. She had no qualms about trying to win her niece over with presents.

Hugh was true to his word. He gave her the choice between him bringing takeout or her coming over for homemade food. Amy didn't hesitate. He was a fantastic cook, and she was dying to have sex in his enormous bed. She could put off the relationship talk for another day.

She had yet to ask Del's advice.

Turned out, his grilled ginger chicken and queen-size bed sex were both better than she could have imagined. She lay on her back, totally relaxed for the first time in days. Hugh was on his side next to her. The gray bed linens made his eyes look even greener in the lamplight.

"I need to get back to my room," she mumbled.

Hugh continued to stroke a circle around her nipple with a fingertip. "OK. But if you want to stay, I can make pancakes for breakfast."

SHE STIFFENED, AND Hugh hated himself for going too far by suggesting she sleep over. He plainly wasn't ready for this fling to be over yet. She looked good in his bed, as possessive as that sounded. He was about to take the invitation back when she asked, "Frozen?"

"Hell, no." He snorted. "Homemade. I may even have some blueberries in the freezer."

She groaned with pleasure. "Sold."

His smile was full of relief, and he turned his head so she couldn't see it. Clearly one way into her good graces was through her stomach. Luckily, he loved cooking for her. Judging by the way she swooned over anything he whipped up, most of her meals came from a box.

"Can I ask you a question?" He hoped his tone sounded light, but she tensed up again. "Why do you dislike oral? I mean, you're fantastic at giving it."

His body stirred, remembering how she'd insisted on getting to know him with her mouth after they had tumbled into bed the first time. The way she'd so eagerly gone down on him ... *wow*. He was dying to reciprocate, but he would never do something she didn't enjoy.

"It's not that I don't like it," she answered. "To me, it's very intimate. It's not something I do until I'm in a longer relationship."

"Ah." He breathed a sigh of relief. "I get it."

He thought he understood, at least. Someone like her would have trust issues. He wondered if he would ever receive the reward of her trust. With the perp caught, how much longer would she be around? He wanted to ask, but she was clearly close to sleep. He should save it for tomorrow and concentrate on the fact that she'd agreed to stay over.

Plus, there was hope. At least, she'd had serious relationships in the past. All he had to do was stay loose, keep it casual for now, and not dump any more of his familial baggage on her.

THE NEXT MORNING, Amy found Hugh in the kitchen with his music turned so loud, she could discern the vocals from her bedroom. He was in front of the stove, and she watched him, totally charmed at how deftly he flipped pancakes. *What a skill!* He jumped in surprise when she came into view.

"I thought loud noise bothered you?" she asked when he turned the music down with a remote.

He shrugged. "Not when it's my music. I think the reason ear buds never worked in the cube farm was that there was also so much movement around me." He smiled self-consciously. "I have few clues to the mystery that is my brain."

She had to kiss him then, didn't she? His mysterious

brain was one of the many facets of him she liked. She grasped his nape and pulled his head down. His mouth tasted of coffee and heat. If she weren't famished, she would have lured him back upstairs.

After they reluctantly parted, she added, "I'm glad you like your tunes turned up to eleven. Me, too."

The pancakes were divine, but she didn't hang around after they cleaned the kitchen. He had to get ready for work, and she needed to get back, check in with DAG, and psyche herself for her afternoon meeting. She still hadn't told him about Chris and Claire.

Not that she feared his reaction. She was almost afraid it would jinx something. She had two possibly good things going right now. Her instinct was to keep them separate until she had a better feel for what could go wrong. They weren't into sharing deep life secrets yet, and probably never would be. It sucked because she found talking to him so easy and relaxing. She desperately hoped they could remain friends after the affair cooled.

A FIENDISH WORKOUT followed by some yoga had Amy as relaxed as she was going to be the day of her meeting with Claire. *Damn it all to hell.* She was still keyed up. Her nerves felt like fragile glass wires.

Babies could be cuddled and would laugh at silly faces. Teenagers could either be ignored or impressed with some martial arts moves. Children and pre-teens, though, were an absolute mystery to her. At least she had the gifts, now resting inside a brightly colored gift bag.

Not that she didn't love Claire – she would die for her without hesitation. Connecting with her was another matter. This was not a situation where she could kick someone's ass to succeed.

The past few years, she'd imagined decimating Chris in a physical fight as an outlet for her anger. That image was no longer tempting, thanks to his recent change of heart. Amy hated to admit it, but she didn't miss that acrid burn in her chest when his name came up. While she thought she might have made different choices in his shoes, now she wasn't so sure.

The bottom line was, if the fate of her future relationship with Claire hinged on forgiving him, she would gladly do it.

She made a mental note to thank Malachai as she pulled into Chris' driveway. Only a pro could spot the guard he'd hired.

This time, Chris wore darker khakis and a green golf shirt when he opened the door. He led her into the living room, not speaking. He gestured for Amy to have a seat on either the tweed patterned sofa or in one of the two gray armchairs, and left the room to find Claire.

The room had been redecorated since she'd last been here. Audrey had favored pastels, and the sofa had been covered in cabbage roses. Amy couldn't blame Chris, though. The room had been overly girly. Now, it looked more like a study.

This was the front room, where guests were parked. There was a den back off of the kitchen where the family hung out. Maybe she would be invited back there again, one day.

She was too nervous to sit. She huffed at the irony. Shove a gun in her face, threaten to kill her, or throw a punch – all those things she could face with calm. But not a nine-year-old girl. Would Claire like her?

She was on the verge of hyperventilating when Chris descended the stairs, followed by Claire. The girl eyed her with open curiosity but hung back when her dad entered the room.

"I know you were little the last time you saw her, but this is your Aunt Amy." Chris gestured, and then went to stand by the bookcase.

Claire nodded, still studying her. "I know. Didi and Grandpa have pictures. They said you catch bad guys by pretending to be other people."

Amy said a quick prayer to thank her parents and nodded. "Yes, that's right. I'm stationed overseas most of the time."

That was a fib, but she hoped it made her sound less neglectful. She'd been anything but! However, she would work with whatever Chris gave her.

"Cool!" Claire's eyes widened. "Have you been to Ireland? Or Germany? We're studying folk tales in school."

"I've been to both." Amy relaxed. They'd been brief vacations, but she had visited. "What do you want to know?"

Claire bounded down the stairs and pulled Amy over to the sofa. After a few minutes, Chris drifted away. Of course, her niece immediately eyed the gift bag. For some reason, Amy waited until Chris left to offer it. She had no doubt he was lurking around the corner, but she wanted this moment to be just the two of them.

"Cool!" Claire exclaimed again as she pulled out a

small wooden figurine of a giraffe.

"That was handmade by a village artisan in Tanzania," Amy explained.

"Wow," Claire responded, her eyes wide. "You went on a safari?"

"Not quite," Amy admitted. "But I saw some animals in the wild."

The other gift – a silly hat that was also a puppet of a chicken with Elvis hair – sent her niece into a fit of giggles. Amy had to chuckle along. Claire's unbridled delight was a balm to her soul. Thus began an hour-long conversation that consisted mostly of Claire peppering her with questions, often going off-topic. Amy struggled to keep up with her energetic and bright niece. She was especially excited when she brought up sports and found out Amy was a fan.

"I mostly play soccer, but I've also been on a swim team and a basketball team."

"I remember you took dance lessons," Amy added, and Claire made a face.

"Yeah, but that was so boring!" she exclaimed. "I like soccer better."

Amy agreed it took skills to play sports and felt a little thrill that they had this in common. Audrey had been the dancer. Claire was a skillful player from what Amy had seen. So much potential.

"Oh!" Claire got to her feet and tugged on Amy's hand. "Come up to my room. I have pictures of you and mom."

While she assumed Chris was still nearby, listening, Amy was surprised he didn't object. She followed Claire to a room that had also been redone since her last visit. Gone were the pink ruffles and floral wallpaper. Now the walls were a cheerful pale yellow set off with sleek white furniture and bold, striped fabrics. Much more appropriate for a pre-teen. Amy smiled at the posters of soccer stars and boy bands that graced the walls.

She took a seat on a padded bench by the main window while Claire pulled a photo album from her short bookcase. Her heart squeezed as the girl joined her on the bench, sitting close enough to where their knees touched. The album was bound in fake mauve leather, and Amy recognized it as one her mother had made. It'd been maybe a year after Audrey's death. Her mom had been heartbroken at Claire's mention of Chris taking down most of the photos. They had understood his grief, but Amy was glad her mom had made the album. It was full of Audrey pictures, from birth to death. Since they came from photos her parents had taken, many of them also included Amy.

"What was this?" Claire flipped to a page that held three photos of the sisters dressed up in sparkly purple costumes.

"Oh, no!" Amy cringed, but in jest. "That was the one year we both took dance lessons. Ugh! I was awful, but your mom was talented."

Claire giggled when Amy pretended to shudder. The next pages held shots of Audrey in better costumes as the years progressed. Once past elementary school, cheerleading uniforms took over.

"This was Homecoming," Amy noted on a snap of them in stylish-for-that-time dresses. "That was my junior year. Audrey was elected into the Homecoming Court."

Claire snickered at some of the outfits, especially her mother's extravagant prom dress. Amy countered that Audrey had worked hard as a cashier to earn the money that paid for it, but she agreed it had far too many ruffles.

"Hey, Aunt Amy," Claire began, but then twisted her lips in distaste. "Wow, that's hard to say."

"Just call me Amy." She honestly didn't care what her niece called her. They were finally connecting. She could call her Moe or Hey You, and she wouldn't mind.

Claire shook her head and bit her lip as she concentrated. Amy caught her breath. That was an Audrey quirk. Had Claire seen it on family videos and copied it? Whether it was from that or her DNA, Amy didn't care. It was beautiful, and she again cursed the fact that Audrey wasn't here to see it.

"Oooh!" Claire's face brightened. "How about AA or Double-A? That sounds spy-like!"

Amy chuckled, delighted. "Either is good. Remember, I'm an investigator, not a CIA agent."

Claire brushed that off with a shrug. "Whatever. Your job is still cool."

The more they looked through the album, the more emotional Amy felt. Not that she would let Claire know. The girl seemed to have a great time hearing the stories behind the photos. So, Amy swallowed her tears and kept smiling. It was worth it to reconnect with Claire. Almost a dream come true.

Before they reached the end, Chris poked his head

around the door to announce they were due for dinner at Laura's soon. *Of course.* Amy wanted to grimace. He would find a way to keep this meeting short.

"Dad!" Claire protested.

Remembering her side of the bargain, Amy butted in. "Hey. Your dad told me about Laura. She sounds cool."

Claire eyed her suspiciously and finally shrugged. "Maybe." Then she switched gears and turned to her dad. "What about our game on Monday? Can AA come watch me play?"

Amy couldn't hide her smile. Devious and crafty! Definitely a kid to watch.

"I'd love to," she answered quickly, and added, "Maybe Laura could come, too? Your Dad can text me the time and place."

Chris kept a straight face and didn't speak, but his body relaxed when Claire agreed. The girl led Amy back downstairs, and they paused at the door. Before Amy stepped over the threshold, Claire grabbed her arm. Before she knew it, the girl flung herself against her, wrapping her arms around Amy's waist. Amy hugged her back without hesitation. One arm held her close, the other hand patted the straight hair she'd inherited from her mother. It was the best few seconds of Amy's recent life.

"See you Monday!" the girl cheerfully exclaimed.

Amy managed a nod and a wave before hurrying down the walk. She pulled up a playlist on her phone – hardcore metal and rap. By the time she'd backed down the driveway, the phone had connected, and loud music filled the compact car. Between that and deep breaths, Amy managed not to cry. By the time she was back at her hotel, her melancholy had lifted enough for her to wonder if Hugh enjoyed any of the bands on her playlist.

Instead of calling her mom and starting a mutual weeping-fest, she texted that the meeting had been a success, and she would call later in the weekend with details. She snorted with affection when her mother replied in a flurry of emojis: hearts, thumbs up, and smiles.

As she contemplated what to do next, her cell buzzed with a text from Peter. *Finally! News from the interrogation!*

But her heart dropped when she read the message: "Need more time with the perp."

Well, that might be good news. Amy hadn't thought the guy would last ten minutes with Daniel, but he must be stronger than she thought. With her report turned in and Mimi "back home," she was at loose ends until DAG finished with Frosted Tips. She still had many local contacts, so perhaps she could help Hugh with another case? He didn't have a dedicated investigator, after all.

They'd planned on meeting later, depending on what happened with the interrogation. She could swing by his office and surprise him. If he had a client, she could chat with Neddra until he was free.

Chapter Seven

THE MOOD IN the conference room at DAG was frustrated. Malachai, Peter, and Daniel gathered to discuss what they'd learned from the interrogation of Amy's perp. While they did that, Mick covered the emergency line.

It was eleven o'clock, and they were beat. The perp had panicked so much on the flight that Whittaker had resorted to a sedative injection. Once at DAG, they'd waited hours for him to wake up before they could begin. It hadn't taken Daniel long with "Skeet" to find out the truth. His actual name was even more ludicrous than his chosen handle: Ryan Campbell. Neither screamed thug or drug dealer.

"He's a dead end. He's too low down to have anything useful on The Duke," Malachai groused. "Amy will be disappointed."

"What about the car bomb?" Daniel ran a hand through his mussed hair. "I know – it could have been directly from The Duke, but it bothers me that this Skeet has no clue. Plus, the denial from Amy's informant was adamant."

"You'd think he'd have given them a head's up about her or Mimi," Peter said. "Something feels off. The odds of Skeet and The Duke being involved in this without either realizing it, is preposterous." He added, "If The Duke even suspected this sort of theft, Skeet would be dead."

Malachai pinched the bridge of his nose. "Just say it. It looks like someone has hit us again."

"What makes you think that?" Daniel's voice was sharp.

"Probably paranoia, but I'm running all the scans. The info on the bomb is due tomorrow."

A few months ago, their inside data banks had been breached, and Mick's girlfriend had been kidnapped, assaulted, and almost killed. The hacker had found the home addresses of everyone on the team. Even now, Malachai wasn't sure it hadn't been an inside job. Yes, they'd taken all personal information out of the system and relocated, but the details of each op were still there.

"That's a long shot, given all the extra security you've added," Daniel replied, downing more coffee.

Malachai shrugged, still glum. "It's not info that Marius had. Amy's location is new."

"Have we checked into the players from her last few ops?" Daniel asked. "I know they weren't high-stakes, but ..."

He trailed off, and Peter jotted it down. He knew the agents laughed at his old school way of using pen and paper. Not that he disliked computers; he was as skilled as Daniel with the machines. Yet writing out notes helped him think. He loved the way heavy, capped pens felt in his hands and the sound they made on paper. His grandfather had equated quality ink pens with success, and Peter abhorred the few times he'd been forced to use a simple ballpoint.

"I need everyone to think. Has anything else odd or unusual happened?" Daniel was getting worked up, his fatigue forgotten. He jumped to his feet and paced. He wasn't very tall, but his energy filled the conference room.

Silence reigned as everyone racked their memories. In the end, they were clueless, and gloom covered the room despite the bright lighting. Malachai stared unseeing at his laptop screen. How had someone gotten behind his latest security measures? True, he wasn't the best hacker around anymore, but DAG upgraded whenever something new came on the black market. They put more cash into their security than the government did.

"I can interrogate the team –" Peter put up a hand as Daniel protested, "—without raising suspicions. Our focus should be on keeping them safe. Daniel, can you arrange a meet with Mateo?"

Mateo was back in his undercover role and currently in a full security federal prison. Whenever DAG had intel for Mateo, Daniel would pose as his lawyer. Whenever Mateo had information for DAG, he would start a fight that would send him to solitary. Since he was helping bring down one of the largest drug gangs in the US, the Feds cooperated and had an inside man in solitary posing as a guard. He would notify DAG, and one of the team would enter through a secret tunnel.

This is also how they arranged for Mateo to have breaks "outside" in order to combat his emotional state for being so deeply undercover.

"We'll meet back as soon as Malachai's results come in." Peter looked everyone in the eyes before adding, "If it is another breach, then we have to assume we have a mole."

Malachai swallowed, feeling a knot of anger work its way down his throat and into his chest. He couldn't imagine anyone on the team doing this. They routinely put their lives on the line for each other. Who could then turn around and try to kill someone?

The first time, they thought that Marius, the man who'd kidnapped Kit, had been behind the breach. That he had hired someone to hack in remotely. But now Marius was penniless and on the run. Could it be that someone on this team was that evil?

Daniel headed for the door – always the first to leave a meeting. Sitting still made him feel like ants were crawling along his limbs. He'd rather be moving, was all. Malachai was always last because he had to pack up his gear, but it was also how he lived – methodically. He felt anxious until he'd peered under every stone. Peter was somewhere in between.

Peter was almost at the door, notes in hand, when the emergency tone went off on Malachai's laptop, and Mick's voice filled the speaker. "You need to see this."

"Shit," Malachai whispered, and tapped a few keys.

By the time the screen was up, Peter was back, looking over his shoulder. The call was from Whittaker, currently on a low-level assignment in Nevada. Instead of his face, the video call showed a packed parking lot with a hotel in the background. Neon lights shimmered in the early morning darkness. The view shifted to a corner of the lot, filled with burning cars. Malachai watched with dread as Whittaker swung the camera around to his frowning face.

"Thanks for the heads up," he shouted over sirens and panicked voices. "I started it with the remote."

"Fuck!" Peter swore, and his stomach bottomed out.

Malachai went into crisis mode, creating a suitable backstory like he had for Amy. He heard Peter gathering specifics from Whittaker but didn't pay attention. This cover up would prove more difficult, due to the witnesses and the extensive damage. *Shit!* Thank Christ they'd informed all the agents to use the remote start until notified.

At some point, Daniel returned, probably hearing their concerned voices or the noise from the call. He stood on the other side of Malachai, grinding his teeth. He was physically sick. He knew how to ferret out a mole, but those techniques were sadistic. Torture techniques from his spook days. He didn't want to use them on his team of bright agents. Who could it be?

BACK IN ATLANTA, Amy arrived to see Neddra exiting the office. She parked the rental, eyeing the older woman enviously. She wished she had the personality to carry off such bright, bold fabrics. Today's outfit was an abstract silky tunic worn over leggings. The yellows and greens matched the warmth in Neddra's smile as she approached.

"Welcome, Amy! Could you give me a hand?"

"Of course," Amy said, and followed her to an older green sedan.

"I wasn't expecting you," Neddra remarked, not trying to hide a knowing smile.

Amy shrugged, hoping it showed nonchalance. "I had free time and decided to drop by."

"Hugh will be pleased. He's due back from the DA's office soon."

Neddra pulled three large bags from the trunk and handed two to Amy. The bags' logo was for a smaller department store chain with stores in the southeast. Amy's bags appeared to be full of clothing, but they were stuffed so densely, it was hard to tell.

She followed Neddra back inside and down the hallway. They passed the copy/supply room on the right. The empty room she'd glimpsed on her previous visit was their destination, specifically a set of folding doors on the right wall. Neddra dumped her bag on the ugly carpet and opened both doors.

It was a closet, half-full with hangers of shirts and pants, separated with homemade size markers. There were even some basic black skirts. Shoeboxes neatly lined the floor.

Neddra smiled at Amy's dumbfounded expression. "The last weekend of every month, a local department store has a special sale – half-off clearance."

She pulled a button-down shirt out of her bag and started settling it on a hanger. "Some clients have no idea how to dress for court. Most can't afford new clothes, so Hugh gives me a budget to keep the closet stocked."

Amy reached into one bag and pulled out several ties. A quick glance at the price tag showed her that Neddra was skilled at finding bargains.

"This is great!" she exclaimed. *Oh, Hugh.* Her heart swelled. Not only providing his expertise, but also this?

"It definitely helps with the judges. Even if they're wearing jeans, a shirt and tie on a young man makes him look more respectable." Neddra nodded to the shoeboxes. "Joshua's Vision lets us pick through any dress shoe donations they get."

Now Amy loved the charity even more. She'd planned to set up a monthly donation, and now was certain of it.

"This was your idea." It wasn't a question. It was clear Neddra had set this with care.

Neddra shrugged, but looked pleased. "Not totally. Hugh mentioned the need. I looked around to find the best deal. He added it to the budget, as long as he didn't have to do any of the shopping."

As the women shared a laugh, Nancy the cat put in an appearance. She meowed and twirled between Neddra's legs. She allowed Amy to scratch behind her ears and rewarded her with purrs. The soft fur reminded Amy of Buttons, the family cat they'd had during her teens. She preferred cats to dogs, but wasn't at home enough to have a pet. A cat was independent and could make do without someone around all the time. Dogs were too needy and dependent. She stifled a laugh when she realized her friends were more like cats. Even Hugh. He had his own gigs and didn't pout when DAG business horned in on their time.

The bell over the front door dinged, interrupting her musings, and she heard Hugh call out, "It's me!"

Her heart pounded in time with his footsteps down the hall. She ran a hand through her hair and straightened her top. When he drew even with the room and saw them, his delighted smile made her feel warm all over. So, her visit had been a good idea, after all.

"Surprise," she whispered, and looked him over.

Sadly, he'd removed his jacket and tie. They hung over one arm while his other hand held the leather messenger bag he used as a briefcase. Not that he didn't look yummy in the tan slacks and white oxford shirt, but Amy would have loved to see him in his full price lawyer get-up.

His hair was different, the sun-streaked brown locks straight and pushed back from his forehead. He had somehow tamed the curls that remained in the back. Yes, she adored the curls, but Business Hugh was equally hot.

"Come on back and tell me what I did to deserve this visit." He smiled and stood aside so she could precede him into his office.

As soon as he dumped his things on a chair and closed the door, Hugh drew her close, holding her face still for an amazing kiss. It wasn't hungry, exactly; it was measured, thorough, and made Amy want to swoon. He ended the kiss, and she stepped back, not wanting to look greedy or desperate.

Hugh continued to smile, hanging his jacket and discarded tie on a coat rack so they wouldn't wrinkle. Good thing Neddra was next door, or she would have jumped him. What would office-desk sex be like with him? *Mmm … another time, maybe.*

"How was your day?" she asked, striving for normality. She hoped before she left she could screw him out of her system. She didn't want to leave with regrets or, even worse, longing.

"Fairly successful," he answered. "We met with an ADA to discuss a plea deal. It's difficult for some to balance a tough-on-crime mindset with individual rights."

"Your clients are lucky to have you as an advocate." She smiled. "You know, if you turned this into a non-profit, you could get plenty of funding. You wouldn't have to risk more of your own money."

He raised his brows. "Then I would be subject to all sorts of headaches, paperwork, and people to answer to." He continued, his tone growing tense. "It would grow, and I would go from being an attorney to a CEO, responsible for everyone. That was fine for my father, but that's not me."

Amy held up her hands. She'd touched a sore spot. The line between his brows was deep. His desire to forge his own path was admirable. He was still working through some daddy issues, but that wasn't so odd. His father had passed away less than a year ago.

She could certainly understand not wanting the responsibility of that many people. Having Del's job would be a nightmare for her, for many of the same reasons Hugh had pointed out. No, she agreed with his vision of keeping his business small, even if it meant helping fewer people.

"Concentrate on the few you can help" was one

credo she believed in. That had been her first hard lesson as a rookie cop. Her first week had ended with her physically ill from stress. Not from all the hours or work, but from witnessing so many lost souls. Most were far beyond saving. Once she'd made peace with the department's and her own limitations, it'd been easier. At least Hugh's efforts might keep some people from ever falling that low.

"Sorry. I get it now." She held up her hands in surrender.

Hugh groaned, walked over to her, and kissed her forehead. "I'm sorry. You were trying to be helpful, and I turned into a grouch." He squeezed her hips and grinned wickedly. "I like that you worry about me. I promise, my finances are stable."

Amy rolled her eyes but leaned in for a hug. It relieved her that she'd not poisoned the mood. He felt so warm and smelled so good; she relaxed, her arms loose around his waist. How long had it been since she'd allowed anyone to hold her like this? She couldn't remember. Most clinches she'd experienced had to do with sex. This was only … affection, concern, caring.

Hugh seemed to enjoy it, too. His hand rubbed a path up and down her back, and she closed her eyes in contentment. The day had been warm for February, and she'd worn a cotton sweater over her jeans. She hadn't wanted to appear too over or under-dressed for Claire.

"I talked to my niece today. First time in three years," she mumbled against his chest.

He stiffened in surprise, but didn't change the embrace. He let her rest against him, in no hurry to move.

"That sounds like a big deal," he finally spoke.

She smiled but didn't open her eyes. Cautious, but interested. She didn't know if it was the attorney in him or only his personality. All she knew was that she wanted to tell someone about her day. Someone with whom she could be matter-of-fact. He didn't know the entire story, and she could share her elation without the tragic emotion.

"It was. Is. She's nine."

"You moved after your sister died." She gave him points for an excellent memory. "You haven't seen her since?"

She sighed and pulled away. She gestured to the chairs in front of his desk, and they sat. His gaze was sharp, but concerned rather than judgmental.

"Chris, Audrey's husband and Claire's father, blamed me for Audrey's death. He cut off all contact," she blurted.

"Wait. Was it literally your fault, or do you solely blame yourself?" He held up a hand. His question was quiet. There was no malice in his tone, only curiosity.

"Little of both," she admitted. "One of my confidential informants was in too deep with a bookie. So, he paid in knowledge and turned on me. A deputy in a drug gang saw a way to get recognized and grabbed me. Unfortunately, the day he and his buddy snatched me was a day I was having lunch with Audrey. Two females with long, blond hair, similar features – they took us both."

"Oh, no," Hugh said, his voice mournful. He didn't ask questions and let her unfold the story at her own pace.

"Yep," she quickly moved on. "We were rescued five hours later, before The Duke arrived."

Hugh sat up straight. "The man linked to the warehouse? The drugs?"

She nodded and embellished the truth. "DAG sent me because I'm familiar with him and how he works."

"OK." Hugh took her at her word. "The experience harmed your sister?"

"Audrey had always been emotionally frail. Therapy didn't work for her. What neither her husband nor I knew was that she'd been taking pills on a semi-regular basis before the attack. Her stash … we found it, after she killed herself a year later." She kept to the original story, where Chris professed he didn't know of his wife's addiction.

"Jesus, Amy, I am so sorry." This time he did touch her, nothing more than a quick squeeze to the knee. It was enough, combined with his next sentence. "A random act wasn't your fault."

"I should have noticed something more was off with her," she insisted.

"It doesn't sound like even her husband noticed?" he asked, and she reluctantly nodded. "Then she must have hidden it well, and you can't take blame for that."

She shrugged, and a silence descended. "I wanted to gut the bastard behind the abduction," she said finally. "I didn't catch him; he seemed to disappear off the face of the earth. Most likely thanks to his boss moving him to another state. After Audrey died, I went too far trying to corner The Duke and was placed on indefinite leave from the force. That's when DAG approached me."

"Your brother-in-law forbade you from seeing your niece?" he asked.

"It was his right. It was my poor decision to have lunch with her mother in public while involved with drug gangs. My parents see Claire regularly, so that was good." She shrugged but didn't keep the pain from her voice.

He kept shaking his head, so she added, "I came down every few months to spy. Check on her from afar."

She smiled and squeezed his hand, still on her knee. "I met with him and his new girlfriend last week. He admitted to some of the blame and agreed that I should be able to have a relationship with Claire. Today was the first visit."

Hugh took a deep breath at the sudden change, then smiled broadly. "What's she like?"

Oh, Lord. That warmth suffused her again. How did he always know the right thing to say? She launched into a much-longer-than-necessary list of ways Claire was exceptional, not wanting to leave out any detail. The topic wound down, and she wondered if she should leave so he could work.

Before she could ask, he broke in with his own question. "I might have an upcoming case you can help me with. Interested?"

"Sure!" Amy jumped at the opportunity. Anything to have something to pass the time while she waited for the interrogation results to come back. Well, anything to spend more time with him.

"A client crashed while driving under the influence.

He pled guilty and did everything required by the court. The problem is that his passenger is now suing him. Says she couldn't keep her waitressing job because of her injuries. I have it on good authority she's faking the extent of her injuries and works at a strip club in another county. Want to be my date?"

She leaned across and kissed his cheek. Bless him for moving to an easier topic.

"I can do better than that." Amy tilted her head, almost smiling. "I could go in posing as a new applicant."

Hugh grinned. "Don't tell me. You were once undercover as a stripper?"

"Nah, you wish." Her smile grew. "A waitress at a strip club."

Hugh mock frowned. "What? Damn. I was looking forward to a private show later."

"Sorry," she said. "I have almost zero dancing ability."

"Was it a topless bar?" He pursed his lips and massaged her knee.

"No." She laughed and leaned in to kiss his cheek again. "But I could pretend it was when I bring you a drink after dinner. As long as you tip well."

Hugh growled in approval and gave her a heated look that made her bones melt. Did she affect him the same way? She must, or he wouldn't be so interested, right? She wasn't sure who this new, playful Amy was, but it was a pleasant break from her normal, angry, business-like self. Must be the afternoon with Claire, she decided. It was enough to brighten anyone's world.

Unfortunately, Hugh still had some work to do, so they agreed to meet later. Amy volunteered to cook the one dish she was good at – spaghetti. Her secret was adding more spices and garlic to a jar of sauce. She gave Hugh points for not laughing when she revealed it.

AFTER AMY LEFT, Hugh dove into paperwork, not looking up until Neddra tapped on his open door.

"At the rate we're going, you'll need to hire a full-time investigator soon," she said as she sat in one of the chairs.

On cue, Nancy bounded in and curled up in Neddra's lap. Hugh wasn't jealous. The cat might spend a couple of hours every day sunbathing on the corner of his desk, but since Neddra dispensed the food and treats, she was the preferred human.

"Oh?" he asked, trying not to smile at her brazen hint.

"I'm just saying." Neddra held up both hands. "She'd be perfect."

"Except for the fact she lives in DC," he replied.

"People move for new jobs all the time." She shrugged, picked up the sleepy cat, and left his office.

Of course, he'd thought about it! Especially now that he knew she had family living here. He wanted to enjoy the present, but he couldn't stop wanting more.

Today had been an epic change, and he hoped he'd downplayed it enough. She had revealed more personal information in those few sentences that he'd ever expected at this point. He wanted to believe it was because her trust in him was building.

For one thing, they made a talented team. They had similar views of race disparity and justice. For another thing, Amy was a skilled operative. The type of investigations he would require would bore her senseless. He might have a challenging job once a month, but most involved only online research.

He needed to face it: she was a spy, not future life partner material.

His hands clenched. When would he learn? The type of women he was attracted to were never the sort to settle down. Their independence and laser focus on careers didn't hold up well in the long term. As with Leigh, when it came down to choosing between him or her political aspirations, she picked the latter. He knew Amy would, too.

She was damned good at her job. Not only that, but it also gave her a reason for being. Her entire demeanor changed when she spoke about it. She lived it, and he understood.

Hugh sat back, rubbing his face. All he could do was enjoy the time with her while it lasted. Sure, he could pull back to avoid heartbreak, but he was in so deep already.

THE AFTERNOON OF Claire's game was overcast and chilly, but the gray sky couldn't dim Amy's excitement. She wore a sweater under her peacoat and a new red wool scarf. The team colors were red and white, so she wanted to look supportive without going overboard.

She spotted Chris and Laura on the metal bleachers and cautiously joined them. Chris had come directly from work and still wore his suit, topped by a long dark coat. Laura's clothes were covered by a stylish black coat with fake red fur trim. That was a bit much, Amy thought, but secretly gave the woman points for trying.

She liked Laura even more when she motioned for Amy to sit beside her. It was a better alternative than sitting by Chris, who still frowned at her. The game had been underway for only minutes, so Laura brought Amy up to speed on what she knew about Claire's teammates and friends.

Whatever guilt she felt about emotionally betraying Audrey was drowned out by the excitement of actually being able to cheer for Claire. Laura wasn't bad, even though she seemed totally different from Amy. However, in some ways, she wasn't unlike Audrey, Amy realized near the end of the game. Her affection for Chris and Claire was undeniable, even to someone as suspicious as Amy.

Afterwards, the three of them greeted Claire as she exited the field house, hyper from the winning game and Amy's presence. Amy had worn her hair in a braid and jumped when Claire yanked on the end.

"Your hair is just like my mom's was," Claire commented.

Amy felt a knife go through her chest. Claire didn't know that this had been a thing between the two sisters. They'd always been very different, but Audrey had pleaded with Amy to keep her hair long so they'd have something that matched. It hadn't been too difficult before she joined DAG. On the force, she always had it pulled back per regulations. But that was also when she was in her twenties and actively dating. Men loved long hair, especially blond hair. She'd used to it her advantage without remorse.

Now, with age and experience came caring less what a man thought of her appearance. The long locks took time to maintain and were often in the way. Hence her frequent messy-bun hairstyles. Yet she canceled every appointment she made to have it cut. With access to Claire cut off, it had been the only thing that still tied her to Audrey.

"I like your hair better," Amy said, running her fingers through Claire's bob.

Claire glowed under the compliment. "Dad lets me tell the stylist what I want. He said as long as it's not a mohawk or a permanent color, anything is OK with him. Last tournament season, he even let me get red streaks! They lasted all through the playoffs!"

Audrey had also kept Claire's hair long. The color was a darker blond shade, like Chris's. The texture came from her mother, however; straight as a board. Amy gave Chris some parenting points, realizing that he'd allowed Claire to pick her own style, not keeping up with what his wife had preferred.

The only negative aspect of being around Claire again was seeing that Chris really wasn't the evil villain she'd created in her mind. *Ugh!* This would take some getting used to.

"If you like mine better, we can go to the place I get my hair cut!" Now Claire was even more animated. She waved her hands around and practically vibrated. "They have this great thing where you download your picture in the computer and you can try on any style you want! It would be so epic, Double A!" Claire pulled on Amy's sleeve. "Please! Let's go tomorrow!"

Amy froze, unsure of how to respond. She looked at Chris, and he was again frowning. Laura's expression was downcast. Amy belatedly realized that Claire hadn't said two words to the woman.

"What if Laura comes with us?" Amy asked, stalling for time to think of a way out.

"OK!" Claire answered quickly, too excited to argue.

Laura's grateful smile and Chris' head tilt showed she'd picked the right tact. Well, she could always get a quick trim. Claire shouldn't be too upset if she backed out of a major cut.

The thing was, she was actually considering it. If it was Claire's idea, then she could break her promise to Audrey, right? She could cut her hair without guilt. Plus, she could help Laura in the process. She had nothing against her, and she seemed like a pleasant woman who really wanted to bond with Claire. As much as she loved her late sister, she knew Audrey would want Claire cared for. Claire deserved a mother, especially heading into the hormonal teen years. Amy couldn't fill that hole.

"OK," she said, and was rewarded with a high-pitched scream from her niece.

Amy luxuriated in the hug as Claire flung herself at her. Too soon, it was over, as Claire pulled out her phone to make the appointment.

When she found out the earliest available appointment wasn't until Saturday morning, the girl's wail was epic and humorous to the adults. Another wail filled the air when Chris reminded her about shopping with Laura that day to pick out a dress for an upcoming chorale concert.

This time, Laura came to the rescue. "I'm sure we can do that after the salon appointment."

Now it was Laura's turn to be the recipient of Claire's cheer and quick hug. *Wow*. It pleasantly surprised Amy that Laura was keeping her end of the bargain. She might be OK, after all.

LAURA AND CLAIRE picked her up at the hotel Saturday morning. Amy was on her third cup of coffee, trying to banish the effects from a restless night.

The past few days had been wonderful and awful. Awful because there wasn't much news from DAG. Only a quick update from Peter saying that they'd paused the interrogation because the perp, "Skeet," had come down with a respiratory infection. So far, according to Del, there was nothing from the bomb investigation that pointed to The Duke, or anyone else for that matter. Of course, they would keep digging deeper.

On the flip side, wonderful had to do with the fact that she'd spent much of her time with Hugh. She'd helped with research on another case, assisted Neddra in assembling a futon in the main room of the office, and spent every night with Hugh. Today, he was meeting her after the haircut so they could shop for paint for the sunroom.

The idea should have filled her with dread – the outing was too familiar, too cozy. If Hugh hadn't mentioned it so nonchalantly, she might not have agreed.

He stated that he was torn between two shades of yellow and wanted her to break the tie. He'd already made the choices; she would merely give an opinion. It wasn't as if they would share a space.

If that reality gave her heart a pang, she ignored it. Today was about her niece, and she was determined to enjoy it. Claire chattered from the backseat all the way to the retail area of a tall condo building north of downtown. Upon arrival, the adults were offered wine while Claire chose a sparkling water. Amy almost asked if they had anything stronger to help combat her jitters, but that would be in poor form around Claire.

Her niece was right – the salon had a state-of-the-art computer system to help clients choose a new cut or color. Claire gushed about how it had helped her pick out her bob. Her excitement infected Amy, and she gathered her hair back in a ponytail for the photo. Even Laura was animated, especially after Claire pointed out that they shared a similar hairstyle.

The hairdresser led them to an ornate desk which held a computer. She snapped a quick picture and uploaded it. Claire immediately took over the mouse, indicating Amy should take the other seat, with Laura looking over her shoulder.

At first, Claire had fun choosing horrific styles – a black shag, an auburn curly perm, and a white-blonde mohawk. Amy didn't rush her, and Laura even encouraged it. Amy enjoyed seeing her niece so silly and carefree. As apprehensive as she was about this idea, it would be worth it for this part alone. Her own anxiety had faded as she enjoyed the company.

"No fake hair shades. That takes too much effort to maintain," Amy finally insisted.

Claire laughed. "OK. Time to get serious."

She then found a swatch close to Amy's true hair color, and clicked on medium length styles.

"I need to be able to still pull it back for work," Amy explained. "It's that or super short," she finished with a horrified grimace at a feathered style.

They found a few styles Amy felt she could live with. Claire bookmarked them and then, with a wicked twinkle in her eye, flipped ahead to some extreme haircuts. They giggled at the first two, but when the third one appeared, Claire gasped.

"This one, Double A!"

Amy looked at the screen in bewilderment, then at Claire. She was shocked to see that her niece wasn't kidding. In fact, Amy could almost see hearts popping out of her blue eyes.

"This would look so good! It would be perfect!" she squealed.

"Really?" Amy wasn't sure if she was that brave.

"It would complement your face," Laura agreed. "But I understand if it's too much of a change."

This haircut would take confidence to pull off. It was the antithesis to any hairstyle she'd ever had. The drastic change appealed to her, though. It would be a clear indicator that she'd moved on from a sad part of her past. It would also be a way to connect with Claire. She looked over at her niece's pleading eyes, full of hope. Before she could wuss out, she stood up.

"Let's do it," she said, and smiled as Claire leaped out

of the chair with an elated cry.

The actual cut seemed to take forever. The first snip was drastic. The stylist lopped off her ponytail, congratulating her that the length would be perfect for donation to a group that made wigs for young cancer patients. After that, Amy asked to be faced away from the mirror. It was too harsh to watch the process. Since the salon was full of mirrors, she also closed her eyes. It was too late to back out now. Plus, she didn't want Claire to see even a hint of trepidation.

"I want to be surprised," she explained with a thumbs up.

Amy felt lightheaded. Literally and figuratively. She'd had no idea that her hair weighed so much. Turning her head felt easier; there was no hair to fall off her shoulder. No messy bun to pull and droop and give her a headache. She felt free.

And horribly guilty. Inhaling, she tried to ease the tightness in her lungs. The suffocating feeling that she had let her sister down one last time. *No.* It couldn't be that, if it meant making her niece happy. That was clearly old guilt trying not to die. This new connection meant more than an old pact.

"Oh, Double A!" Claire's squeal brought her back to the present. Amy peeked to see her niece smiling at her in delight. "You look like a fairy princess!"

Amy choked out a laugh and lifted a hand to touch the short strands at the side of her head. She looked at Laura, who smiled with a hand over her heart. Hopefully, her stunned look was a good sign.

Claire bounced up and down with excitement,

thrilled at how well her plan had turned out. Perhaps it was worth it, then. Audrey would rather have her daughter happy than hold Amy to an old promise. She was certain.

Taking a deep breath, she nodded for the hairdresser to turn the chair around to the mirror. A different person stared back at her. The pixie cut highlighted her cheeks and made her eyes look larger. She couldn't decide if it made her look younger or older. In a way, it did both. She felt light enough to float away.

"Do you like it?" Claire whispered from the side of the chair.

"I do." Amy spoke the truth and hugged her niece. "Thank you for talking me into this."

Relieved and full of importance, Claire chatted through the checkout process and during the walk to Laura's car. Amy tried to follow the conversation, but her mind wandered to Hugh. Not that she cared. *No*. It was her hair. If he found the haircut unflattering, then it was proof he was a shallow bubba that didn't deserve her notice. Not something she should stress over. Who cared what the hulking man thought?

She said goodbye and then entered the coffee shop. Everything fell away, and all she could see was Hugh rising from his chair, his hand over his sternum, in a gesture much like Laura's. His mouth was open in shock, but he was also smiling.

"Damn! You look stunning, Tink," he said as she joined him.

Amy's bones liquefied, and she held onto the back of a chair in order to remain standing. He meant it. The gaze that roamed over her was appreciative … and hot. Her knees threatened to buckle again. Oh, she couldn't wait until they were alone!

Somehow, Amy managed small talk as they drank coffee. Hugh mentioned that he needed to stop back by his house. He'd forgotten a part for the lawn mower he needed to match while they were waiting on the paint to be mixed.

While she was still conscious of every move Hugh made, lustful ideas had taken a backseat to the sudden buzzing that filled her head.

What was it? Nothing was amiss, according to her investigator senses. Claire seemed to have enjoyed the day and was acting more openly with Laura. Hugh was his normal, charming self. So, what was off? Why did she want to run and hide? Her muscles strained from holding back.

She was puzzled, and allowed Hugh to lead her to his SUV. She focused on trying to find the source of her apprehension, but came up empty. Before she knew it, they were parked at his house. She had to move, now! Once he unlocked the door, she brushed past him and darted up the stairs, her heart thudding in her ears.

BACK AT THE offices of DAG, it wasn't long before shit hit the fan. It happened as soon as Malachai walked into Peter's office and laid out his findings with a grim expression on his normally placid face. They needed Daniel in on this, so Peter dialed the partner directly.

"I'm heading to the airfield. Archie's flying me to Houston." Daniel's voice was tinny in Peter's ear, meaning he was on speakerphone inside the car. Peter rubbed his forehead and reluctantly shot down those plans.

"Cancel that and come in. We have the results from the car bombs."

"Got it." Daniel's voice was grim before he disconnected.

"What should we do with the kid?" Malachai asked from his seat across from Peter.

Peter shrugged. "He's not useful to the feds. We can ask Amy if she wants to turn him over to the local cops. Or to The Duke. Maybe she can trade?"

"Call her later." Malachai nodded and pulled an antacid from his half-empty roll.

"Do those come super-sized?" Peter joked.

"I wish," Malachai replied and handed him what remained.

Peter was drinking water, and Malachai had a cup of hot herbal tea. Waiting on this info had been keeping them up at night. Now that it was here, their morning coffees had turned to gravel in their stomachs. They'd skimmed the reports and immediately placed the call to Daniel after moving into the secured conference room. They swept it daily for bugs, and there were no windows. They fortified all areas from floor to ceiling with shielding materials. The air and heat ran on its own system and could only be accessed through an inside wall panel. Even if one of them somehow brought in a bug, nothing could be transmitted out or recorded. It was the ultimate safe room.

By the time Daniel arrived, they'd polished off the

roll of antacid tablets. After Daniel took a seat, Malachai tossed him a new pack. Daniel's already serious face grew even darker. Peter passed him copies of the reports and summarized the findings.

"As we suspected, the bombs were identical. The labs matched them to three other bombings in the last few years. These instances, however, did not target specific people."

Daniel's eyebrows went up. "No way was this random!"

Peter shook his head. "No. The other instances, the bombs were placed to do the most damage to a building. All three buildings housed companies who had once been part of Allegro International."

"Fucking Bertram Hess? Are you kidding me?!" Daniel shouted and threw the papers on the tabletop. He pulled off his bomber jacket, his movements clumsy with frustration.

"Fill me in?" Malachai requested as the other two men exchanged a look.

"Bertram Hess was the founder and head of Allegro, a medical equipment company. As they grew, he bought up smaller companies all over the world. He was greedy and egotistical, so naturally, he turned to smuggling. It was easy, until he turned from drugs to biological weapons. That put him on the CIA radar," Peter said. "Daniel brought him down. Allegro was broken up and sold off. Unfortunately, Hess was released from prison in Italy two years ago."

"What else has he been doing other than targeting former branches of Allegro?" Daniel asked.

"And why?" asked Malachai.

"He's a psychotic narcissist?" Daniel shrugged. "Revenge? His own little pissing party?"

"That's all we know so far." Peter sighed. "Malachai has internet feelers out."

"This can't be a coincidence." Malachai's fist slammed on the tabletop. "We get hit by two old enemies this close together, after decades?"

"We have a mole," Daniel whispered and swallowed hard. "No way they breached our systems both times."

"There has to be a way to find the mole without torturing our agents," Malachai insisted. "I'm aware you two know all the awful ways to get intel. There's got to be another way!"

He rubbed his gray beard, wanting to throw up. He knew violence was sometimes necessary in their business, but to have it used on their own agents? That was unacceptable! He looked at his two partners, his mouth set in a thin line.

"Let's start with what we know." Peter rubbed his bald head and wished he had a drink. He turned to a fresh page in his notebook and wrote: *Mattias.*

"We know that one person targeted us for revenge, using our agents' personal info. It now looks like another person connected to our CIA days is targeting our agents based on internal data about their cases and whereabouts."

"Despite a complete overhaul of our systems security," Malachai added bitterly. He knew in his gut someone hadn't hacked him externally.

Peter nodded his head. "And you are the best, Malachai. We all know that."

"So, it has to be internal," Daniel summed up, throwing an ink pen against the wall in anger.

"All the main team has access," Peter continued. "That includes us. No matter our personal feelings, we need to consider every agent a potential mole."

Malachai shot him a sympathetic look but nodded. "This is fucked up."

"Mick and Mateo work more with Malachai," Daniel pointed out.

Malachai had been training them both. Mateo especially, since he had so much time on his hands when he was believed to be incarcerated. They were also the newest recruits.

"But we can't take the focus off the others," Peter said. "This could be a long con. It could still be Del, Amy, Archie, or Whittaker."

"Whittaker is the most dissatisfied," Daniel pointed out, blunt as ever.

Peter rubbed his head again. "I know, I know. Even though he's family, I'll admit he's also our worst agent. This recent bomb could be to throw us off."

"Is there a way we can trap the mole?" Daniel looked at Malachai.

"Nothing I've set up has worked so far. Too many people with access, too many operations going on," Malachai answered.

"First, we need to scale back our jobs." Peter held up a hand to stop Daniel from arguing. "We can afford to miss the income. We can finish ones in progress and keep the agents working on low-level ones. Right now, only Mateo is involved in one long-term. Their safety has to come first."

"Agreed." Malachai sighed. "That would also lessen traffic on the system. I could always quit," he quipped after a moment. "That would definitely slow it down."

"Yes!" exclaimed Daniel, and the other two men looked at him in horror.

"Not actually quit." Daniel frowned, insulted that they took him seriously. "Take a sabbatical or something. That would be a great cover for stepping back on jobs. Is there a way to create a shadow system? Where you're able to run the actual one off-site, and the agents have access to what they thought was the real one?"

Malachai pepped up at the challenge. "Yes. It would take some work, but it's possible."

"Perhaps this will encourage the mole to take more risks when accessing our data." Peter almost smiled. "This is great, Daniel."

"I could say I'm taking time off to finally teach that course for the CIA," Malachai suggested.

"Very believable." Daniel grinned. "Everyone here knows they've been after you for years."

Malachai wanted to smile, but he still felt sick. One of their teammates, friends, was a mole. This person had supplied intel that had harmed Kit, as well as Peter's son, John. To a smaller extent, they had harmed Mick. Now, they could add Amy and Whittaker to the list. Yet, it was impossible to feel good about what they were planning to do. At least this idea took torture off the table, for now. He'd work his ass off on a new system if it meant that could be avoided.

"Give me a few weeks to create this with no one suspecting," Malachai said. "Then we can launch this operation."

The other two men nodded, their smiles fading. No one ever thought this would happen. They always put so much thought into hiring agents at this level. Their background checks rivaled the CIA or NSA. Who in their midst was not who they seemed?

"What about Hess?" Daniel asked. "We need to take him out."

Peter nodded. "Agreed. But who can we trust?"

Daniel's smile was wide and wicked. "I say we do it ourselves."

Peter started to chuckle, but saw the man was serious. Not only that, but almost salivating at the idea. And, oh God, was the idea appealing. It had been years since he'd been out in the field. That was also the reason he shouldn't go. These days, his adrenaline came from guiding the teams through their ops. While he prided himself on staying fit, he was nowhere near tactical shape.

"Let's take Del. She's the last agent who would turn against us," he suggested. Not only was she a skilled operative, but she was also a medic. Just in case their older-than-they-wished bodies refused to cooperate.

Malachai nodded. "Plus, we can keep this op separate from our own internal one."

Daniel drummed his hands dramatically on the tabletop. "Let's get this planned, gentleman! With Malachai's skills, he'll locate Hess in no time. Let's be ready."

Chapter Eight

HUGH FOUND AMY in the bedroom, staring at her reflection in the dresser mirror. He watched as she touched the short tendrils of hair on her forehead and then rubbed her bare neck. Her face was blank, even though her body radiated tension. He could almost see her vibrating.

"You look beautiful," he offered, leaning on the door frame.

He wasn't sure what she needed right now. He hung back, waiting on a clue from her. She'd been beaming when she confessed Claire had chosen the style. It really suited Amy's face and frame, too. Of course, she could be bald, and he would still find her attractive.

Finally, she turned toward him. Then she startled him by bursting into tears. On instinct, he marched into the bedroom and gathered her in his arms. He held her close as she made a damp area on his sweatshirt. Her loud sobs threatened to break him. He rubbed her back, kissed the side of her head, and felt his heart swell.

"Let it out," he whispered.

She was absolutely not the type of person to cry on anyone's shoulder. Her being this exposed to him was a gift, and he cherished it. He would stand here for hours if she needed him. Had something happened with Claire? They'd seemed happy. Was it seeing another woman with her niece? Was she regretting the drastic change in her hair?

One thing was certain, it wouldn't be something frivolous.

BY THE TIME her sobs tapered off into sniffles, Amy felt like a crybaby. Yet she loathed to pull away. This embrace felt so comfortable and nonjudgmental. She wanted to stay this way for hours, but the independent part of her protested. Hugh must have felt the shift, for he tousled the strands that fell over her forehead.

"You are utterly beautiful and sexy, Tink."

Amy pulled back to return his smile as best she could. She wanted to explain to him why she had unloaded so suddenly. She'd destroyed a link to Audrey. But she'd also reclaimed herself and strengthened her new relationship with her niece. So much emotional work for one morning! She should explain the hair story that tied her to Audrey, she figured.

"Before they rescued us, Audrey and I were sexually assaulted."

Whoa! The words were out before she even thought about them. What the hell was her mouth doing? Almost no one knew this part of the story. It wasn't anything she'd ever confessed to a sexual partner. Why now, and why him?

She backed up a few steps and could see Hugh as he froze. His eyebrows raised, and he blinked several times as he digested what she'd said. He looked at the far wall as he leaned on the dresser, digesting her bombshell.

Amy shifted her weight on her feet, something she did when preparing for a fight. *Wait. A fight?* Is that what she wanted? Had she said that to provoke a skirmish? To push him away?

Maybe. Her shoulders drooped as she admitted the truth. It was so much easier to fight than to cry. He'd gotten closer than she'd suspected, and while she wanted to hug him close, one part of her wanted to push him far away. Yeah, she was more comfortable with away.

Finally, after blowing out a breath and shaking his head, Hugh spoke. "Why didn't you tell me, before …?"

He waved his hand in the bed's direction. God, his entire face radiated pain and confusion. Yes, she was a bitch, but it was better to do this now than later. Later, it would hurt more.

She shrugged and looked away. "If I had, you would have been careful, gentle, and I would have hated it."

"OK, I CAN see that." Hugh nodded slowly.

So much now made sense to him. Why she concentrated on sex being fun and daring, but not intimate.

He had so many questions, but no idea how to ask them. A minute ago, she'd been in his arms, shaking with stark anguish. Then she'd gone on the offensive, finding a perfect way to push him back. She was even showing it. Her chin was thrust up, and her poker face hid her emotions.

He must have looked confused, because she huffed out a frustrated breath and turned away before explaining. Her voice was low and matter of fact. "The guy with the plan, Ajax, sent the other one to get The Duke. Unfortunately, that took time. Ajax grew bored. He started in on how attractive we were for white narcs. I told him he could do whatever he wanted to me, as long as he didn't touch Audrey."

She rubbed her collarbone before continuing. "Later … I could hear her crying, but they tied me up. I lost most of my voice, screaming about all the different ways I was going to kill him because he was hurting her."

Even though she wasn't facing him, Hugh turned on his heel. Jesus, she would hate him if she saw the tears in his eyes. Amy the Warrior. Protector of her sister to the detriment of herself. In his mind, he could see his tough, tiny Tink single-handedly defeat the room full of bad guys. But in reality … the worst had happened.

His heart broke for her. He swallowed past the lump in his throat. He desperately needed to say the right thing. He gave up trying to hide his emotions and turned back to her.

She was facing him, braced for a hit, her legs apart and arms loose by her sides. He swallowed again and tried to smile.

"Amy Stuart, you are the bravest, ballsiest woman I've ever known."

He wanted to cheer as she relaxed a bit. But her blue eyes were still full of suspicion. What more could he say?

Hoping it was the right thing, he added, "And nothing you've said makes me want you any less."

"Really?" she whispered.

Hugh gathered her in his arms before she had time to fight him. After endless minutes, she even relaxed against him and returned the embrace. He rubbed his cheek against her short hair and gave a sigh of thanks that he'd chosen correctly.

"I promise not to treat you as anything fragile." He added a pinch to her bottom. "Remember, I know you can kick my ass if I do."

The joke worked. She snuggled closer. Hugh's knees went weak with relief. How he was going to accomplish that, he didn't know. All he wanted to do the next time they were intimate, was to make love to her slowly and thoroughly, worshiping her body and her mind. He also knew she wouldn't stand for that.

He jumped when she pinched his butt in return. "C'mon. Let's go buy some paint. I'll redo my makeup while you grab that part you need to match."

Later, he was glad she'd ended the moment before he did something colossally stupid, like tell her how he felt. Yet surely, she was developing deeper feelings for him. *Right?* He doubted many people knew the secret she'd bestowed on him. As much as he wanted to proclaim his love from the rooftops and beg her to stay, he knew it would result only in her running away. He had to be patient.

Plus, he had a secret of his own. *How would she react?* His worst fear was that it would transform things between them, just as it had affected every relationship he'd had until now.

IT AMAZED AMY that the day ended up being a good one, after all. The home store had been fairly deserted this time of year, even though it was a Saturday. Hugh confessed he normally shopped at large stores early in the morning or late at night to avoid the crowds. Their trip was uncomplicated and easy.

By late afternoon, they had the sunroom prepped for painting. They clustered the furniture in the middle and covered them with a tarp. Taping off the door and windows took so much time that Amy's shoulders were stiff when they finished. She rolled them, easing the tension, feeling pleased by their work.

During the task, they listened to music and periodically chatted about topics ranging from politics to childhood toys. Earlier, she'd been hell bent on pushing him away. She recalled no conscious change of plan. Being around him was like standing in the sun. She'd been cold for so long, it wouldn't hurt to thaw a little, would it? She was made of stern stuff. She deserved to relax for once, didn't she?

How could she feel so peaceful after the morning's upheaval? The cry had surely been cathartic, judging by how she felt afterward. That must be it. A tremendous step in accepting what had happened to her sister, plus connecting with Claire. That was why she felt good. Normally, she'd hide in a closet, wrapped in her guilt and anger. Well, there was still a chance of that happening once she was alone, she knew.

She also knew that she had no intention of going back to her hotel room tonight. Along with the stillness she felt was also a giant dose of lust. While they worked, she couldn't keep her eyes off Hugh. His long fingers gracefully smoothing the blue tape in place. The bulge of the muscles in his forearms when they moved the sofa. Even how sweat caused his hair to curl. *Those damned rakish curls!*

She let the electricity move through her veins, drawing it out. It felt healthy to be horny. This feeling she knew, comfortably. Her body craved an outlet. *Not that different from crying*, she thought. Merely another form of release. Plus, this guy hit all her buttons. All the times they'd been together, and she wasn't bored yet. Far from it.

Later in the afternoon, they were sitting around the kitchen table, discussing dinner options, when she couldn't hold back any longer. In one easy move, she straddled Hugh's lap, grinding herself against the beginnings of the erection she could feel through his jeans. *Ah!* Maybe he'd been eyeing her all day, too.

His firm hands grasped her hips, slowly dragging her back and forth against his crotch. All the while, he kept eye contact. His lips parted as his breathing deepened. It was sexy as hell, and Amy wanted to come immediately. Her fingers dug into his shoulders as she pressed herself closer.

"Oh, McCoy! I feel the need to bang you like a screen door in a tornado," she drawled, trying for the right amount of Southern twang.

Well, now. She'd actually shocked him speechless. Hugh gaped at her for a long moment, then raised his brows and giggled. Out came the adorable dimple.

"I don't think I've ever had that pleasure. Your wish

is my command, slugger."

He kissed her – a hot, passionate kiss – while trying to stand. He swayed, off-balance with her weight. She smiled and wiggled free. He moved to kiss her again, but she held up a hand.

"Bedroom. Naked. Now."

She raced up the steps, laughing as she heard him stomping behind her. She knew she would get there first, thanks to her head start and his bad knee. By the time he entered the room, she was by the bed, pulling off her top. He stumbled as she unhooked her bra and let it fall. She moved on to unlacing her boots, but Hugh still only watched. As sexy as that made her feel, she was too far gone.

"Need to hurry, babe." She gestured to his clothing.

The giggle she so adored burst out of him again as he quickly toed off his sneakers and whipped his t-shirt over his head. By the time she'd slipped out of her leggings, he was gloriously naked and on the bed. One arm was behind his head, while his other hand loosely stroked his hard cock. This time, Amy froze. If she wasn't already turned on, seeing him touch himself was sufficient.

"Ready to show me the banging?" he whispered, and pulled on a condom.

Without delay, she climbed on the bed, straddling him. She ran his cock from her clit to her opening and back again. A full-body shiver wracked her. *Damn.* She could do this for hours, but she needed him inside, now. Lining them up, she lowered herself with a loud moan.

"AMY!" HUGH CRIED her name, partly for the way he felt

sliding inside her, and partly because of the look of ecstasy on her face.

He wasn't under any illusions that he was the best lover on earth, but damn, if she didn't make him feel that way. She leaned forward to place her hands on his chest. This caused her breasts to sway enticingly, and he couldn't resist touching them. When he pinched her perfect nipples, she ground against him, and he pushed back. Too soon, she sat back with a wicked grin.

She arched her back and began to raise and lower herself slowly. It was maddening; it was perfect. Her body undulated like she was dancing. Hugh swore she had never looked sexier – her eyes half-lidded and full of need. Her mouth parted as she gasped every time he filled her. She was so wet and hot around him. She was close, he could tell.

He reached out and circled her clit, but she pulled his hand away with a teasing smile. "Oh, no. You just watch."

She touched herself, and Hugh threw his hands back to find his pillow. He needed something to hold on to; Jesus, this might kill him. What a way to go, though. He frantically attempted to fill his head with case laws, anything not to come too soon. She was the epitome of sexy – one hand stroked her clit, and the other rolled a nipple. She threw her head back and moved faster.

HUGH'S FACE WAS a sweaty grimace. Amy felt him trying to move under her, to thrust into her as she pushed back. Lord have mercy – his arms! He was clutching the pillow with all his might, and his biceps bulged.

She had the urge to bite one, but before she could lean forward, Hugh licked his lips. Then a different urge overcame her, and she froze.

Hugh's face immediately switched to concern. "What is it?"

"I want your mouth on me," she gasped.

She'd expected him to hesitate, to make sure he knew exactly what she wanted, but he surprised her once again. As she finished the sentence, his hands were on her hips, lifting her off and bouncing her onto the mattress next to him. Another two seconds, and he had a pillow wedged under her butt and his shoulders between her legs.

His first contact was not slow or careful. Fingers took the place of his cock, and then his mouth and tongue devoured her. She screeched in delight, bowing her back in response. It was difficult for her feet to find purchase on the sheet, splayed open as she was. Consuming; that was the correct word. His mouth, his tongue, even his teeth, consumed her. It'd been so long since she'd enjoyed this, and he obliterated her past experiences in the first few seconds. *Lord, he was good at this!*

She moaned, gasped, and cried, "Jesus, Hugh! Fuck! That's so good. I can't … don't stop, Hugh!"

She managed to get one hand in his hair that was curled with sweat. Then he focused with intensity on the right spots, and she came with almost a scream. He prolonged the orgasm with precisely enough pressure, and Amy wondered if it would last forever. It was like touching a live wire. Her body buzzed with reaction, yet she couldn't move for anything.

ONLY WHEN SHE was a shaking, shuddering, incoherent work of art, did Hugh sit back on his haunches. *Fuck*, he'd never seen her more beautiful. He felt like a king. He had done this to her. God, it had been all he'd dreamed and more. Her taste was exquisite, and he could have stayed between her thighs for hours.

But as much as he'd like to sit and stare, his cock was aching like never before. He wanted to fuck her so hard, she would never forget today. He wanted to mark her with love bites, tattoo his kisses all over her.

He flipped her over, so the pillow was under her hips, her ass raised. He covered her with his body and slipped back inside her. She arched her back, taking him deeper.

"Fuck, baby. That's perfect," he groaned, and began moving with long, slow strokes.

"More," she gasped, and shifted underneath him.

He moved onto his elbows so he wasn't crushing her. "More what, Amy? Faster? Harder?"

"Everything!" she cried. "I want you to come as hard as I did."

That did it. She was a strong woman; he knew that. He also knew she would kick his ass if he held back out of fear of hurting her. He levered himself up, grasping her hands in his, and let go. The bed frame creaked as he pounded away, driven on by her encouraging cries.

When his release came, he feared he screamed as loud as she had. He tried to shift his body, taking some weight off of her, but the truth was, he couldn't move any further if his life depended on it. He felt her thumbs rubbing the sides of his now relaxed fists. She turned her head to face him.

So gorgeous, he thought, seeing her half-lidded eyes. It wasn't just that she looked thoroughly fucked. She did, indeed. It was the warmth in her face that did him in. She'd let down one more wall, and he'd been welcomed in a few feet more. He was suffused with lust, male pride, and another emotion that he quickly pushed away. Another time. If he knew anything about the luscious Ms. Stuart, it was to keep things light.

By God, he'd use that to his advantage and hope it helped worm his way into her heart. It was worth a try. If the relationship failed, at least he'd know he'd given it his all. She was worth a bruised heart.

Somehow, he was able to move to take care of the condom, and then made it back to the bed. Amy curled into his side, rubbing her face against his chest like a cat. Her satisfied smile made him happy. A moment later, he yelped in surprise as she pinched him.

"What was that for?" he asked, not too concerned since she was still smiling.

"I admit – you have skills," she mumbled against his skin.

He felt his face actually heat. "Well, I wanted to tell you I was world-renowned, but I thought you might not believe me, since I misplaced the trophy."

He felt the breath from her chuckle tickle his pecs. "Oh, really?"

"Absolutely. Experience and enthusiasm, baby. I even do daily tongue exercises." The exaggeration tapered off into giggles. "But I can always use more practice." He hugged her closer. "Actually, that was a piss-poor example. You came too quickly. I demand a do-over."

She tilted her head back to smile up at him. "I think I can handle that."

He wanted her to know that he'd been dying for a taste of her. He was dying to do it again. He wanted more time with her, both in and out of bed. He could spend hours staring at her. Yep, he was in so deep, there was no sign of the shore. But thanks to everything that had happened today, she must be at least in the same ocean, even if only up to her knees. He was perfectly at peace in this moment with her.

Telling her how he felt would be an idiot decision, he knew. So, he held his tongue, not wanting to mess up the moment. She must have read his mind, for they stayed there, smiling at each other for the longest time.

DANIEL HAD BEEN correct: Malachai located Bertram Hess within eight hours. The former billionaire smuggler mustn't have anyone tech savvy in his remaining circle. Malachai caught him emailing from an unsecured cell phone. By the time DAG triangulated his location, Daniel, Del, and Peter were packed and ready to go.

Peter ignored all the silent side-eye questions from Del during the flight to LA. She hadn't asked for specifics when they informed her that Archie was flying them out for a meeting with a high-profile client. As team leader, she frequently attended such interviews. She'd only raised her eyebrows when, at the last minute, Peter told her to bring her go-bag.

Every agent had one, in case a last-minute op came up. It held basic weapons, communication gear, tactical clothing, and boots. Not anything you would need for a simple client meeting.

But Del was a pro and held her tongue until the three of them were alone in the rental car. The West Coast heat was a shock for this time of year, and she'd already tossed her suit jacket aside.

"OK, spill." She glared back at Peter, sitting in the backseat.

Daniel chuckled, but kept his eyes on the road. Tension was high. Combined with the heat, they were all edgy. He'd half expected Del to corner them on the plane, but he should have known not to underestimate her restraint. He had very little of that ability and didn't care to cultivate more. Which was why she led the agents, and he worked recruitment alone.

"We're here to find the man who planted the bombs," Peter explained.

"You mean we're here to find out how he knew where our agents were working." Del sat back with a frown.

"Bingo!" shouted Daniel.

Peter rolled his eyes at his partner's exuberance. "Yes."

Daniel was similar to a ferret: he had only two speeds, which were "high" and "off." It amazed Peter how Daniel's energy hadn't diminished in thirty years. Personally, Peter felt his own age, despite regular workouts. His internal energy focused inward, turning puzzles and data over in his head. Perhaps that was why they worked so well together. Total opposites, attacking issues from different angles.

Peter preferred to be in-between, like Malachai. The man was calm, centered, and worked in front of a computer for hours. Yet, he was laid-back only out from behind his desk. While working, Peter almost expected to see sparks flying off the technical guru.

Currently, Malachai must be generating an electrical storm back at the office, setting up the shadow network. Whatever they needed in order to lay a trap. Peter swallowed past the knot in his throat and turned his attention back to Del.

"Why the cover story?" she asked, and then her eyes widened. "You think there's a mole?"

Could it have been something in his expression, or was she that astute? He and Daniel had agreed to level with her. She was the least likely candidate, after all.

"We're not sure. We're banking that it isn't you." He gave her a pointed look when she turned back.

"This time." She rolled her eyes. "You know better."

Peter grinned back, but nausea rose in Del's throat at the idea of a rat. The team covered each other in life-or-death situations. Surely, none of them could be behind this! She knew her team, damn it!

She'd been there when they'd tried to rescue Kit. Saw how traumatized Peter's son had been.

And even though Amy and Whittaker seemed to have recovered from their close calls, Amy would have been killed if not for her remote start key fob. These people were her family, and the mere thought of a traitor was inconceivable.

Nevertheless, they must find the truth. She cringed, an awful thought shifting through her brain.

Why were both Peter and Daniel here?

"You brought the red case?" she asked, even though she already knew the answer.

Peter nodded, and her heart fell like a stone. He must have it tucked inside his go-bag. While she hadn't seen the pair in action, she had heard the stories, the rumors, and even some of the lies.

The red case was a holdover from their CIA days. It was updated every time new tools became available, but rarely used. Peter hated to use his skills to extract information if it went beyond the psychological. Daniel, however, was an adrenaline junkie and didn't mind using physical torture for the sake of the op. He never went too far, nor did he seem to enjoy inflicting pain, as far as she could discern. He just enjoyed pitting himself against a bad guy to get intel.

Since they were under a time constraint, several forms of extracting a confession were automatically taken off the table. No confining the perp to a small box or waterboarding. Del was fairly sure they hadn't practiced either for years. Luckily, there were pharmaceutical tools that worked within the psyche of whoever they dosed. Quick, effective, and efficient.

"Give me the details, then," she said, and listened while they explained on the way to the empty office building Malachai had rented.

CAPTURING HESS SHOULD have been easy. Turned out, he could afford to employ only two low-rent security guards to watch his back. It would have been a piece of cake, if any of her teammates had been there with Del.

Unfortunately, Peter's and Daniel's reflexes had aged along with their bodies. One of the guards managed to get off a shot as Peter pinned him down. The bullet went wild, heading toward Del. The only way to avoid it was to let go of the other guard and dive for the pavement.

Luckily, no one was hurt, but that guard managed to escape, heading out to the street from the hotel's underground parking garage. Del was glad she'd disabled the cameras beforehand. She doubted he would flag any sort of cop or security. He'd allowed his boss to be taken, so his best bet was to disappear.

"Fuck!" Peter swore as he cuffed the man and taped his mouth. "We need to hurry!"

Daniel had Hess in the van by the time Del and Peter joined him, the guard in tow. Hess had been easy — he was older and rotund. He didn't even attempt to run. With the four men hunkered down in the back, Del drove the family van out of the deck as if she didn't have a care in the world.

Once they were back in the office building, they dumped the guard in one room and dragged Hess to the other space they'd prepared. Del strapped him to the chair and then stepped back. Peter still wore an angry and embarrassed red flush on his face. She knew he needed to take over now to restore his pride. As they began, she stepped outside to find the case of bottled water they had stashed earlier. As much as she adored and respected these two men, she had no desire to watch this part.

PETER, FOR ONE, was happy she'd left. He was still

smarting from his earlier fuck-up. Bad enough it happened at all, but in front of Del? What a blow to his ego.

Despite his miserable physical state, Hess's mind was as sharp as ever. It took Peter almost an hour to get the answers they needed. It helped that Daniel had started to remove and polish some of his shiny, stainless steel tools. The ones with cutting edges were especially scary in the bright fluorescent lights.

"I bought it! I bought the info," Hess finally wheezed.

"We knew that," Peter said, as Daniel pulled a bone saw out of the red bag. "We need to know who from."

Hess didn't speak, and Peter sighed. "Looks like it's your turn." He nodded to Daniel.

It was Daniel's excited grin that did Hess in. It was his secret weapon. People saw it and immediately thought he was bat-shit crazy. It had probably saved his life on more occasions than a gun ever had. He'd started perfecting it after interrogating a serial killer early in his career. The trick was the dead eyes. That was the hardest part to fake.

He was proud that Amy had copied the smile. He hoped she would never perfect the soulless eyes, though. She was too full of life, even if she denied it. Damn, he hoped she hadn't turned. He'd been rooting for her ever since they met.

Daniel wanted to rage at the idea of a mole. It must have shown in his body language, because Hess began to squeal.

"OK! OK! Elliott Essa!" Hess cried.

"Who the fuck is he?" Peter asked, bewildered. That name wasn't on their radar.

"Middle-Eastern, a royal cousin or something. Runs a terrorist group, Red Winter."

Now that was a name familiar to them. Red Winter was not only a global terrorist organization, but they also financed themselves through heroin production. A large percentage of heroin sold in the US originated from them.

Peter and Daniel exchanged a perplexed look. Neither of the heads of Red Winter were named Essa. Nor were they any relation to a royal family. Peter nodded for Daniel to proceed. Daniel approached the man, wielding a pair of shiny pliers.

"No! It's the truth!" Hess began to cry, saliva flying as he spoke. "I paid him $2 million!"

"How did he get this info?" Daniel grasped Hess's hand that was strapped to the arm of the chair and carefully inserted thin pliers under his thumbnail.

"Someone on the inside!" Hess sobbed. "Essa said he was selling intel cheap in order to get revenge! I'm not the only one he sold to!"

Hess swore that was all he knew. He had no clue who the inside person was, who else bought information, or where Essa was located. They'd met in public at a bar in San Francisco. After an hour with Daniel and another shot of truth serum, Peter assumed the man had given up everything of note.

While Daniel packed up and wiped down the room, Peter called Malachai and delivered the news. Now they knew more about how Marius had found Peter's son and

Mick's girlfriend months ago. Same seller of inside intel.

"Elliott Essa. Got it." Malachai's voice was all business. "No idea why he wants revenge?"

"No clue. Essa might be an alias, or someone lying about being with Red Winter. All we can trust is that there is an inside operative. We need to activate the idea we had." Peter sighed.

"Everything is in place. Want me to wait until you two are back to announce my leave of absence?" Malachai's tone was heavy with despair. Unlike his two partners, he had no skills to hide his feelings.

"Let's wait a couple of weeks when the other ops end. Archie is waiting for us at the airport. We'll keep this new info to ourselves for now," Peter stated.

"Understood." Malachai hung up the phone, sorrow choking his voice.

AFTER SPENDING THE weekend together, Amy felt at loose ends on Monday. Hugh was in court most of the day, and that evening, he was meeting former frat buddies for dinner. She wasn't due to see Claire again until tomorrow afternoon.

As always, she'd been up early, gnashing her teeth over the lack of news from Skeet. She really didn't give a damn about his illness. She wanted closure, damn it.

Especially now that she had something in her life to look forward to – Claire. She sand her niece didn't need her guilt hanging over them like a thundercloud. Once she had Ajax in her custody, she could do what needed to be done and then move on with her life. Every second she spent waiting seemed like an eternity, and she was tired of it.

She decided a trip to the High Museum of Art or the Georgia Aquarium would keep her busy and entertained that afternoon. She rarely had time for such mundane escapades, but it would keep her brain and her feet active.

After a hasty breakfast, she worked her frustration out at the gym and was a sweaty mess when her cell chimed. Her stomach dropped when she realized it wasn't DAG with an update. But it was a text from Hugh, so she had to smile.

Hugh: *"I have time for lunch, if you want to meet?"*

Amy: *"Name the time."*

Hugh: *"1pm. Come to the courthouse? Plenty of restaurants nearby."*

Amy: *"Sure."*

Hugh: *"Wait for me outside. The less time I spend in the busy atrium, the better."*

Amy: *"See you then!"*

She had just enough time to shower, change, drive, and, hopefully, get lucky finding a place to park. She could be a tourist after lunch. She'd much rather see hunky McCoy than a sculpture or a shark.

THROUGH THE ENTRANCE to the courthouse, Amy saw a room filled with people busily moving from one place to another. She milled about outside, looking for a sight of Hugh. She was anxious to see him in attorney mode.

She paused as if her boot had encountered a big

puddle of tar when he walked into view from out of the crowd. She may have even gasped, but she would never admit it.

His navy suit must be custom made, the way it fit his shoulders and thighs. Ditto the white shirt that stretched across his chest. Even the red-striped tie screamed money, somehow. Brown leather shoes showed enough wear to be taken seriously, as did the long tan coat slung over his arm. His hair was gelled away from his face, even the back curls tamed. He was business-hot hotness personified.

She touched her messy bangs. *Damn*, she should have made more of an effort, knowing they were meeting at the courthouse. Her faded jeans and thick sweater were not dressy enough, but she'd been in a hurry to get here on time. *Oh, well.* At least the slow traffic had allowed her enough time to apply lipstick.

He exited the building, stopping to take a deep breath. She knew braving that crowded gauntlet was difficult for him. Her chest swelled with pride as he seemed to shake it off and began looking for her.

He found her, and she locked her knees at his brilliant smile. Hugh walked over, and she finally noticed the young man who was accompanying him. He was as tall as Hugh and rail thin, like many guys in their late teens. She noted the pressed shirt and tie that must have come from Neddra's closet. His eyes were wide, and she saw perspiration along his hairline. *Poor guy.* She knew court could be overwhelming.

"Amy, this is Todd, my client. Todd, this is my friend, Amy."

"Hi, Todd." She smiled and extended her hand.

"Ma'am." He was soft-spoken, and his palm was wet with sweat.

Hugh nodded to a bench on the far wall. "I'll be free in a sec."

Amy took the cue, leaving him to confer with his client. She watched as he braced a steadying hand on Todd's shoulder and spoke with his head low. Between his words and his body language, Todd relaxed and nodded along. After a handshake, Todd bolted for the street.

She stood as Hugh approached, and they walked from the shade of the building out into the sunshine. Hugh's mouth was tight, and his eyes shadowed. Was it a response to the loud bustle of the courthouse, or something else?

"Trouble with your case?" she asked, and hastily added, "Not that it's any of my business!"

Hugh sighed, but gave her a quick smile. "I'm simply frustrated. So many kids make one mistake and can't afford help. No one deserves to go to prison for a little pot, or a busted taillight, or stealing food."

Anyone else might have expressed indignation, but Amy had been a cop. School-to-prison pipelines and racism were realities, no matter how many good cops she'd known. Court-appointed attorneys often had no time to advise their clients about how to speak in court, and that could put another mark against a defendant who was belligerent only out of fear. Factor in the corrupt cops, the racist cops, and the cops who were lazy, and it often spelled doom for those they encountered.

While she'd known many good cops and some gung-ho public defenders, she'd never met anyone like Hugh. He could be making big bucks working in business or tax law. That he'd picked to fight for justice instead made him a kindred spirit. In a way, she was in awe because his path was more on the ground than hers was. A pang of envy zinged into her chest, but she couldn't see herself as an attorney. No way.

Amy opened her mouth to agree, but before she could speak, someone called out Hugh's name.

She turned to see a woman sauntering toward them on tasteful and expensive-looking high heels. Amy tugged on her baggy sweater, again cursing herself for not doing her hair.

This woman was gorgeous, flat-out beautiful. Yet she downplayed it with her dark suit and conservative blouse. She probably had amazingly thick hair, but the dark strands were pulled back in a flawless twist. The opposite of Amy's own air-dried pixie cut. The worst part was that she seemed genuinely thrilled to see Hugh. He probably wore a similar expression, but Amy refused to look. *What you don't know, can't hurt you.*

"Leigh!" Hugh returned the woman's hug. "What brings you to the courthouse?"

"Having lunch with my cousin. He just joined the DA's office." She waved an elegant hand, and her gold bracelet glittered in the sunlight.

Hugh turned to introduce them. Amy prayed she had dug the last of the paint out from under her nails. Thank God she was skilled at oozing confidence in tough situations. It was automatic, so she shouldn't worry. But then, why was she so anxious?

"Leigh Baker, this is Amy Stuart. Amy, Leigh represents Atlanta on the state Senate. Amy is helping me with a case."

The women shook hands, and Amy forced her arms to hang casually by her sides afterward. She wanted to cross her arms or pull them behind her back. The instinct made her furious. She had experience dealing with powerful people. Why was she feeling like this?

You know why, she mentally slapped herself. It appeared that Leigh and Hugh had been involved at some point. Intimately involved. The woman was practically devouring him with her eyes, her hand possessive on his arm.

"Do you remember Cait Thompson?" the woman asked, stepping closer to Hugh. "We once stayed at her cabin in Vail?"

Oh, fuck you, Amy thought. She tuned out the conversation, not needing any more proof that this woman had once screwed Hugh. Why flaunt it to Amy? She would admit to a little jealousy. Maybe a small bit. Not a deep, clawing beast that wanted to pry itself free and maul this woman. Certainly not.

Amy was so intent on not glaring at the couple, she jumped when Hugh put a hand on her back.

"Great to see you." He nodded to Leigh. "Congrats on your cousin's new job."

The woman wagged her fingers in goodbye and sauntered off. She spared not even a glance at Amy. Which made her equally relieved and furious. She couldn't fault Hugh – he'd behaved like a gentleman. The hand on her back had been a subtle way to show that they were more than colleagues. If she weren't so mature, she would have smirked. The hunky lawyer was leaving with her. Not the gorgeous, rich woman from his past. If he wanted Leigh back, he could always wait until after Amy went back to DC.

That thought plunged a knife into her back. OK, *now* she might be a little jealous. They had no future, and why should she care what he did after she left? This was only a temporary affair.

She needed to remind herself of reality. Her perceptions became tangled around this man. In his presence, she could almost forget her own name and the fact she wanted nothing lasting.

"There's a great cafe right around the corner." Hugh pointed to his right.

"Sounds good," she replied, trying to sound aloof and composed.

Luckily, they'd missed the lunch rush. They ordered at the counter and took the numbered disc to place on their table. Hugh took off his jacket and loosened his tie before grinning ruefully across at her.

"Leigh was part of my father's grand plan."

Amy held up a hand. "Hey. You don't have to explain anything to me."

She knew from practice that she looked and sounded unconcerned. How he saw through that, she hadn't a clue. She'd lost count of how many perps and operatives she had fooled over the years. It was damned unsettling how he'd guessed that she was a tiny bit jealous.

He shook his head, smiling, and grabbed her hand.

"Leigh is on track to run for Lt. Governor. We were together until I wanted to give up politics. She picked her career, and there were no hard feelings."

Amy hmphed but didn't pull her hand away. "She wanted to jump you."

Hugh blushed. Lord, he was sexy when he did that. Especially when he twisted his mouth and the elusive dimple made an appearance.

"Well, the feeling wasn't mutual." His voice dipped, and he stroked the side of her hand with his thumb. "If the relationship had been that intense, we couldn't have parted as friends."

Amy rolled her eyes but decided to believe him. She didn't think he was bullshitting her; rather it was the nice guy code: *love the one you're with*. Not that the L-word belonged here. It was just a saying.

HUGH WAS IN deep. He stared at the woman across the table, stunned by how pretty she was. Her thick sweater made him want to snuggle her in front of a fire. Her jealousy over Leigh was also charming. Why would he prefer a woman who was mainly interested in amassing power? Amy also lived her job, but she was focused on making the world better.

Their food arrived, and they dug in. During the meal, Hugh received several messages, but he ignored them until one came from Neddra. He apologized to Amy and called the office.

"The printer crashed again." Neddra repeated what she'd texted.

"Shit. I don't have time to come and fix it. Can you

use the one at the grocery again?"

"I can." Neddra's voice was peeved.

"I know, I know." Hugh sighed. "I'll make a decision soon."

He groaned and ended the call. He pinched the bridge of his nose and answered Amy's inquisitive look.

"The office copier is old and has hang-ups. So far, I've been able to fix it myself. Neddra thinks we need a new one, but they are pricey to even lease."

"Ah," Amy said. "Why agree to a lease when you might decide not to stay?"

"Yeah! I know, I need to make a decision!" Hugh snapped.

When she sat back in surprise, he knew he was over-reacting. This morning, he'd felt so torn. He had a solid case with Todd. He'd felt centered until chatting with two guys he had worked with as ADAs. They teased him about selling out, leaving a job where the bad guys were sent to jail to go help low life's skate on pot charges. He swallowed the bile of second guesses that now sat heavily in his gut.

"Deciding to keep the office? You've barely begun. Why not agree to give it at least another year? I hate to think of you losing too much money if this isn't what you want, but you need to give it time before you give up," she suggested.

His mouth compressed into a thin, peeved line. She was trying to help, but she had no idea. She'd trusted him with some of her mysteries; it was time he divulged his own. He knew it was a risk – she would see and treat him differently after she found out the truth. It was human nature.

He looked around to make sure no one was nearby and divulged his secret. "It's not the commitment. Not really. The issue is, I would have to use money from my inheritance." He sighed. "I bought my house while I was still employed. Everything about the office, I used my own savings. I have enough for a year or so with no enormous expenses, and a copier would be an enormous expense."

"The inheritance is your money now. What's wrong with taking some? With your low rates, you'll need to eventually, right?" Amy's brow knitted with confusion.

"Yeah." Hugh sighed again and blinked against a sudden headache. "I don't want to touch it until I have a plan for all the money."

"I don't understand. Why do you need a plan? Use some, save the rest. Why does that upset you?"

Hugh looked at her in suspicion, but she seemed genuinely dumbfounded. She reached across the table and grasped his hand. He looked at her short, unpainted nails, so different and preferable over Leigh's manicured talons. He adored the way she looked gorgeous even when it was clear she wasn't trying. He was crazy about her and ready to end it all with his confession.

"You don't have to tell me. I only want to help, Hugh. Something about this has you in knots. It can't only be about money." Her blue eyes shone with concern, and that did him in.

"Amy. My father left me $18 million," he whispered.

"Whoa. Well, shit." Her mouth fell open.

Hugh slumped in his seat, pushing the remains of his

meal away. The secret was out. He tried to brace himself for a change in Amy. How differently would she treat him? How hard would she scold him for not doing what his father had wanted?

That had been Leigh's reaction. The money would have gone a long way to securing his place in state politics. When he had informed her of his decision to go his own way, she'd been mature enough to not ask for a campaign contribution. Unlike so many of his contemporaries, who'd rushed to set up meetings after his father's death. Women came out of the woodwork, all of them fake and insincere. The memories made him itch. He sat back and held his breath, waiting for her response.

Chapter Nine

YES, SHE KNEW her initial response was inane, but that was … unexpected. She had assumed his inheritance was a couple million or so. *I mean, look at his office. Look at Hugh!* Other than the snazzy SUV, he lived middle-class at best. She had assumed his mother had been the principal beneficiary. Perhaps she still was, since Amy had no clue the extent of the entire family's fortune. Fortune looked to be the correct word, and it spun around her head, making her dizzy.

Wow. She honestly had no clue how to proceed, other than keeping hold of his hand. He looked desperate, in need of a lifeline. Plus, she simply loved touching him.

"I'm paralyzed at deciding how to use it," he admitted. "The amount … most days I can't even wrap my head around it."

"Who said you had to decide right away?" she finally asked, wondering if she'd missed part of his declaration. Was there a time limit? She had no clue how inheritances worked.

"No one," he mumbled. "Just me. I guess it's guilt."

He shifted in his seat and finally looked up at her. "I tried to give it to my mother. She refused. I started plans to split it between charities, but once I started researching, it was overwhelming. I didn't want to support an organization that spent most of its money on staff salaries and bonuses. Amado has refused all but one million because of their endowment."

He shrugged. "I'm stuck. I've been stuck. I feel like if I touch a part of it, it will be a slippery slope that I can't come back from. I do *not* want my family's money to finance my life. I want to make my own way. But before I know it, a copier could lead to new carpets, or a new roof for my house. Then before I know it, I'm relying on it and hating myself."

"I understand," she whispered.

She thought she did, at least. She could certainly understand the fierce independence they shared. She had worked hard, saved money and invested so that she never had to ask her parents for money. That was an enormous source of pride for her. Who knows? That massive amount of money might tie her in knots, too.

All she knew was that this dilemma caused him pain, and she wanted to help. His normally sparkling eyes were shadowed, and she could see a muscle jump where he clenched his jaw. How could she make him happy again?

"I can loan you the money for a copier," she began, hoping to lighten the mood, but he shook his head. "Hey, I have a good deal saved up. DAG pays well, I don't own a car, and I rent."

"Thank you." He managed a smile that didn't quite

reach his eyes.

"Well, you love that shitty office." She grinned, forging ahead. She could fix this for him. "You provide a needed service that makes you feel good. What's the problem with me blowing money on a copier to help you out?"

Hugh shook his head. "Nice to know you believe in my work. The copier is only the symptom. No, I have to solve this on my own. And my office isn't shitty." This time his eyes twinkled with humor.

"Yes, it is." She smiled back. "But it's that way on purpose."

"True," he admitted. "When can I see you next?"

She held back her frustration as he changed the subject. There was so much more she wanted to know about him and why he was so torn over the money. Yet, she knew this was his call, and she had to follow his lead. They could discuss it later, in private. Of course, the word private brought to mind more carnal thoughts, like how amazing he felt moving inside her.

"You aren't tired of me yet?" she laughed, a thrill shooting down her spine.

"I think I could stand you forever," Hugh responded immediately.

As soon as the sentence was out, he froze. Amy, of course, panicked. *Was he serious?* This was too much, too fast, despite her possessive feelings an hour ago.

She frantically searched for a way to let him know when his smile widened. "What's not to like about hot-as-hell sex? Plus, anyone puts a hit out on me, I have my very own bodyguard."

Amy relaxed. *Good, he didn't mean it that way,* she thought.

"Why would someone put a hit on you?" she asked, scrambling to match his teasing tone.

Hugh shrugged, a mock sad expression on his face. "No one. Sadly, I'm not that exciting. But if it ever happened, could I pay you in homemade meals?"

"Yes," she laughed.

LUNCH ENDED ON an upbeat note, despite his inheritance bombshell. Ever the gentleman, he insisted on walking her to her car. His goodbye kiss was thorough, but with an edge of sweetness. His long fingers slid into her short strands of hair, holding her face immobile. She breathed in his subtle cologne that reminded her of a rainstorm. *Ever the water baby*, she thought. The embrace ended when he brushed his lips over each of her eyelids before dropping his hands. She smiled up at him, squinting in the sunlight, thrilled that she'd helped salvage his bad day.

She wished she could solve his dilemma. It was so frustrating not being able to swoop in and solve a problem. She had to wait for him to find a solution. That didn't mean she couldn't do some research on her own to find a way to help. She should ask Malachai or Mateo about the best ways to narrow down a list of beneficial charities.

At least Hugh was being practical, in that with his low rates, he knew he would eventually need some of the money, and he'd rather do that than raise his fees. As always, her heart fluttered at his choice of how to use his degrees. In her line of work, she frequently dealt with people on the opposite extreme – greedy, selfish, and cruel. It was heartening to know she and her team were not alone in the fight to help.

Back at her room, she messaged Malachai first since she wasn't sure whether or not Mateo was currently in prison. She couldn't imagine what his ordeal was like. He was a double agent, undercover in his own dangerous and violent past. He was an enigma to most of the team. He was fairly new, very quiet, and not available for most group ops. Yet there was something trustworthy about him. She knew DAG's background investigations were extensive and even included personality testing. Anything to make the team better.

She frowned. Maybe she should suggest adding a test to the mix that might have warned Mick would be a shitty boyfriend. She snagged a bottle of water from the fridge, her spirit rising when she realized it'd been days since she had last thought of the bastard.

Her phone pinged with an alert, and she expected to see an answer from Malachai. Instead, the message instructed her to phone Peter.

Was she finally being updated? Her day was looking up in other ways now. She hit the contact button and tapped her foot while it rang once before he answered.

Peter wasn't one for pleasantries. "Skeet's a dead end, Amy."

Damn it. She sighed and sat on the sofa, her tasty lunch now weighing heavily in her gut.

"He's low in the hierarchy, and I doubt The Duke even knows his name," he explained.

"But he is part of the gang, right?" Her tone was sharp.

"Yes," Peter replied. "So, if you want to trade him for info –"

"Yes!" Amy interrupted, her heart racing. "You know what I want to trade for, Peter."

Of course, he knew. She'd made sure they had written it into her employment contract, just in case, so that Peter couldn't later change his mind. It was brutal, but necessary to her mental health. Hell, even to her survival, if being able to stay in contact with Claire counted.

"Very well," Peter conceded without emotion. "Give us a day to arrange transport."

"Will do," she replied, her heart banging in her chest like a jackhammer.

Amy ended the call, unsure if the knot in her stomach was from excitement or dread. Peter had approved the trade. Skeet knew nothing of value past some basics of The Duke's enterprises. Moreover, according to an email sent this weekend, they now had confirmation that the bomb was unrelated to her op. Like Kit's abduction, it was just another way to shake up DAG.

Amy hadn't asked questions. She guessed she should have, but Peter had pointed out the obvious: Hess would go after the other agents now. She and Whittaker were in the clear. Del, Mick, and Archie were tracking every move Hess made online, in person, and over the phone.

Normally, she would have itched to be part of such an op. Now her endgame was here, and that was all she could focus on. Within the hour, she had the details.

Peter used the contact info obtained from Skeet to

arrange a meet with The Duke. There would be a trade, and Amy would be their representative. Surely, he would remember her – she'd made his life such hell after her kidnapping.

The Duke's only reply was to name a time and place: tomorrow, 2pm, at a small park in Brookhaven. Del would deliver Skeet and act as her backup.

Amy blew out a breath. Lordy, Hugh would hate her if he found out what she was planning. If this was to be what ended their relationship, then so be it, she thought with a heavy heart. It would end, regardless. Whatever relationship or fling they had was nothing compared to what she owed Audrey.

She would make up some story about why she couldn't see him tomorrow. She would claim work. He shouldn't be suspicious. She would feel a small pang as she lied to him, but justice for Audrey was paramount to her. She hesitated to cancel her plans with Claire. She would have to wait and see.

THE NEXT DAY, Amy was waiting outside impatiently when Del pulled up in a white panel van. Amy hopped in, sat her backpack between her feet, and they sped off. She glanced in the back after she buckled her seat belt to see Skeet tied up and gagged on the bare floor. He looked to be asleep.

"Had to drug him," Del explained. "I drove him down. He should come around soon."

"Are you flying back?" How could she sound so normal when her heart was thundering in her chest?

"I haven't decided yet. Things are quiet in the office.

I may drive back and stop in Virginia, see some friends." Del squinted, even though she wore sunglasses.

Amy directed her to turn at the next intersection. She was grateful for the seatbelt that held her steady. She was so pumped, she wanted to bounce with anticipation.

"What's the plan?" Del asked, and Amy was again grateful Peter had sent her. Del was all about the details, zero bullshit.

"We're making a trade. Frosted Tips here for Audrey's rapist. The Duke has been hiding him since the abduction."

"Oh!" Del's eyebrows went up. "I see. Your plan for him is…?" She took her eyes off the road to give Amy a pointed look.

"Probably just shoot him. Then celebrate," Amy replied matter-of-factly. "I've had fantasies of torturing him in all sorts of ways, but now I just want quick closure. I have the opportunity for a relationship with Claire, and I want to be done with this part of my past."

Del was silent for a bit, as Amy continued to give directions. Del shouldn't be shocked; Amy had spoken of this before. Not that she herself had any qualms about today. How could she? She'd planned this for three years. The only change being the manner in which Ajax would die.

Not only had she imagined the torture, but she'd also investigated techniques and outcomes. She'd wanted Ajax to know the same agony he'd put her family through. Suddenly, though, that part wasn't important. One shot and done, then on with the rest of her life. Justice would be served.

"Amy, you've never killed anyone. It changes you. I know you have it in your head that it'll sweep away the guilt you feel, but there's no guarantee it'll work that way." Her friend kept her tone even.

"Del, I appreciate the warning, but I'm not changing my mind." Of course, Del would warn her. She also knew her friend would back her decision, whatever it was. Amy didn't fault her, especially considering Del's past and the reason she joined DAG. Killing left a mark, even when it was justified.

Quiet descended, and finally Del nodded. "I should have time to help with disposal before meeting Archie."

That horrible, crude offer brought tears to Amy's eyes. What a good friend Del was. In a big city, there were endless places to hide a dead body. Amy also knew of abandoned homes within twenty minutes of the park where she could finish off Ajax. A quick death was better than he deserved, but she no longer felt the need to draw it out.

"I found a perfect spot to park last night," Amy explained. "Clear view of the meet spot. Don't show the guy until I wave my hat."

She took off her red baseball cap and showed it to Del. Yes; it was Hugh's hat, which she'd been meaning to return ever since the night of the bar fight. She'd kept it for some reason she couldn't explain. Wearing it today for good luck? An apology? After this, it would be tainted, and she would trash it.

"Whoa!" Del exclaimed, sending her several surprised glances while also steering the van. "Big change!"

Oh, her hair. Amy blushed and fixed the cap back

over her short hair. She'd grown used to it, even after three days. The feel of air on her neck made her feel more alive, more connected to the world. She never realized how her messy knots had caused her head to ache all the time. The absence was striking.

"I love it. It suits you," Del said.

"How so?" she chuckled, curious.

Del laughed. "Down to business. I always figured you kept the long hair for undercover work, to look innocent. It didn't match your demeanor. *This* style screams, you're here to take no shit."

Amy actually laughed in delight. They were quiet until Skeet twisted in his restraints and moaned as the sedative began to wear off. In response, Del turned up the radio, blasting the interior with classical music.

Brookhaven was at the top of the perimeter, near Lenox Mall, where Amy had shopped and not too far from Chris's home in Buckhead. They turned down a residential street where original brick homes were slowly being replaced by McMansions. Amy wrinkled her nose in distaste. She much preferred where Hugh lived. The extra drive was worth the privacy. Here, she could almost reach out her window and touch the neighboring house.

The park began at the end of the street. As they approached, she could make out a single man sitting at one of the picnic tables under a covered structure. There were too many vehicles with tinted windows nearby to tell which ones held his posse. Mothers with children swarmed the nearby playground. The tennis courts were empty. The air was filled with the sound of kids screaming in delight and traffic noise from the nearby parkway.

Calm descended over her as she made her way to the picnic table, replacing her earlier frenetic energy. Yes, this was an op, but it was the ultimate op for her. The accumulation of three years of excruciating guilt, over not only what had happened to Audrey, but also her own inability to bring the man responsible to justice. Time seemed to slow to a crawl as she approached. She savored each second, knowing her moment of triumph was at hand.

The Duke sat there, facing her with both hands flat on the concrete top. The fact that he watched her added to her determination. *That's right*, she thought; *I'm finally coming for you, and you have to give up what you owe me.*

She sat across from him, mimicking his hand placement. The dark red wood felt uneven under her fingertips. He looked older than she'd expected. Technically, he wasn't much older than she was, but the years had been harder on him. The Duke was tall and slight, but with the beginnings of a beer gut. Gray sparkled in his hair and beard. There were more lines in his face now, his complexion more ashen. *Running a drug empire takes its toll*, she thought, without a shred of sympathy.

"It surprised me when you asked for a trade," he began. "I'd have thought that you'd prefer to take me down."

Amy shrugged. "Next time, perhaps."

He grinned, showing off a gold tooth embedded with a diamond. He nodded to the van where Del was watching them intently.

"Skeet in there?"

"Yes." Amy nodded. "Where's Ajax?"

The Duke sighed and shook his head. "You won't like this, Ms. Stuart."

Amy's hands balled into fists, and she glared across the table. She wanted to pull the gun out from behind her back, but knew he had people watching, just as Del was. No, it had to be a lie. Damned bastard was trying to renege on their agreement! He should know DAG could tear him to pieces.

The Duke folded his hands and actually shot her a look of apology. "He's dead. He's been dead for years. As soon as I found out what happened, I took care of him, personally."

Amy was numb. *What?* Ajax was dead? Pain, fury, and confusion rendered her mute, and The Duke filled the silence with his deep voice.

"He disobeyed me. He thought by kidnapping you, it would please me." He shook his head. "Fucking idiot. And then, he availed himself to you and your sister. You know I couldn't let that insolence stand."

"Why agree to this meet, then?" she snapped.

"I want that traitor back." He nodded toward the van.

She laughed. "You have nothing to trade!"

She rose, but he motioned for her to wait. She hesitated before sitting back down. Her instincts said to either scream and rage or shoot him. Neither was a good option right now. They were in public. She took a deep breath to regain her composure and waited.

"I would not presume to nullify a deal with DAG." He smiled. "I've met Daniel before. I know better."

Interesting, she thought, but she was too angry to reason now. Ajax was dead. This blew through all her training. She knew how to separate from a situation and clear her mind. None of her skills were working now. If she couldn't kill Ajax, where did that leave her? Nowhere. Nowhere, and with nothing left to avenge her sister. Her vision narrowed to focus only on the man across from her.

"I have information to trade you. On the Dominican gangs that are trying to move into the Bluff. Neither Papa G nor myself condone their methods."

It would be solid intel, Amy knew. She clenched her teeth, torn. She could keep Skeet. Use him as a stand in for Ajax, and put a bullet in his head. She doubted The Duke would mind. The greedy dude was dead, either way. Peter would support whatever course of action she took, so her job was safe. But the possibility of diluting the heroin trade and stemming some deaths? The Dominicans didn't care about collateral damage and had taken out many innocent people, as well as people merely looking to score. A headache began to form at the base of her skull, and she felt overheated in her peacoat, even though the temperature was still low. The Duke waited as she struggled over her decision.

ON THE WAY back to Amy's hotel, Del made two stops. Amy remained slumped in the passenger seat, frozen yet limp. She'd stuffed the baseball cap in her backpack, next to the supplies she'd brought along. The receipt for the tarp and duct tape was long gone. She hadn't imagined she'd be returning the purchases. Her plan had been fine-tuned over the last three years, and she'd refused to consider it could be upended, unsuccessful.

Was she bereft, angry, or what? She had no clue. She felt like she'd turned into a sizeable chunk of stone. It was as if the sky was now green and the grass was blue. Nothing made sense anymore. Her only chance at redemption, and justice for Audrey, was gone. The monster monkey on her back would never leave. The specter of living with this monster of her own making for the rest of her life was too much to take in. Better to shut down for now.

All she was conscious of was Del. Her friend led her back to the suite, sat her down, and then started making drinks. When they were out with the team, they usually drank beer. But alone, their private joke was to choose girly drinks. Del even kept paper umbrellas and fancy toothpicks at her apartment solely for that. Neither of them was overly feminine; one couldn't be in their chosen field, and besides, they weren't built that way. Yet sometimes it was fun to embrace that part of them. Last time, Del even wore a maxi dress to set the tone.

Luckily, the micro kitchen came equipped with a blender and tall glasses. Amy barely heard the machine chewing up ice cubes. Del mixed margaritas with fresh strawberries, heavy on the tequila. It was so strong, Amy gasped at her first sip. The alcohol burned away some of the fog surrounding her. That was both good and bad news. She didn't want to face reality. Not at all. But it would be better to digest it while her friend was here, she knew. If she waited until she was alone, it would stay buried. She still had mandatory therapy lessons scheduled, and it would be worse for it to come out there.

"Drink up, and then tell me what happened," Del ordered. "I can leave in the morning."

Amy blinked back tears and drank half the glass before speaking. Time to metaphorically stab herself. At least the alcohol was now buzzing through her system, leaving her limbs looser. Her head had yet to start spinning, but she still had half a glass left.

"Ajax is dead. The Duke killed him three years ago," she whispered.

"I assumed something like that when you handed Skeet over with nothing in return." Del frowned.

"Not nothing." Amy shook her head. It still felt odd to not feel her hair brush along her shoulders and back when she moved.

"He called DAG from the meeting. Gave them all sorts of intel on the two violent gangs trying to move in on his territory. He handed the phone to me, and Peter verified it was worthy data. So, that's what I traded for." She took another gulp of her drink.

"That's good, though!" Del exclaimed. "More violence and drugs off the street, yeah?"

Amy drank more and shrugged. "Yeah."

"I know it's tough to have your plan crushed." Del's voice was quiet.

"You were probably right. It might not have made a dent in my guilt. Nevertheless, I still wanted to do it. Premeditated murder." Amy had to smirk.

"If you'd had a gun during the abduction, I can see

you doing it. It would have been justified, too. However, I think you were a cop too long to carry out your plan. You have to find other ways of atonement, like being with Claire. Amy, it wasn't your fault, but I know that won't take away the guilt you feel." Del reached over and squeezed her arm.

Amy shook her head, and the dim room swam. *Nope.* Del was wrong; she would have done it. Not because she was that hardened, but because it had been the only solution to atonement. *What now?* Damn, she needed more liquor.

She held up her glass and saw that it was almost empty. Del noticed and went back to the kitchen to make another batch, even though she'd finished only half her own glass.

"Girl, you need to talk. Let it all out." Del eyed her knowingly over the counter. "Luckily, I know how to make that happen."

"Ugh!" Amy stuck out her tongue. "We agreed! No bringing up Puerto Rico! I can still taste that hangover."

"So, spill, and I won't mention it again." Del winked.

During one of their first ops together, they had celebrated too much at the conclusion. It'd been a fun, crazy night where they had talked until they passed out. The next day, however, was horrific. Amy had woken up on the bathroom floor and found Del snoring on the coffee table. They'd flown home, commercial, with massive hangovers.

Del handed her a full glass and shot her another pointed look. *OK.* Amy went to the other issue weighing on her mind. She would sort out her feelings about the trade later, when she was thoroughly intoxicated.

"There's this guy. Hugh." She focused on the blank television set across the room.

"The charity lawyer who hired us," Del filled in, and Amy nodded.

"He's such a good guy. He loves his mom, he's fighting to make a difference in the world, he's restoring an old house, he has a cat …" Amy's train of attributes trailed off, and then she shouted, "How can I be hung up on someone like that?"

"He sounds fucking perfect." Del chuckled, and Amy raised her free hand in response.

"Egg-zactly!" she slurred the word. "Which isn't for me."

"Who says you don't deserve that?" Del looked askance.

"Me." Amy sighed. "I like bad boys with no strings attached."

"Tastes change," Del pointed out. "I used to be like that, too."

"OK, you managed to find your Mr. Right and settle down, but he supports your job. Hugh wouldn't, not for long."

"Ah." Del nodded. "He wants a normal wife?"

Amy's face screwed up. "Yeah. I dunno. He wouldn't want a wife to be gone that much. Not that I would marry anyone. Eww! I must be drunker than I thought to even mention that word."

Del poked her good-naturedly. "There are compromises in any relationship."

"He's too good," Amy pronounced flatly. "And I'm despondent because I didn't get to murder someone. That doesn't match, Del. His heart is pure, and mine is black."

"You haven't killed anyone," Del reminded, but Amy waved it away as inconsequential.

"Well." Del attempted another tactic. "If he's as nice as you say, he probably sucks in bed. You'd get bored before long."

This sent Amy into a fit of giggles, and she saw Del trying to repress a smile.

"I see what you're trying to do. No, Mr. Attorney has mad skills. There's nothing fucking sweet about the way he fucks." The absurdity of the wording in that sentence sent her off into more giggles.

Del laughed along. "He doesn't like your job? He's too macho? Too afraid for you?"

Amy snorted so loudly, she had to laugh at the silly noise she made. "I'll have you know he congratulated me after I kicked his ass, literally. And he let me crush a Nazi's balls one night, instead of stepping in. But don't think he's a pussy. He's strong, athletic, and he outscored me at a shooting range.

"He mumbles in his sleep. Leaving dirty dishes in the sink makes him cranky. He'd never be able to enjoy a big music festival because of the noise and crowds. He's not perfect," Amy finished.

"Those don't sound like deal breakers to me. Oh, Amy." Del sighed. "He sounds like a keeper. Don't give up on him yet."

But Amy was shaking her head so violently, her gorge

rose in her throat. She paused for another sip of her almost empty glass. Comparing herself to Hugh showed how incompatible they truly were. He was such an incredibly good guy, and she was demented. The attack hadn't soiled her, but her thirst for vengeance had. Her bottomless pit of hatred would never make sense to someone so nice. Who could have a normal relationship with someone who carried around their own private monster? Hugh deserved better.

"Nope. The op is over. Better to cut it off now than later." She verbally formed one last thought.

From far away, she heard Del speaking, but it was easier to lay her head back and drift off than to argue any longer. Her heart ached, and she didn't like it. Escaping was a wussy way out, but all the fight had left her, and she was oh-so tired.

DEL HAD PAINKILLERS and a giant pot of coffee waiting when Amy finally struggled out of bed the next morning. One glance at the mirror, and she ducked in the shower to wash away the smeared makeup and tone down the hair that stuck straight up.

"I'm stopping in Virginia on my way back," Del announced, keeping her voice down. "My phone will be on if you need to talk."

Amy hugged her. "Thanks. For everything, except the hangover."

"Oh, you." Del chuckled. "Remember. Think about moving from revenge to ways to honor Audrey's memory."

"I will." Amy nodded carefully so her head wouldn't

throb more. "I'm seeing Claire later."

"Don't just walk away from the man." Del scowled. "Think about what I said."

"I will!" Amy promised, not exactly lying. She would think about Hugh; she couldn't help it. But her mind was made up. She wasn't walking away. She would be flat-out running from him. It was for his own good.

It occurred to her that she hadn't mentioned anything about his money to Del. It hadn't really hit her yet that he was *that* wealthy. Not that it mattered – he had no plans to keep it. His mother had raised him well, since he didn't act like he came from money. The inheritance was his secret, and she didn't feel like it was something to share. She normally told Del everything, but the money wasn't anything that defined him.

Del helped her pack up the disguise, cameras, her gun, and knives. There wasn't enough space in the van, and Archie wasn't available, so Amy would have to fly back commercial.

"Call me when you get back," Del ordered.

Another quick hug, then Amy was alone with her thoughts and hangover. The headache was receding, so she concentrated on water and food to settle her stomach. She might never drink tequila again, even if this wasn't the worst hangover she'd had.

Instead of more coffee, she opted to lie down with a cool washcloth on her face. She turned to a meditative playlist on her phone and pushed everything out of her mind. She had plenty of time before meeting Claire after school, and she wanted to be alert and positive.

CHRIS GREETED HER at the door, and her stomach fell to her feet at the uneasy look on his face. Had he changed his mind? Wouldn't that be typical! Give her hope only to snatch it away. Yesterday was awful enough; she might not survive another setback.

Nevertheless, she squared her shoulders and swallowed her fears as she walked past him into the house. The air smelled of coffee and wood smoke from the small fire in the fireplace.

"I wanted to thank you for last week," he began after she entered. "Claire has done a total 180 towards Laura."

"Oh. Good. I'm glad." Amy feigned nonchalance while her heartbeat surged, and she tried to calm her roiling insides.

"Again, I'm sorry for not letting you visit." He looked uncomfortably around the foyer. "I really don't blame you anymore, Amy. You tried to help Audrey as much as I did."

Amy stayed silent as her heartbeat returned to normal. While she felt better physically, the past two days had been a roller coaster of emotions. She felt her stomach bottom out as the free fall continued. Should she raise her arms and celebrate this part? His admission was shocking and acted as a balm on her soul. Yes, she had done her damnedest to help Audrey. Yet she never imagined him admitting that.

"Anyway." Chris cleared his throat. "Claire hoped you might like to go out for ice cream."

"Sure," she answered. If Claire asked to go to the moon, Amy would contact NASA. "Did you want to drive, or should we take my car?"

Chris actually smiled slightly. "No. She wants to go with you. Only you."

Amy swayed on her feet as the truth hit her. He was allowing her to take Claire out. He trusted her that much. It was so monumental. Amy didn't snap back to herself until Claire bounded downstairs. She wore jeans and a tie-dyed sweatshirt that proclaimed "Girls Rule the World."

"Double A!" she squealed. "Do you still like your hair? It looks fab!"

"I love it," Amy answered, and sent one last cautious look at Chris, to make sure. "I suppose you can direct me to your favorite ice cream place?"

"Duh." Claire rolled her eyes and grinned.

The small shop was in Buckhead, around the corner from the mall. Claire ordered a double scoop of mint chocolate and moose tracks. Minding her recently upset stomach, Amy stuck with a small vanilla caramel.

She asked the tired question of how her school day had gone, but Claire was vocal about the details. She was like Audrey in that regard – chatty and exuberant. Unlike her mother, though, Claire loved math and hated English.

They talked about her favorite teacher and how excited she was for the next block of science class because it focused on geology. Amy remembered seeing a gem and mineral shop near her dentist's office and put it on her list of places to shop from when she returned home. It sent a thrill down her spine. She could actually send Claire the gifts she bought now. No more hoarding them, praying for an opportunity.

"Do you have a boyfriend?" Claire's unexpected question caused her to jolt.

Her mind went immediately to Hugh. *Boyfriend? No.* He'd been more than, and also less than that. There was that damned past-tense, running a sword through her heart. She sighed and saw that Claire was biting her lip with worry. Lord, what happened to her poker face? All her life, it had been automatic. She smiled and shook her head.

"Not really. I travel too much right now." Her airy tone was fake, but Claire relaxed, so it worked. "When I lived here, I dated a man who was finishing his medical residency. Your mom adored him and wanted us to get married, but when Amir was offered a job in California, we picked our careers over each other."

They finished their cones, and Amy gathered their trash and stood up to throw it away. She fervently hoped that that would end this line of questioning. Lord, she hadn't thought of Amir in ages. They'd parted amicably, which was another sign she was damaged goods. To be with someone for over a year and not cry when the breakup happened? Her heart was truly black.

Claire, however, wasn't finished. "Do you think Dad and Miss Laura will get married?"

Ah, *this* was what she'd been leading up to! While part of her job depended on being able to think fast on her feet, this personal question made Amy hesitate. Truthfully, the answer was probably. But she wasn't sure how much honesty to give her niece.

She sat back down slowly, stalling. "I don't know. How would you feel if they wanted to?"

Yes, it was a wuss-out, but her experience dealing with kids was very slim. Claire shrugged and fidgeted with her cup of water. Her nose crinkled as she contemplated.

"What about Didi and Grandpa? Would they be mad?"

Now that she was asking about Amy's parents, Amy might have a clue as to what the real question was. Oh, this girl was so sweet, she wanted to weep.

"Well," she strove for nonchalance, "I think they want you and your dad to be happy. It's not like Laura would be replacing your mom. No one wants that, not even your dad."

That got Claire's attention, and she looked up, surprise in her wide eyes. Oh, they were so blue! Amy swallowed a chunk of love so large her throat hurt.

"Your mom loved you and your dad, and she wouldn't want either of you to be alone," Amy continued. "I do know that. It would make her very sad." She added, "I think she would want you to have a stepmom to help with all the girly teenager things."

"But you can do that," Claire pouted.

Amy nodded. "True. But I can't be here all the time. And I can't help your dad be less lonely."

Claire sighed and shrugged again. They went back to sitting in silence for a bit. What else could she say? How would she feel in Claire's shoes?

"Talk to your dad." Amy finally spoke. "Let him know about your concerns. You can call Didi and Grandpa, too. Any of us are happy to talk to you about your mom. And think really hard about your feelings over this. If you were to sort of like Laura, it wouldn't mean you didn't love your mom."

It looked like Claire was blinking back tears, so maybe she said the right thing? Damn, she had no close friends who were parents. She decided to ask her mother later and let her know Claire was struggling. She owed her parents an update, anyway.

Amy waited until they were back home to break her news to Claire and Chris. They had joined Chris back in the den to watch a video of Claire's science project presentation. The afternoon had been wonderful, and Amy hated to mar it. She waited until it was time to leave to drop the bomb.

"My op is over, so I need to leave soon," she announced.

Claire pouted and wailed until Chris held up his hand. "We both hope you can come back soon, right, Claire?"

She nodded, but kept her lower lip out. She clung to Amy's waist with surprising strength. Amy stroked her fine hair, feeling the hug down to her bones. Today was becoming the antithesis of the previous day and all its shittyness.

"I promise it won't be long," Amy said. "Plus, I'm not far from Grandpa and Didi's. We can meet there, too. You have my number, my email, and my Skype info."

Amy held her breath, praying that Claire wouldn't cry. If she did, Amy would join her, and she had already cried far too much this trip. It wasn't normally her thing, especially over the last few years.

"I bet we can FaceTime during games, too," Chris said. "Or at least record them."

That seemed to placate the girl, and Amy was able to leave after half a dozen hugs from her niece. Why she felt lighter rather than sadder, she had no idea. She even managed a half-hug with Chris.

One down, she thought as she drove away. Only the toughest one remained. She didn't want to think about that, so she turned up the music and began composing her final report to DAG in her head.

THE REPORT TOOK less time to write than she'd hoped. She should pack, but there wasn't much left. She had sent everything from the op back with Del. Archie wasn't available tomorrow, so she would fly coach. All she had to do was re-pack her backpack.

You're stalling! she shook her head. *Get it over with!*

She and Hugh had made loose plans to meet after her time with Claire. It was up to her to let him know she was free. She started the call, but hung up before it connected. She was a person who didn't shy away from confrontation, but this time was different. She took the coward's way and sent a text: "With the op complete, I'm due back in DC tomorrow."

She cringed, cursing herself, and held her breath, waiting for his reply. Surprisingly, he didn't respond immediately. She'd expected a confused phone call. For five minutes she sat, her stomach threatening to discharge the ice cream she'd eaten earlier. Finally, her cell buzzed with a text. Her hands were shaking, so it took three tries before she could sign on.

Hugh: *"I'll be there in 20 minutes."*

He must be at the office, she guessed. It would take longer than that to drive from his house. She threw her phone down and hunched over, her arms around her torso. Of course, she knew it would have to be in person. He would be angry and hurt. Oh, God, how could she bear seeing him wounded?

Would he see it was for the best? If they tried to sustain this, it would be more excruciating when the inevitable happened. She was doing them both a kindness. Between him and Claire, she was too full of emotions. It was plainly too much, after years of being numb and unconcerned.

She needed to ease slowly back into being human again. Of course, she would choose Claire over a fling. It would be better for Hugh, too. This way, he wouldn't get his hopes up. He deserved so much better than an emotionally-stunted, would-be revenge killer.

Prepare. Her training kicked in, and she almost wept with relief. *Handle this like an op,* she thought. Great idea in theory, but how could she remain stoic with so much feeling making her body ache? *One step at a time*, she told herself. First, set the scene with safety in mind. Her safety, to be exact.

Should she sit or stand? Simple decisions flummoxed her. The bedroom was out – too much temptation. She dug her clothing out of the closet and drawers, flinging them onto the sofa. No sitting close, either. If she sat in one chair and stayed busy packing, he could either stand or take the other chair across the long coffee table. Yes, that sounded safe. No proximity and something to do with her hands.

His knock was softer than she'd expected, and she prayed it was a good sign. She opened the door and managed a smiling, "Hi." She gestured to the mess and indicated the empty chair. "Sorry. I'm a messy packer."

He threw her a look that said he doubted her statement, but he sat. He was wearing loose cargo pants and a black V-neck t-shirt with an unzipped, faded navy hoodie. He looked luscious, as always. He must have been at the office pouring over research, for his hair was mussed. He always ran his hands through it whenever he tackled a problem. The action released the natural curls from the gel he used to keep them straight. *God, his curls!*

Hugh clasped his hands between his knees and frowned. She returned to her seat and pulled over her backpack, trying to look busy. She swallowed and tried to breathe through the tension, not wanting to speak first.

"I don't want this to be over." He finally spoke and looked up at her, his hazel eyes earnest. "I know long distance isn't ideal, but it's not impossible."

Fuck, fuck, fuck, she wanted to cry. Damn him for speaking his mind and throwing out a practical solution. *Fuck.* Now she had to hurt him.

She shook her head. "Not a good idea."

"You have feelings for me." His jaw was set, his teeth gritted. Veins popped on the back of his hands as he tightened them in frustration.

"Yes, but ..." She racked her brain for the right words. *Oh, God!* Why had she admitted that?

Hugh jumped out of the seat and paced to the breakfast bar and back. The evening felt suddenly unreal, like a bad dream. Had he stepped into an alternate universe? How had things gone sideways so quickly?

He hadn't seen her since their lunch date the day before, and she'd seemed fine. Had meeting Leigh set something off? Was it his inheritance? Most women liked him more, knowing he was wealthy – they expected extravagant gifts, pricey dinners. That had been his fear with Amy – how she would change toward him. This … this was the opposite of what he'd expected. But based on the timing, he thought maybe his money had ruined it, somehow. *What in the fuck is happening?*

Where had he screwed up? Had he been too forceful in bed? Not enough? Too caring when she'd cried? Not enough? *Jesus!*

He paused to take a few deep breaths when he became dizzy. Hyperventilating now would be very uncool. He needed to control his emotions, but this scenario was a complete surprise. He was unprepared for it and his emotional response. He was off-balance by the depth of his anger and sorrow.

He turned, spreading his arms out, and shouted, "This was more than just a fling! I know you care about me!" His voice softened when she flinched at his temper. "What did I do wrong?"

Her façade cracked, and he saw honest emotion for the first time. Her mouth curved down, and her eyes filled with pain. *Good*, he thought; *feel what I'm feeling.*

"Nothing." She shook her head, and then the mask was back. "You did nothing wrong. We both knew I would leave when the op was over."

"You're acting like there was nothing between us. That's bullshit," he said flatly, and braced his legs apart, waiting for her reply.

"I'm not denying that." She shook her head, not looking at him. "We're too different, and to drag it out would only be more painful and stressful."

You knew it was coming, sucker, his brain spit out. *The women you go for aren't the type to settle down.* It had to be the money. Something had made her change between yesterday's lunch and today.

Hugh wanted to argue with his common sense. He'd been so sure she almost loved him. But he must have pegged it wrong. He had honestly expected her to agree to long-distance, when the op was over. Sap that he was, he'd seen it developing until one of them caved and relocated. He felt his cheeks tinge with shame. What a fucking idiot he'd been.

Amy raised her head and maintained eye contact, even though every second shredded his heart more. There wasn't a shred of warmth or humanity in her expression. Hugh didn't try to hide his pain and disappointment. His hands ached, and he realized he had them clenched into fists. *Save yourself*, his brain whispered. *There's no changing her mind. At least leave with your balls intact.*

Finally, he dropped his head and took a deep breath before facing her one last time. "OK, then." He raised his eyebrows and nodded. "Be safe. Have a nice life."

BEFORE SHE COULD speak, he was out the door. He

didn't even slam it – merely closed it with a quiet click.

She wasn't sure how long she sat, frozen. Her mind tumbling over everything he'd said. Shocked at his capitulation. Why was she sad that he hadn't put up more of a fight? Ridiculous! He'd let her off easy, and she should be grateful.

When she finally moved, it was to dig her phone out from the pile of clothing on the couch. She tapped the airline app and paid too much money to switch her flight from ten in the morning tomorrow to eleven tonight. She needed to leave, now. She shoved the rest of her belongings into her backpack and headed for the airport. She could return the rental and spend the rest of the time speed-walking through the vast terminals. She needed the exercise.

Just her luck, the flight was delayed, but she made it back to her apartment around three in the morning. As soon as she walked in, despair surpassed her relief at being home. Compared to Hugh's house, even with all the rooms undone, her place looked barren. She had the basics, but she hadn't yet added any paint or objects to make it look like someone actually lived there.

She needed sleep, she decided. Things would look better in the morning. They had to.

SHE AWOKE AROUND eight. Unfortunately, her surroundings looked bleaker in the sunlight. Nothing she could do about that now, so she quickly dressed and headed to work. At least her cubicle had a bit more personality. Plus, the thought of seeing her teammates – except for Mick – was a bright thought.

Malachai was the first person she encountered. He stopped short and gaped at her. Did she look that beaten down? *Oh, the haircut*, she belatedly remembered.

She touched the short strands and explained, "Made a big change."

"That looks great," he was quick to respond. "But you look like shit. Go sit, and I'll bring you some tea."

She should have attempted some makeup. It didn't help that the only clean clothing she had was either too dressy, or what her mother called "sick clothes." What she wore when she was too sick to leave the house, and no one was going to see her. For Amy, that comprised an old, oversized sweater with moth holes and faded leggings. It wasn't as if DAG had a dress code for the office, she reasoned. Making an effort was beyond her today.

She sat at her desk and booted up her desktop. She saw Malachai re-enter the room, followed by Del. Of course, he'd snitched. But she was happy to see Del, even though she knew to expect a dressing down.

"Let's go into the conference room," Del suggested when Whittaker entered shortly after.

They sat at the table, and Amy thanked Malachai for the tea. It was strong and sweet, hopefully loaded with caffeine. He moved to leave, but Amy motioned for him to stay. She felt in need of his mothering today.

"What happened? Did Chris revert back to an ass-hole?" Del asked.

"No, actually. He trusted me to take Claire out, and I'll be seeing her over Spring Break at my parents," Amy explained.

"Ah, so it's the guy, then." Del shook her head, her mouth in a thin line of disapproval. "You dumped him, didn't you?"

Malachai looked at her in confusion, and Del explained, "The lawyer that hired us for the op is in love with her."

Amy protested with a snort and a shake of her head. But she didn't speak. She refused to cry at work.

Del added after seeing Malachai's shocked face, "She doesn't think she deserves him, so she kicked him to the curb." She turned back to Amy. "Right?"

Amy shrugged glumly and sipped her tea. "It was for the best. We're too different."

Malachai squeezed her hand. "Different isn't always a bad thing. I have some chicken soup in the freezer to send home with you."

She had to smile and return the squeeze. He was the best. Chicken soup was also one of the few things he could make from scratch. He surprised her when he rose to leave instead of staying and comforting her. She didn't take it personally. Like the rest of them, he could become obsessed with certain projects.

"I think you two need to talk alone. Del, I do have a question for you when you're done." Malachai exited after patting Amy on the hand.

"Oh, Amy. Which part of you do you think he'll come to dislike?" Del smiled sadly.

Amy wanted to recite a list, but couldn't come up with anything concrete, at first. While she pondered, Del rattled off likely items.

"The rape? Bad things from when you were a cop?

All the illegal acts DAG has committed? How desperately you wanted a relationship with Claire? The guilt over the suicide? The fact you enjoy kicking a man's ass in combat? He doesn't seem the type to ask you to give up your job."

Amy shook her head, peeved that her friend could so easily list her failings. But that's what friends do, right? Stick with you no matter how shitty you are. No, Hugh knew all of them. He'd seen her at her best, and he'd stuck around for some of her worst.

"What else are you afraid he'll find out?" Del's voice was quiet. "That you planned to kill Ajax?"

"Yes! I don't know!" Amy burst out, honest. "You already found Mr. Right. You're so lucky." Amy pouted and flopped back against the chair, causing it to squeak on its wheels.

Del abruptly sat her mug on the table and laughed. Hard. Amy's frown thinned; she was confused why her friend was laughing as if she'd heard the best joke in the world.

Trying to catch her breath, Del shook her head. "Oh, no, sweetheart! Luck has nothing to do with it. Well, maybe lucky we crossed paths."

She turned to face her and grabbed one of the hands Amy had been twisting in her lap. "It's hard work, making a relationship successful. It's hard as hell for people like us to let someone in. To let someone love us every day. To feel worthy."

Tears filled Amy's eyes as she saw the truth in Del's words. She wasn't afraid of Hugh and his seeming perfection. She was afraid of not measuring up to the

Amy in his mind. It seemed impossible that someone like him could care for someone like her, the Revenge Killer.

"When you let yourself trust someone, and that confidence is returned, it's exactly like finding Mr. Right." Del smiled again. "You have to decide if you're brave enough, and if the man is worthy."

"Well, I'm not brave enough," Amy said flatly. "Plus, I'm still too fucked up over Audrey's death. Especially now that there's no way to avenge her."

"The info that The Duke provided – it will save lives. That sounds like a mighty fine tribute to Audrey, then. Something from which you can feel a sense of justice. Much more meaningful than one dead scumbag. I'm going to keep pounding that into your head. You need to move away from revenge toward ways that you can honor Audrey." Del kept eye contact and spoke slowly, so Amy could hear each word.

Amy nodded and looked down at her tea. "I'll think about it. I have an upcoming session with Ella, and Peter will kill me if I miss it."

"Excellent." Del hugged her. "You know I'm always here for you."

Chapter Ten

AFTER VERIFYING THAT Mick wouldn't be in today, Del walked Amy back to her cubicle and then went searching for Malachai. His office was empty, so she checked the server room. He was bent over, fiddling with some wires, wearing a coat over his sweater. She wrapped her arms around her thin shirt and suit jacket. They kept the room at an arctic temperature to combat the heat emitted by all the hardware.

"That charity lawyer requested a full report this morning," Malachai told her, his eyes twinkling. "I know Amy already turned in her part. Would you like the honor of writing the final statement?"

Del playfully punched him in the arm, her smile radiant. "I would, thank you."

"You can't reveal too much," he cautioned, and straightened up. "Is meddling worth it? Are you sure Amy won't come to her senses?"

Del shrugged. Her friend still didn't realize how hard she'd actually fallen for this guy. She wanted to shake some sense into her, but that wouldn't work with Amy.

For her inner life, she rarely took advice, and heaven forbid you lay down a gauntlet. No, she had to come to terms with it herself. All Del could do was keep reiterating what she'd said earlier. That and, perhaps, spur some movement with Mr. Bainbridge.

"She may. I'll give her a few days, while I work on some delicate wording for this report." Del bit her lip, planning to proceed carefully.

AMY'S HOPES FOR accepting a new assignment far away were dashed the next day. They called all available agents into the office, and the others were added via conference video. Peter announced they would scale back for a couple of months while Malachai taught a class for the CIA cyber terrorist unit. Mateo would be the only agent to continue his current op, but he'd be in solitary confinement where he had access to a private server and laptop. The rest of them would help the legitimate side of the company conduct research and background checks, since business was booming in that department. They could do this from home, or come into the office. Amy would be stuck at home, because the alternative was sitting near Mick.

That Whittaker asked for time off instead surprised no one. Normal business bored him, and he felt little loyalty to the company. If DAG asked Amy to plant flowers or dig a ditch, she'd do it gladly.

She gritted her teeth and wanted to scream. *Great.* More time alone with her guilt and regrets. Maybe she should take some time off, too. Go to Europe, or learn skydiving. It was awful that, if not for Hugh, she could go back to Atlanta and hang out with Claire. If she went, she wouldn't be able to stop thinking about him, so that was a no-go idea.

She needed a way to exorcise him from her brain before she returned to visit Claire. *How?* There was one way, she realized. Some token of apology so that he wouldn't hate her.

She caught Malachai on his way out and described the bones of the concept she'd had. Why did he have to teach this stupid class now? She doubted his protégé was up to the challenge, but it didn't hurt to ask.

"Since you'll have your hands full, do you think it's something Mateo has the skills to do?"

"Probably." He nodded. "He's been a quick study. Send him the details, and let him know I'm available if he has any questions."

Amy gave him a fierce hug. "Thanks. I'll miss you."

She sighed in relief. Hopefully, this project could help occupy her mind and lessen some of her guilt. Get Hugh out of her mind for good.

HUGH FOUND BELIEVABLE excuses to avoid the office for the rest of the week. If he needed documents or books, he retrieved them during the middle of the night. He was awake most of those hours, anyway.

He'd let Neddra know that Amy was back in DC. Luckily, she made no comment about it or his lack of office days. He didn't want sympathy, pity, or even her raging on his behalf. He wanted only to forget.

Which was difficult to do while stuck at home. He had taken back the pale-yellow paint they'd chosen for the sunroom, switching it for a lime sherbet that the clerk swore was the "happiest" shade they carried. He also spent an entire day searching antique houses for the perfect bed, finally settling on an oak four-poster style that had a matching chest. Some fresh paint, bedding, and curtains made the bedroom different enough for him to be comfortable. No ghosts of Amy or their spectacular sex.

When he wasn't working on a case or on the house, he was at the gym. His physical therapist had pronounced him good-to-go on his last visit, and Hugh was thankful to run again. The pain kept his mind off his fucked up emotional life. Later, he would study it to see where he went wrong. Right now, he was focused on avoidance.

Hugh was buried in case law research when his cell phone trilled that Saturday. It was his mother's tone, so he quickly answered. *Had she fallen again? Had the check engine light come on in her car?*

"Hey, Mom. Everything OK?"

"Hugh." Her exasperation was loud and clear. "Everything is fine. I wanted to check on my son. We haven't talked since Sunday."

Hugh relaxed, leaning back in his chair. He glanced at his monitor and immediately felt guilty. *Shit.* Had he not checked on her in almost a week?

"I'm so sorry, Mom." He mentally slapped himself.

To his surprise, she laughed. "I assume you've been working or spending time with Ms. Stuart."

"Just work. Amy's back in DC, now that the case is finished."

"Oh."

He felt a guilty blush creep up his cheeks. How did moms always know? It was as if she had some sort of secret portal to a part of his mind. Especially as a kid. She had a way of knowing when he was upset or if he was trying to lie.

"Yes, work has been crazy, but that's no excuse for me not to call." He hoped to change the subject.

"Hugh." Her sigh was pronounced, and her tone sharpened. "Before your father passed, we normally talked about once a week. I love hearing from you, but not because you think I'm lonely or feeble."

Shit. She was almost never angry. Like him, Candace was low-key, but when she became pissed, watch out. How could he get through to her that he wasn't used to her living alone? That she was getting older? The mention of either didn't sound like a way to calm her down. Of course, he worried!

"I know. I'm overprotective." He took the blame, even though he didn't believe it. He'd rather not get into a fight right now. Better to diffuse the conversation.

"I'll have you know, this week the dishwasher flooded, and I handled it myself."

Her tone was smug but pointed. Hugh straightened in his seat. He pinched the bridge of his nose as he felt the beginnings of a headache forming. Had she called a random plumber? What about the water damage? Had the kitchen floor been checked?

"Why didn't you call me?" Was he hurt or angry? More hurt, if he was being honest. His mother had cared for him all her life, and he was proud to help her now.

He considered it his job as an only child. Why hadn't she called?

"Son, I can't call you every time something goes wrong."

Yes, you can, he thought, but instead he asked, "What did you do?"

"First, I called Bessie to get a recommendation." Bessie was her friend that lived in the same condo complex. OK, that was sensible. "Then I asked Amado over to work on some funding papers while the plumber was here."

Damn. Hugh had to smile. That had been a smart move. He'd never realized his mom was so aware.

"Amado gave me the number of a company that deals with water damage, and they're coming Monday to check the tile. Bessie is coming to play cards then."

Damn, he thought again. She'd done it. And without his help. Should he feel proud or useless? Truth was, he felt both.

"Wow, Mom. You handled that perfectly," he admitted.

"Thank you." Her voice was back to warm. "I feel like I could take on any disaster now."

"I'm sorry for acting overprotective. I guess I've been standing in your way." Hugh felt like shit as he realized that.

"Nonsense! You were doing it out of love." His mother was insistent. "Now, you have permission to love me a little less closely."

A laugh burst out of him. "Yes, ma'am."

It felt good to laugh. Damn it, he should have called

his mother days ago. She then asked about the cases he was working on. She knew he could give her only the broad strokes, but it gave her an opportunity to reinforce her encouragement.

"Thanks, Mom. It means the world to me that you support this. Especially since it wasn't what Dad wanted."

His mother clucked her tongue. "Sweetie, it may not have been what he'd planned, but I wouldn't say it wasn't what he wanted."

"Mom, I turned my back on three generations of leaders!" he protested, his voice rising.

"At base, the idea was always to strike out and find your own path. Is that not what you're doing? Yes, they all made a fortune, but that wasn't the point. The point was to be different, to create something new. The money came from their business sense and work ethic."

Hugh wanted to argue, but all his words fled. She made an excellent point. Since he stayed quiet, his mother continued.

"The political aspirations came to your father later in life. Yes, we signed you up for volunteer opportunities to look good on your college applications. Plus, I enjoyed it when you tagged along with me to shelters. When he saw how excitedly you took to it, he envisioned you doing it on a grand scale, because that was how he was wired. He never thought small." She ended with, "I'm so proud of what you're doing, and I think he would have come to that same conclusion."

How he sounded normal for the rest of the call, Hugh didn't know. He hit the end button with a chest full of emotion as he digested this epiphany. Was he fulfilling "the plan" by doing what he wanted? He absolutely would never be wealthy from it, but he could keep it going with just a fraction of his inheritance.

His chest felt tight, considering everything his mother had said. He wished he had Amy to talk to; he wanted to get her read on it. As soon as the thought came, he shoved it away. No, she didn't deserve any space in his head now. He swept the foolish yearning away and texted his group of friends. Hopefully, someone was up to hanging out tonight. Then, he needed to head to work and face things there.

THE ONLY CONCESSION Neddra made to his return was the addition of a hanging plant in his office. She had followed him back, her arms full of mail, Nancy on her heels.

Hugh eyed the giant fern quizzically. "What's this?"

"It's supposed to help clear the air," she explained with an innocent smile.

"Ah. Thanks," he said, and bent down to give Nancy an ear scratch.

"Welcome back," she said, and this time smiled broadly. "We missed you."

She turned to leave and tossed one last comment over her shoulder. "There's no need to put on a brave face for me. I'll give you another week to wallow."

With that, she left Hugh alone with his mail. Her concern and understanding choked his chest to the point he had to cough. Nancy jumped up to curl on top of his lap. That was new, but Hugh figured some animals could pick up on human emotional states.

"Thanks, girl," he whispered to Nancy. "I need a lap full of warmth today."

He quickly sorted through the stack, grateful to Neddra for always removing the junk mail. He found what he was searching for near the bottom. The last report from DAG was inside a priority envelope. He hesitated. Did he even want to read it now? The past week had given him some much-needed distance and clarity. He should wait before ripping off the band-aid.

His hesitation lasted almost two hours. Then he had time to waver – the next appointment wasn't until this afternoon, and it was too early for lunch. *Get it over with*, he told himself, and tore open the folder.

He flipped quickly through the first few pages, which detailed the evidence, Mimi, etc. He was only interested in what had happened after that final normal lunch they'd shared. What had caused the shift in Amy? Was it more than just finding out about his money?

Of course, he hoped that her sudden turn wasn't his doing. Why it mattered so much, he wasn't entirely sure. They were still over, either way. It wasn't as if she would come running back if he gave the money away tomorrow.

He read with interest about how Skeet had proved useless except as a trade. For some reason, DAG had allowed Amy to make that decision. It seemed far above her pay grade, but Atlanta had been her area when she was a cop. Could it have something to do with the abduction of her and her sister?

Hugh abandoned the file to place a call to the investigator he contracted when he needed police reports. Even the basics would help shed light. If he were right, it would make sense.

The author of the report included more details than he should have. Surely, they had a legal department to vet these official reports. He turned back to the cover page and saw a D.L. Paich had compiled it. Was he administration, or an executive?

He continued to read. Amy had agreed to trade Skeet to The Duke in exchange for Adrian "Ajax" Post. However, the deal was amended to replace Ajax with information regarding another drug gang. That intel was subsequently turned over to the DEA, who were confident it would lead to many arrests.

This trade had happened the day before Amy left. He sat back and considered this new revelation. He looked forward to reporting back to Joshua's Vision that their problem had led to such a take down in the drug trade. It would thrill Roderick to know that the bomb's disarray had had a happy ending. Even though the car bomb hadn't been connected after all, according to this report. DAG was sure it was a mistake; they'd investigated and uncovered an intense dispute between two rival gangs. Their target had the same car as Amy's rental, even with a similar tag. That was a relief. Hugh's chest still ached whenever he thought back to that night and how badly Amy could have been hurt, or worse.

Not that he cared now, he thought. He checked his email, opening the most recent one with anticipation. *Bingo!* His hunch had been correct! He felt like a voyeur, even though the police report was public record. He scanned the email, searching for the names of those involved.

They had indeed identified Ajax as the rapist. And he'd been part of The Duke's crew.

Why hadn't she told him? The meeting had evidently turned her inside out. He wondered why the trade had changed, and if that was what had upset her the most. If The Duke had made her choose between the perp and the information, that would have been an excruciating choice for her. Hell, since it concerned her sister, any of it would have been difficult for her.

He pinched the bridge of his nose, his heart breaking for her. Jesus, he could have been less angry that night. But she'd been a different person, an ice queen determined to cut the cord no matter how much he bled.

Her incredible guilt could have been at work, but why take it out on him? Convenience? He hadn't a clue. This might be proof that her leaving had little to do with him. Not that the realization helped his bruised feelings. She hadn't asked for a break, for time to think clearly. She'd chosen to rip out his heart and shred what remained to pieces. That was what he had to keep foremost in his mind.

Not the way she had fit perfectly into his life. Or the way her hair smelled like wildflowers. Especially not how she had accepted the way his brain goofed up, like the night at the bar. He shouldn't think or go there. That led to memories of that damned push-up bra and how she'd welcomed his touch later that night. Fuck, she had been hot, soft, and wet.

He reached up, took two fistfuls of hair, and pulled.

Stop! He absolutely did not need to think of their last time together, which had been the best sex of his life. It attained that designation because of the emotional connection, as much as the physical effect. How could she open up to him like that, and then just leave?

Yes, of course, he considered going after her. A million times a day. Yet something held him back. Probably pride, but damn it, she needed to explain. He'd be damned if he'd beg her. If she wasn't hurting as badly as he was, then that said it all. She was probably fine, off on another case, not thinking about him at all.

He let the report fall from his hand into the wastebasket. Enough of that. He had cases that needed his attention.

AMY SPENT THE rest of the week at home, mindlessly compiling background reports. She would have preferred working at the bustling office, but Mick was there. Maybe he didn't want to be at home, either, because it gave him too much time to think about Kit. Amy snorted. She was projecting; their situations were nothing alike.

She couldn't hate him as much as she had weeks ago. No room left in her mind, perhaps. An errant thought floated through her mind. Had she not ended things with Hugh the same way Mick had with Kit? Eww! That was an unpleasant idea. Yet it was accurate, she acknowledged with a sick stomach. At least Hugh hadn't been in a traumatized state, recovering from a horrific assault. That still made her not quite as much a bastard as Mick. She brushed all thoughts of him away and tried to concentrate on boring reports.

Being confined to her apartment wasn't a party. She dreamed about Hugh every night. Some dreams replayed how cruel she'd been, and others were soaked with sex. She would awaken from those aching and gasping, knowing that she would never experience anything that perfect again. The worst ones contained tidbits of the times he'd held her hand or made her laugh. His concern had never been overpowering; he had offered an understanding ear rather than a solution.

A change was what she needed, she decided. Her apartment should look lived in, homey. She hit her local big-box retailer and left with some framed travel posters and two more fake plants. She printed out some of the new pictures she'd taken of Claire and covered her corkboard and fridge with them. After a brief hesitation, she added an old picture of her, Claire, and Audrey to the mix. *There.* That looked better, she decided.

Her afternoon was spent researching fun outings for her, her parents, and Claire to take during Spring Break next month. Even better than winning the lottery, she was either speaking to or texting with Claire almost every other day. What a mood elevator that was. If she could only stop thinking of Hugh and be assigned a new op, preferably undercover. She desperately needed to become someone else now, even superficially. While conducting an op, she was always on guard. There was no downtime needing to be filled with constant activity.

The happy text alert she'd assigned for Del trilled, almost lost in the action movie soundtrack she had playing as she worked. She snatched it up only to see a line of thumbs-up emojis. Too impatient to wait for a response, she called instead.

"Good news? Are we going back to work?" Amy asked.

"What? No." Del sounded taken aback. "No jobs until Malachai comes back. This news is even better!"

Amy had no clue what she might be referring to, since no new ops was bad news.

Del rushed on, her voice exuberant. "The DEA was able to take down three stash houses based on the info from The Duke. They arrested one gang's mixer and confiscated a total of $15 million worth of heroin. As a bonus, one gang was also dealing pills, and they had a room full of black-market uppers and downers."

"Wow." Amy was stunned. "That's much more than I'd hoped for. I didn't know the heroin dealers had added pills to their business."

"DEA suspected one gang, and that's why they were thrilled with the intel," Del supplied. "Audrey would be proud."

Amy sat quietly, her mind fitting the pieces together. Neither she nor Chris had any idea where Audrey had obtained the meds she'd abused. There wasn't a doctor trail, and the bottle had been unmarked, so the assumption had been black-market stock. Sure, there'd been dozens of dealers and sources in such a large city, but what if …

"What if Audrey's dealer was affiliated with them?" she finished in a whisper.

"Highly possible. You know that all illicit trade connects on one level or another. Does that make you feel better about the deal with The Duke?"

Amy shrugged, even though Del couldn't see. She was too emotional to speak. She needed time to process this revelation.

"You OK?" Del asked. "Need me to come over?"

"I'm OK," Amy answered through a tight throat. "I'm going to hit the gym. Think on this some more. This is incredible news, Del. Thanks for letting me know."

Well, wouldn't that be some kick-in-the-ass irony of the year – by not getting to put a bullet between Ajax's eyes, she'd actually helped to stop something else connected to Audrey's death. Her addiction had been a minor player in the tragedy, but she might not have died if she hadn't found access to the pills. It hadn't been an accidental overdose. Audrey had swallowed half the bottle.

It delighted the former narc in her that the raids had dismantled drug gangs. Sure, other players would rush to fill the void, but perhaps Papa G would be one of them. At least, he wouldn't bring the level of violence or badly doctored drugs that the past group had.

She stood up and shook herself. Enough brooding! She'd head for the gym, then check in with her mom as planned. If she let her thoughts ruminate on Atlanta, they would inevitably turn to Hugh. That was too much to take right now.

The intense workout was exactly what she needed. Her mind and body felt strong and ready. Adding a blistering cold shower and some food, she almost felt in top shape. At her desk, she pulled up the homepage for a theme park near her parents and dialed her mom. She wanted to ensure there were enough rides there to interest Claire before booking the tickets.

She put the call on speaker so she could click through the site while they talked. In the end, they agreed the park would be an excellent choice for an outing. Her mother asked what was new, and before she realized it, Amy was telling her about the DEA bust. As always, she used only general terms when referring to her job, so the story was that she'd come across some information during the Atlanta job which had led to the raid. She expected "congratulations" or "good job" from her mother, and was stunned when the woman burst into tears.

Tapping off the speaker, she brought the phone to her ear. "Mom? Mom! What happened? Are you OK?"

Her mother sniffled. "Yes. Give me a moment."

Amy waited, fidgeting with a pen. That wasn't enough, so she stood and paced to the living room and back.

"Sorry, dear." Her mother cleared her throat. "It's … miraculous, that your information led to such an, um, event."

"That's exaggerating it, Mom." Amy frowned. "I'm not a miracle worker. I had no part in the raid."

"I know." Her heart eased when her mother chuckled. "Oh, your sister would be so proud! Your dad and I certainly are, always have been. Because of this, other people might not end up as Audrey did. You helped this happen! I can't wait to explain this to Claire when she's older. You'll be such a hero to her!"

It struck Amy mute, so her mother continued. "I know you'll always feel guilty, dear, even though you shouldn't. Between this amazing news, everything you learned from Chris, and your new bond with Claire, I hope you can finally heal. Audrey would want that. Honestly, do you really think she'd want you to feel so badly? You know she wouldn't. Maybe this is the universe's way of telling you it's time."

Amy found her voice and ended the call as quickly as she could, without making her mom suspicious. She should call Del or Ella, the DAG shrink. The awful part was that she desperately wanted to call Hugh. Which was impossible, no thanks to her.

She could see his face, full of pride and joy at her news. The sudden pain was so sharp, she gasped and bent over in her chair. When would the thought of him not feel so excruciating? Surely, it wasn't normal to miss someone this much. To remember exactly how he smelled, what his touch felt like. How she had memorized so much about him in such a short time was a mystery. She could even recall the pattern of faint freckles on his face.

She cried out in frustration. She didn't want to keep thinking of him!

Grabbing her cell, she texted Archie: *"You in town? Knife-throwing or target range? Your pick."*

By the time his reply arrived, she'd scrubbed the shit out of her bathtub. Needing to stay busy was her primary goal, but the smell of the cleaning solution also helped her feel productive. Clean was good, as was breaking a sweat. She read his text, panting from exertion: "Axes and beer, darlin! Pick you up in an hour."

AMY WAS CHARMED to see they'd set up the business similar to a bowling alley, except here the lanes had full walls on either side. *Good idea for safety,* she thought. The bar also covered their ass when it came to alcohol. No ordering from the bar until after the game was concluded.

They had five throws each. Archie went first, and undoubtedly had been practicing, for his small ax landed in the bulls-eye every time. Amy returned his smirk with a one-finger salute before stepping up to the line. This differed from knife-throwing, which she wasn't quite an expert at yet. A whoop of joy escaped her when her ax actually landed in the target. She'd expected it to glance off or fall short.

"I'm an outstanding teacher." Archie swaggered back up, making her laugh.

This was what she needed. Fun, activity, and no room to ruminate. The match ended 5-3, Archie's favor. She vowed to come back and practice before challenging him again. Not that she ever minded being bested by him. He was the king of blades and long-distance shooting. Good teammate that he was, he enjoyed sharing his talents. And even when he touted his mastery, it was with good humor and self-deprecation.

When she saw that the bar also served food, she insisted on buying dinner. It would delay her going home and also satisfy the growling in her stomach. They found a table in the corner and sipped their beer while waiting for the burgers.

Archie hoisted his mug. "Here's to you. Heard about the DEA raid."

She clicked her glass with his. "Thanks. That was a surprise bonus."

She expected the conversation to continue with more work-related topics, but he surprised her. "Think that was where your sister got the pills?"

Amy slowly set down her glass. She wasn't offended; everyone at DAG knew her story and had contributed any knowledge they had on the drug trade in Atlanta after she joined.

"I don't know," she answered honestly. "I want to think so."

"You did good." His smile was slight, filled with empathy. "Feel proud, Amy. Maybe it's time to put the avenging angel to rest."

"Avenging angel?" she snorted, a lick of anger tickling her spine. "What the hell, Archie?"

He shook his head, his longer hair flowing around his neck. "I assume it's hard to let go when you've planned righteous vengeance for so long. What was your plan for after you'd settled the score?"

Her mouth worked as she struggled to find an answer. Truthfully, she'd never thought that far ahead. At basic, her goal had been to have as normal a life as she could. Continue catching bad guys, spying on Claire, and ...

A frown filled her face as she glared at her friend. *Damn it!*

"Not too late to figure out what happens next," he

pointed out, his eyes kind.

She blew out a breath. Well, no more spying on Claire. That problem had been solved. Too bad ops were stalled at present. She'd love to take down a few dozen bad guys right now, wouldn't she?

Not necessarily, she realized with a jolt. She snorted. It must be the emotional toll from today. Or the beer. She doubted her mellow mood would last.

"You're assuming I'm done with The Duke," she pointed out. "How do you know I'm finished avenging?"

"Because it's time," he whispered, his blue eyes earnest. "The rapist is dead, the drug trade disrupted, the violent gangs apprehended. You did your sister proud, darlin'. Time to let it go."

She swallowed past the knot in her throat and blinked back tears. "Maybe."

"Just think about it." He smiled and sat back as the waiter brought their food. "Doesn't mean you're going soft. Think of it as another layer of armor. You slayed that dragon, and now you're ready for the next one. Until then, it's OK to relax."

Archie's words swirled through her head for the rest of the evening. The four beers she'd drank helped the swirl, too. What he'd imparted had been just like what her mother had said. Could it be true? Could she have finally found enough justice for Audrey to dissolve some of her guilt? It didn't seem possible.

SHE AWOKE WITH a slight headache, the concept still foremost in her mind. After two cups of coffee, she looked at the picture of her, Audrey, and Claire that she'd pinned on the wall. She stared at it for so long, she had to shift in her chair when her leg fell asleep. Could it be true?

The lightness she'd felt since reuniting with Claire still infused her. Yes, Chris's admission and apology had something to do with that. She searched her psyche, looking for sore spots to poke. In the past, it had been a way to find motivation. Firing up the guilt had urged her on for years. Could she still be Amy without that?

She didn't feel any less confident this morning, any less capable. Her anger was banked for now. The guilt was still there, but she realized it was smaller, less volatile. If she didn't add fuel, it wouldn't combust. She ruefully shook her head. No, she didn't want the guilt to completely disappear. The remorse kept her on her toes.

Now she saw there might be a way to use it to her advantage. To make her time with Claire count. To help her sister by being a proper part of Claire's life. To do that, she needed to still the storm inside of her.

Her phone buzzed with a reminder, breaking her deep thoughts. A laugh burst out when she read it. She'd forgotten that she had a session with Ella this morning. Well, damn. She sure had a breakthrough to discuss.

Sometime during the last few months, she'd begun to not really look forward to the sessions, but not to dread them, either. It was impossible to look forward to an hour of mentally and verbally gutting yourself. But something was working, just like it had after the assault. Her animosity towards Mick was receding, and she'd done a complete 180 on Chris. All in all, she was less focused on the past and more excited for the future.

She should discuss the news from DAG and her mother's reaction that had tilted her world on its axis. Her inability to get justice for Audrey was the reason behind the rage that drove her to these appointments. Not Mick; she knew that now. While she still considered him a low-life bastard, his personal life was his own. Now, if Kit showed up and asked her to kick his ass, she would do it gladly.

At first, coming to therapy had been about keeping her job, following Peter's command, despite the fact that it had saved her before. Over time, the intense anger had diminished slightly. Of course, the Atlanta op and a chance for redemption had done part of that work.

So much news to cover. She shocked herself when she responded to Ella's question of what she wanted to focus on today.

"I can't understand why I miss him so much," she blurted, then set her mouth in a thin line.

Ella, ever the professional, gave her a sympathetic look. "Him, meaning Hugh? What do you mean by 'so much'?"

Amy sighed and sat back in the plush gray armchair. Ella's smaller office was decorated with soothing neutrals and muted patterns in soft blues and deep greens. It looked like a small living room at a furniture store, but homier. The psychiatrist kept her desk, files, and diplomas in her principal office. This room was strictly for sessions. Amy appreciated the attention to detail. The space exuded peace, although it routinely saw powerful emotions.

"I don't know. I think about him too often," she

admitted with a scowl.

"More than any past lovers?" Ella asked.

Amy shrugged. "Yeah. More than my friends, too. I guess it's guilt."

Ella smiled slightly. Amy had truthfully recounted the breakup at an earlier appointment. The doctor shifted in her seat and clasped her hands. She never took notes, since she recorded the sessions. The doctor was maybe a decade older than Amy, with short dark hair and a round face dotted with freckles. Amy liked the fact that Ella must have little fashion sense, for she always wore interchangeable classic pieces in navy, white, and brown. It was so like Amy's own work wardrobe, except she preferred basic black and white. No worrying about what might or might not coordinate.

"What part do you feel most guilty about, Amy?" Ella asked gently.

"I don't think I broke his heart, but I definitely left some cracks." Amy felt tears welling in her throat, making her voice thick.

"Are you sure what you feel is guilt?"

This question caused Amy's head to snap up. "What do you mean? What else could it be?" She laughed without humor. "Remember, guilt and I are old friends."

"Guilt may indeed play a part," Ella began. "But could another emotion be remorse?"

Amy narrowed her eyes. Her first thought was, *fuck no*. She rarely had regrets about anything. She made her choices and stood by them, even when things went to shit. Like her failed attempt to bring down The Duke after Audrey's death. She knew personality tests tagged her as cocky, overconfident. Peter had been the one who made her see how much thought went into her actions, even ones made on the fly.

Before being invited to join DAG, she'd undergone behavior testing. The one that sealed the job had been deciding options during a firefight. It had been in real time, using agents and paint guns inside an empty house. Later, Peter had played the tape for her, pointing out each step and asking why she had picked each tactic.

She'd been left in awe of herself and her abilities. Now she wore the cocky moniker with pride. Ella must be mistaken, she reasoned. While Amy fucked up sometimes, that wasn't the case here. It had been for his own good. Still, she'd been a mean bitch about it.

"I could have let him down easier," she grudgingly admitted. "I was certain he wouldn't give up unless I made things clear."

Ella raised her eyebrows. "So, your intention was to push him as far away as possible. Wasn't that a bit extreme for such a short fling?"

Amy ground her teeth, a huff of anger escaping. OK, Ella was right. It had been extreme and cruel. At the time, it'd made all the sense in the world. The only option. But being that bitchy was not like her. So, why had she treated him like that?

She shrugged her shoulders, refusing to face the therapist. Silence descended over the room as Amy tried desperately not to think. Her leg jumped. She wanted to stand up and pace, but she forced herself to stay seated. Pacing would show that she was disturbed, upset.

"Amy, it sounds like you connected on a deep level

with this man." Ella's voice was soft. "Something that hasn't happened in a long time, if ever. What if your intention to push him away came from fear?"

Now the anger was back. Amy met her gaze, furious that she would say such a thing. *How dare you!*

"I'm not afraid of Hugh!" she shouted, heat rising in her torso.

Undisturbed, Ella said, "Not of the man, but of the potential of the relationship."

"See! That's where you're wrong." Amy grinned in triumph. "The relationship was doomed. You know! You know I was set on killing Ajax. Hugh would never see me the same if he found out. Why would I want to be with someone who would look at me with horror?"

"Amy, are you truly horrible, or is guilt still speaking for you?"

"What?" Amy narrowed her eyes, her tone full of warning.

"Vengeance, justice, revenge, are all common feelings, desires. Shouldering the blame for Audrey's death shaped your perception of yourself. Now that you realize no one blames you – not your parents, not Chris, not even Claire – it's time to reclaim yourself," Ella explained patiently. "You're not a monster who caused your sister's death." After a brief pause, she continued. "What if Hugh actually understood and accepted you? Perhaps he saw the true you all along. Could you have used your revenge plan as an excuse?"

Amy shook her head violently, tears filling her eyes this time. Too emotional to speak, she kept shaking her head. Hugh was too good, too virtuous to condone murder, that was true. Yet she hadn't actually murdered anyone. All her plans for Ajax had evaporated that afternoon in the park. Had it been an easy excuse?

Her burden of guilt was lighter now. Had it been so massive, then, that it'd kept her from exploring a relationship? *Oh, shit.*

The pressure inside her head swelled until she couldn't stop the tears. She clenched her jaw, struggling to keep control of herself. Jesus! What was it with her and tears lately? She'd cried more in the past few weeks than in the past few years! She wasn't a whiny crybaby!

"Perhaps that was the actual fear. Having someone you love think badly of you."

I don't love him! Amy started to shout, but when she opened her mouth, only sobs emerged. Ella came over, knelt beside her chair, and held her hand as she cried. Jeez, two bawling sessions twice in a month! What was her life coming to with so much emotion flying around? She did not love him. Falling in love that fast was illogical and doomed. Sure, in a few short weeks, he'd become a close friend, and the sex had been spectacular. But that didn't equal love.

Her sobs tapered off enough for her to blubber, "He could never love me."

So, she'd made it easy for him. After such a ruthless send off, he would stop mooning over her. It was the last act of friendship she could offer him, or so she'd been certain of at the time. But now, the Amy who wasn't a murderer and wasn't solely responsible for her sister's death, was second-guessing herself. Had she purposefully pushed Hugh away because she felt unworthy?

"How do you know?" Ella asked gently. "Are you willing to risk wondering the rest of your life? You've faced gunfire, bombs, hitmen, drug dealers. You might find you're brave enough to ask this man this one question."

No way, Amy thought. Then the faint tone signaled that the session time was up. She'd never been so grateful for a noise before. She flew from the office, not stopping to even put on her coat until she was halfway down the block.

Chapter Eleven

THE JOURNEY BACK to her apartment passed in a blur. After locking the heavy door behind her, she dropped her coat on the floor and didn't stop until she was lying across her bed. She closed her eyes, inhaled, and then let the rest of the flood loose. Her own wails of misery hurt her ears, so she buried her face in a pillow. The bed moved underneath her as she jerked with each sob.

For once, she didn't even try to stop or calm herself down. She wasn't sure if she even could, so she just let go. It felt like hours passed before the storm tapered off to random tears. Too exhausted to even raise her head, she wiped her nose on the pillowcase and coasted into an exhausted sleep.

It was late afternoon when she roused herself. She felt stuffy, spacey, and achy, as if she was recovering from the flu. Maybe it was a new strain, she thought. Fucked-up-life flu or excessive-guilt virus. She dragged herself to the shower and stood there until the hot water ran cold.

She heated a can of soup and forced it down solely

because her body needed fuel. Too bad it wasn't Malachai's chicken noodle soup. She could use that and one of his burly hugs right now. She should go to the gym, but lethargy still ruled her body, so she substituted with some stretches and yoga poses.

In the middle of a downward dog, her phone went off. She almost didn't answer, but saw it was Mateo. He had limited access to calling, so it must be important. Could even be about the favor she'd requested.

"Hey Mateo! How's it coming with the program?" She forced excitement into her voice.

"Actually, I think it's complete," he replied.

She finally was used to his quiet, accented voice. It was at odds with his looks. In person, he looked like a stone-cold hitman with long hair, covered with gang tattoos. When he'd first joined DAG, she had been put off by the deadness in his eyes. But hope and opportunity had enacted a makeover, and within a few weeks, his eyes showed sparks of life. He'd never failed to have their backs, and everyone at DAG knew how perilous his undercover work was, and admired him for it.

"That's amazing!" she exclaimed. Honestly, she hadn't expected delivery for a few more weeks. Mateo must be more of a prodigy than Malachai had let on.

"If you're free, I can show you how it works," he added. "I'm in town, on break from solitary."

"That would be fantastic." Her heart soared, and then she hesitated. "Would it be too much trouble to meet outside the office?"

"Not at all," he replied. "I can come to you."

By the time she had neatened up herself and her

office corner, he arrived bearing his laptop and a six-pack of craft beer. Ah! Archie must have snitched about their mutual love of unusual brews.

"Hey! I should treat you," she argued as she accepted the beer.

"You can owe me." He smiled, accepting a bottle, and followed her into the bedroom. She had pulled in an extra chair, and now sat back as he booted up his thin, state-of-the-art laptop.

"I admit," he said while they waited, "I'm dying to know why you asked for this."

Of course, he would want to know. She had studiously avoided thinking about Hugh and her feelings during therapy since she'd awoken. She owed Mateo for all his hard work. She could put on her poker face and keep to general terms.

Yet she was so exhausted from doing that. This morning must have used up all of her energy. Shielding herself was natural in their line of work. Why was it taking so much more effort today?

She looked to the side. "It's to help a friend. He inherited some money and doesn't need it."

"Must be nice." Mateo shook his head. "But good for him. Most people would waste it on stupid shit."

"Yeah, he's a good guy." Her voice was sad, and Mateo turned to look at her.

"How so?" Now it was her turn to spear him with a sharp glance. He held up his hands. "Not my business, huh?"

"Sorry." She sighed and gave him the full story. "You can feel good about the time this took to create. He's a lawyer who deals with low-income clients, mostly teens and young adults. He helps them get out from dumb mistakes or terrible choices that would ruin their lives and send them to prison."

"Fuuuck." He drawled out the word. "That's amazing. Wish I'd had someone like that back when I was a stupid punk. Would have saved me some terrible years."

He was busily typing commands into the computer, so she took a chance and asked, "So, what changed? What made you switch teams?"

It was a puzzle she and Del had pondered. All anyone besides the owners knew was that he was heartsick about the path he had taken and was willing to become a double agent in order to set things right. No one wakes up prepared and eager to change his or her life that way. Plus, he'd been set up for life as his gang's hitman. Something drastic must have changed his mindset.

She thought the stone-cold killer blushed, but it was hard to tell with his beard and the bad lighting. She started to say, never mind, it wasn't her business. Then he actually answered.

"A girl." He smiled sadly and looked down at the keyboard. "One day, I was in the prison yard. It was visiting day, and a woman walked by. At first glance, I was sure it was Janey. I ran over to make sure, but realized the woman's nose was wrong."

He looked up, a rueful twist to his mouth. "Janey and I, we lived in the same building growing up. I was pals with her brother. The neighborhood never got her. She was smart enough for a private school scholarship and moved away for college. I was so proud. And relieved, because after that I really fucked up my life. Glad she wasn't around to witness."

His brown eyes filled with regret. "That day I thought I saw her, all I could think about was how disappointed she would be in me. She wanted me to get away from that life. She was the only person who believed I could be more." He cleared his throat. "Daniel had given me his card years before. Don't know why I kept it. I knew that life had me trapped. But thinking about her … I reached out. Turns out, it wasn't too late. Maybe when my stint ends, I can find her and thank her," he finished with a shrug.

"I promise to help you," Amy vowed, touched at his confession. A girl. That was the last reason she would have guessed for him to change. She realized he had held back big chunks of the story, but so had she with Hugh.

"Might not be too late for you, either." He slid her a sneaky glance. "Don't underestimate what this lawyer's work can accomplish. I for one am blessed to be able to help."

Amy opened her mouth to argue, but instead gestured to the laptop. "Ready to show me how this works?"

The lesson was short and sweet, thanks to Mateo's attention to detail and programming abilities. At the end, Amy sat back, her throat clogged with intensity. It was perfect. She reached out and squeezed his arm. Suddenly, what she needed to do was crystal clear.

"Can I ask you for one last favor?"

MALACHAI MASSAGED HIS sternum. There wasn't enough antacid in the world to tame the burning in his chest. He stared at his computer screen, praying his eyes were deceiving him. No matter how hard he blinked, the images remained the same.

He picked up his phone to call Peter and Daniel, then realized he didn't even want to voice the message he had to impart. He punched the text icon and typed: "Our plan worked, to an extent. It narrowed the list of suspects down to two."

Almost five minutes passed until a response lit the screen. The other two men were probably as stunned as he was. Despite all the proof, they'd all secretly hoped there had been another explanation. Some cosmic anomaly to explain all that had gone wrong. But no; the sabotage, the pain caused to the team, had all been deliberate.

Why? Who knew? There was no explanation that could satisfy Malachai, and he was the least offended of the trio.

> **Peter:** *"I can be there within the hour to initiate the next step."*
>
> **Daniel:** *"Fuck. Fuck. Fuck. Give me 45 minutes."*
>
> **Malachai:** *"Understood."*

They knew he wouldn't divulge the identities of the suspected moles until they met in person. Until then, it was his own burden to bear. He rested his head in his hands. The weeks ahead would be hard and painful.

"YOUR LAST APPOINTMENT, Mateo Diaz, is here." Neddra stuck her head inside Hugh's office.

"Good." He sighed, ready to be done for the day.

He'd not slept well, his hope for a plea deal had been rejected, and he'd missed lunch. He was weary. "I'll meet him in the conference room."

He had turned the remaining empty room into a client space by adding an oval table and six chairs. Not that he would ever need that much seating, but it helped his practice look official. His own office had become a wreck over the last five weeks. He didn't have the energy to clean up. There were books and files everywhere, and he had opted to create another room to meet clients in rather than attempt to bring order here.

Eventually, he knew he would bounce back. His caseload was filling up nicely. His mother was doing well with her newfound independence. As for his feelings for Amy, he'd moved from despair to anger, and he thought acceptance couldn't be far off. Surely. He couldn't manage living with such sorrow and regret much longer.

Armed with a legal pad and his favorite pen, he set off to meet his potential client.

Mateo Diaz was older and better dressed than most of his potential clients, Hugh realized with surprise. However, the black tattoos that covered his hands and peeked out from the edge of his gray turtleneck told a darker story.

Mateo rose to shake hands, and he was taller than Hugh had guessed, perhaps 5'10" or so. He was lean under his sport coat, but his handshake was firm and strong. The shaggy dark hair tucked behind his ears matched his beard.

"What can I help you with, Mr. Diaz?" Hugh asked as they sat.

"I'm actually here to help you." Mateo's voice was gentle and heavily accented.

Hugh raised his eyebrows and silently cursed Neddra. Normally, she was skilled at weeding out people who wanted to sell him something. Before he could tell Mateo he wasn't interested, the man dropped a bombshell.

"I work for DAG. Amy asked me to build something for you. I'm here to show you how it works."

Hugh's heavy fountain pen hit the pad with a thunk as his fingers went numb.

"Whatever it is, I'm not interested," he said flatly, and started to rise. At least he would, as soon as he could feel his legs again.

"Please, Mr. Bainbridge, I worked very hard on this. At least allow me to demonstrate its use."

While Hugh was taller and broader than the man was, something in his face made him pause. Mateo maintained a small smile, but something in his eyes telegraphed danger. Hugh wasn't frightened; the man was from DAG, and he trusted every one of their agents. Yet instinct had him staying in his seat and nodding. OK, he would admit to being mildly curious, as well.

Mateo turned his open laptop toward Hugh and punched some keys.

"To get started, you designate an amount and tie it to a separate account. I would suggest an offshore bank to avoid questions. You then select individual amounts from $10 to $100. Going any higher would also provoke questions."

Mateo switched to another screen. "You can select as

many categories as you want. Amy thought you might be more interested in individuals rather than charities, so here are some choices to start."

Hugh realized Mateo was referring to GoFundMe. The list of choices included medical, memorial, educational, emergency, and more. His mind raced as Mateo kept speaking.

"Once you load in your starting amounts and frequency, the program will disperse money. It's hack-proof and totally anonymous, if you employ offshore banking."

This was about his inheritance, that stone around his neck. She had found a way … *Jesus!* Why would she have done this? If he meant nothing to her, why …?

Hugh sat back, shocked down to his bones. "Amy asked you to do this?"

"I had some time on my hands." Mateo responded with a shrug. "She said you needed to donate money without worrying that it might go to waste. The program weeds out anything that might be suspicious, but there will always be people who game the system. Another reason to keep your amounts under $100."

"For example, if you loaded in a million dollars and set the program to select ten accounts a day for $10, it would run for over twenty-seven years. The only time you would need to log in would be to change amounts, frequencies, or preferences. Otherwise, sit back and let it run."

Hugh was speechless. The money could go away, helping thousands of people. If this worked, it would be perfect. A godsend. Except for the fact it had come from Amy. His shriveled heart sank lower in his chest. He wanted nothing to remind him of her. He especially didn't want to accept this guilty conscience gift, no matter how amazing it was.

Mateo saw Hugh's face darken and held up his hands. "I'm here to show you how it operates. Any other questions, you'll have to ask Amy."

"So, this is an apology? A farewell gift?" Hugh snorted derisively, pushing his pad away with a force that caused it to career off the table and flutter down to the ugly carpet. "I want nothing from her. How much do I owe you?"

Mateo smiled and shook his head. "I made this as a favor for a teammate. Even if it weren't for that, it would still be free. Amy told me what you do here. How you focus on teens and young adults, helping them before it's too late. Wish someone had been there to talk sense into me at that age. My life would have been very different."

Mateo rose, and his eyes twinkled for a split second. "Like I said, any other questions, you need to ask Amy. She's in your waiting room."

The smaller man left the room while Hugh froze in place. He inhaled an endless breath and jumped out of the chair before stopping to think. He made it down the hall in time to see Mateo and Neddra leaving.

He'd been set up! He heard the metallic scrape as Neddra locked the door. *Damn her!*

Amy stood in the center of the room. Late afternoon sun broke through the filmy curtains, highlighting her blond hair and the uncertainty in her eyes. She was wearing the pink angora sweater of sex, and Hugh felt doomed. One hand fidgeted with the hem; her other hand slid into the front pocket of her jeans. He could see her pulse pounding in her throat, near the mole that had enticed him at first glance. *Why was she here?*

"YOU GREW A beard!" she said, cursing herself for stating the obvious. That was not how she'd planned to start.

He must have stopped shaving after she left. The beard was well-kept and full, even the left side, which was normally patchy when he had stubble. He looked older and less approachable, which may have been deliberate. He'd also cut his hair, she saw when he turned his head. A little length remained on top, enough to curl against his forehead, while the back and sides were almost shaved away. Her heart hurt as she realized it served her right. There was no way to go back, only forward.

He must've had court today. He was wearing the expensive watch his parents had given him for law school graduation. He only wore it on court days, for luck. Otherwise, he wore a plain Timex that was a fraction of the cost. He'd ditched the tie and rolled up the sleeves of a sage green shirt that highlighted his eye color.

He stood there, silent, hands on his hips, feet braced apart. His head was tilted back in challenge. She well deserved his aloofness.

All the speeches she had planned vanished, and she desperately searched for the right words. Now that she was here, no words seemed adequate. He was so much more beautiful than she remembered. How could that be?

"What's that for?" he asked, tipping his head toward

the back of the office.

"The program? Just trying to help." She swallowed; her throat dry. "No matter what happens, I hope you can use it."

"Anything else?" He crossed his arms, the cotton fabric straining at his shoulders.

He had a right to make this difficult. She'd hurt him without giving a reason. If he didn't look so enticing, she might be able to concentrate. *One man, one question,* had been Ella's solution. Great, but for the fact the question needed an explanation and an apology.

"I'm sorry. The way I acted, the things I said. They were wrong and awful. I listened to my guilt and my fear," she blurted.

"What fear?" he asked, mockingly. "Of me?"

"No!" She held her hands up and moved forward a pace before halting. "You never made me feel unsafe! It's a long story, but it messed me up that day because I didn't get to kill someone." She sighed. "I was heartbroken because the opportunity to murder someone, what I had waited three years for, didn't happen."

Her toes curled in her shoes as she made herself look at him. "Ajax – the man who assaulted my sister and me – worked for The Duke. The agreement was to trade him for the guy we caught at the warehouse. I spent three years deciding exactly how I was going to torture him to death. I don't mean only imagining. I mean learning actual techniques, buying supplies. My hands itched to be covered in his blood."

Hugh's expression was still blank, but his face went pale. A corner of her mouth kicked up in a humorless smile. Now he knew what kind of monster she was.

"By the time I made it to the trade, my plan had changed. I was merely going to shoot him." She shook her head in disgust. "Then I found out The Duke had already killed him, right after the assault. Bastard. Anyway." She took another deep breath. "I'm sorry I was so cruel to you the next day. I knew the truth would be … revolting to you. I didn't think I could bear it, so I took a coward's way out. I wanted to hurt you enough that you wouldn't ask questions. All I could think was that you didn't deserve a horrible person like me. Especially on top of my guilt, my anger, and all the other shit, from what happened to me and Audrey." Her shoulders fell, and she let her hands fall. "And that I didn't deserve someone as perfect as you."

"I'm far from perfect." He snorted. "What changed your mind? Why did you nix the torture?" he asked before she could disagree with his statement.

What? Why was he asking a question instead of blasting her, as she justly deserved?

She shrugged her shoulders so hard, her arms flapped against her hips. "I don't know! After spending time with Claire and Chris, my anger and guilt … changed. But I fully intended to kill him, so why does that matter?"

"It matters." His voice was softer.

Afraid to look up, she kept her gaze on a matted section of brown carpet near Neddra's desk. "For once, I wanted to get on with my life," she said. "Then The Duke gave us intel that led to a takedown of a violent gang trying to conquer the Bluff. The DEA seized an insane amount of heroin, and pills, too. My mother, my friends, have pointed out that that was the ultimate tribute to Audrey. And my relationship with Claire would mean more to her memory than revenge. You said so yourself. I finally realized the truth."

"It wasn't me? The inheritance?"

She looked at him with confusion. "What would that have to do with anything?"

"Never mind. Nothing." He shook his head. His shoulders dropped as he exhaled silently. Did he truly think she would have held that against him? That it would change her feelings for him at all?

"What now?" His voice was softer, and she forced herself not to be a wussy and look him in the eye. "Is an explanation really why you're here?"

His face was impassive, but now his hands were in the pockets of his slacks, and his stance was looser. She gathered all of her courage, praying her voice wouldn't crack.

"I know hearing the truth about that day is revolting. I think my cruelty was more to hurt myself than to hurt you. To make sure you stayed away. So much has changed since then, both inside my head and with my outlook." She swallowed hard. "I only hope you can accept my apology."

"What do you really want, Amy?" His voice was so low, he was almost whispering. His eyes were shadowed, but his gaze was intense.

"You," she answered honestly, without thinking. A thrill shook her, and she realized how freeing it was to tell the truth after so long. To be open. This was her last chance, and she found she might have the strength enough to take it. In her mind, she extended her foot over the abyss, then let herself fall. "I'm going to be spending at least half my time here in Atlanta going forward. I wonder if we could … or if you still need an investigator … If …" Her voice trailed off into a whisper when he shook his head.

Fuck. She let her head fall once more. It was too late. Her bravery thudded to the ground with a sickening crash. She swallowed something that felt like a boulder. *Fuck!* Hot tears burned behind her eyes. *Again?* Would she ever stop weeping? She'd rather die than break down in front of him now. She should turn and leave, but she felt rooted to the spot in despair.

"I don't need an investigator," he said, and she saw him slowly approach until his shoes stopped a foot away. "What I want is a partner."

Her head jerked up, certain she'd misheard him. There was a tiny smile amid his new facial hair, and his eyes made her want to faint. They were full of love and a surprising sheen of tears.

"I want someone who isn't afraid of letting me see everything – the good, the bad, and the ugly. Someone who trusts me with their heart. Someone who will love all the fucked-up parts of me, too. I'll sell you half the business for a dollar," he added, and reached out a hand.

With a watery cry, she launched herself into his arms and wrapped herself around him. He hugged her so tight, his arms felt like iron bands around her back. She wrapped her legs around his waist so that she could relax her hold on his shoulders and leaned back to rain kisses over his now-grinning face.

"I love you. I'm so sorry," she cried. "I was such a bitch. I love you so much."

"Hush," he whispered. "I love you, too. Everything is fine now."

"I've never kissed a man with a beard before," she joked through her tears.

"I've been lazy. You can decide if it stays or goes." His smile was devastating, and her broken heart restarted as he leaned in for a kiss.

By the time the kiss ended, they were both breathless and flushed. Hugh shifted his hold so she wouldn't slide down and turned toward the back. After two steps, he stopped and reversed directions.

"Where are we going?" she laughed.

"I was going to ravage you on my desk. After that, we can decide how to divide the office space." He glanced down at her, eyes glowing with emotion. "But I think we should go home first."

"Home?" More tears clogged her throat.

"Yeah. Our home." He nodded. "We're going to make love in our bed. It will be slow and sweet, and we'll both cry."

She wanted to say "good plan," but was too full of love and happy sobs to speak. So, she tightened her grip on his shoulders, never wanting to let go.

Epilogue

THE BELL ON the door dinged, followed by Hugh's voice. "Just me, Amy."

Amy smiled at his thoughtfulness and executed another search on the computer. She was close to finding a bastard deadbeat dad that was behind on his payments. Knowing that the bell didn't signal a visitor allowed her to keep her concentration.

She was focused on tying up this one last loose end before they left for vacation in two days. Even though Candace declined to keep the family mansion, she'd retained the beach house on Hilton Head Island. The three of them would host Chris, Laura, and Claire for the first four days before having the place to themselves for the rest of the week.

The house had not only a private beach, but also an Olympic-sized swimming pool. With Hugh's promise to show her his competition moves, Amy had ordered a Speedo in his size. She wanted the full effect, damn it. The thought of watching the muscles below his tattoo move as he swam made her tingle all over.

She heard Hugh enter the office, but she didn't look up until he laughed.

He raised his hands at her annoyed glance. "Hey! I have a surprise for you."

Annoyance gave way to suspicion. Now that a small chunk of his inheritance was funding the office, Hugh had tried to buy her a car with his savings. She'd protested and bought herself an older muscle car. The unrestored exterior allowed her to move through the rougher neighborhoods unnoticed, while the stellar engine made fleeing easier. Since then, he hadn't stopped trying to spoil her. She leaned back in his last purchase, an ergonomic office chair built especially for her height and build.

Hugh threw back his head with a laugh. "Relax! This surprise didn't cost a dime!"

She blushed, grateful that he kept smiling. Her suspicions, insecurities, and bad moods rolled off him like water. The past few weeks were full of discoveries about themselves as a couple, and she even loved every tiny flaw she'd uncovered about Hugh.

The program that Mateo had designed worked flawlessly. Hugh had kept a fraction of his inheritance and invested it. There was more than enough to keep the business afloat and for retirement. Amy's savings had been similarly designated, save for the amount put into Claire's college fund. The house restoration was coming along, and they were almost ready to tackle the landscaping.

Amy saw Claire at least once a week. Chris had proposed to Laura, after clearing it with his daughter. Claire was over the moon about helping plan the small wedding. Hugh had been accepted at once, especially when he proudly admitted to following women's soccer.

Amy had been worried about fitting in with Hugh's friends, but she soon found them to be a diverse group who were stoked to introduce her to alumni tailgating at college football games in the fall. Besides her work with Hugh, she volunteered at Joshua's Vision a few hours a month with Candace.

At DAG, Peter refused her resignation, moving her to contract work only when needed. Ops were starting back up, now that Malachai had returned from sabbatical. She didn't complain. This way, she had the best of all worlds.

"Hurry up!" Hugh said.

She left the desk as he motioned for her to follow him into the waiting area.

The first person she saw was Del, and she squealed in delight. She rushed over for a hug, but halted when she saw Mick. *Shit. Why was he here?* It couldn't be DAG-related, not with Hugh looking so pleased with himself.

To her utter surprise, a dark head popped out from behind Mick's back.

She stopped. *It couldn't be!*

Horrified, Amy spoke. "Kit! What …? You shouldn't be here! It's too dangerous!"

Kit raced across the room and engulfed her in a hug. Amy returned the embrace, both thrilled and dismayed.

"Marius is dead. There's no more bounty," Kit explained.

Amy cut her eyes to Mick. Smug bastard. Great

news, but why was she back with *him?*

"He didn't know." Kit identified the disgust on Amy's face. "Amy, he didn't know what happened to me."

"Doesn't make me any less of a bloody imbecile," Mick chimed in with a half-smile.

"We know that, dude," Del quipped.

Kit rolled her eyes and pulled Mick forward, interlinking their hands. "He lied in an idiotic attempt to keep me safe. He knew I wouldn't leave if I thought he loved me, which he did, the asshole. All he knew was that I'd been battered and poisoned. He only wanted me safe."

Wow, they look happy, Amy noticed. Actually, they looked disgustingly in love. She knew what that looked like, thanks to a thing called a mirror.

She felt Hugh's hands squeeze her shoulders. She smiled back at him, letting him know his surprise was a good one, after all.

"I'm sorry," she said to Mick, and nodded her head at Kit. "I treated him like shit after you left."

"You were sticking up for Kit." Mick shook his head. "I understand that. Even more so once I learned her secret."

"Anyway." Kit nodded, her curls bouncing. "We came to invite you to our wedding."

"What?" Amy almost screamed in shock.

"I'm not letting her go again," Mick explained, his deep voice serious.

"Of course, we'll come," Amy began to accept, but stopped.

Fuck! Horror washed over her, and she was glad Hugh's hands were still on her. She needed him. Why he had not run for the hills when he'd found out her little secret tidbit about accidentally stabbing Mick, was beyond her. Instead, the man she loved had laughed and sworn to never mention it to anyone.

"Shit, Mick," she began, and cringed. "I am so sorry."

Everyone but Hugh looked at her, confused. He squeezed her shoulders, giving her strength. She huffed out a breath, and confessed in a rush, "I stabbed you – that op we did last fall. Not on purpose! I didn't realize it was you!" She finished with a shrug. "But I didn't feel bad about it, afterwards. I swear it was an accident, but it felt like karma."

Del muffled laughter behind her hand as Kit looked to Mick for an explanation.

"The scar on my back." He actually chuckled.

Kit's mouth formed an O and she looked at Amy in shock. After a moment, she looked back at Mick. "You need to be on your toes, then, buster. You try to ditch me again, and I'll sic Amy on you."

Everyone laughed but Amy. "It truly was an accident, Mick."

"I believe you. All is forgiven and forgotten." He actually bowed to her, his hand over his heart. "And I'm glad my fiancé has such a friend."

"When is the wedding?" Hugh asked, and straightened in surprise as Mick burst out laughing.

"Um … tomorrow," Kit admitted sheepishly. "And no, I am not knocked up. Just eager to be Mrs. Harris. If you two want to pack a bag, Archie can fly back to pick you up in two hours," she explained. "Please? Please?"

Amy looked at Hugh, who shrugged with an easy smile. "Nothing on our agenda that Neddra can't postpone. We were winding down for our beach trip, anyway. If we pack for both, we can fly back the next day and drive straight down."

"Looks like we're in," Amy announced, and grabbed Hugh's hand. Making decisions as a couple had started to feel natural, she realized. Even after such a short amount of time. This man was being woven into every aspect of her life, accentuating the good parts, helping her to deal with the bad parts. She prayed she did the same for him.

As if he heard her unspoken question, Hugh squeezed her hand, mouthing, "I love you," when she looked up.

Unmindful of anyone else in the room, and with her heart in her eyes, she mouthed back, "I love you, too."

THE END

Get exclusive, never-before-published content when you
sign up for my mailing list.

Go to the link below, sign up and receive a
free DAG Bonus Scene: the wedding of Mick and Kit!
https://dl.bookfunnel.com/n0er9f8tnd

Stay tuned for Book 3 in the DAG Team Series featuring
Mateo coming soon.

*To authors, reviews are priceless. Please consider leaving an
honest review/rating of this book on Goodreads, Amazon,
B&N, etc. Thank you!*

Acknowledgements

I owe the idea of Amy to all the many strong, magnificent women who I've had the privilege of knowing through the years. The ones who fought their way through fire and yet exited with their hearts intact. That's the trick, you see. It takes strength to not lose your true self through struggles. Being a badass means being vulnerable and asking for help when you need it.

I dedicated this book to four women who have inspired, encouraged and believed in me the last 25-30 years – The bridesmaids: Julie, Bonnie, Dee and Angie. I am in awe of you all and I will never feel worthy of your wonderful friendships!

As always, no writing would be possible without the support and unending belief from Jimmy, Elisabeth and Sam. Even when things were rough the last few years, you would not let me quit. Thanks for kicking my ass when I deserved it and hugging me when I needed it!

A massive thank you to others who lent their expertise and assistance – Cady, Tammy, Abby, Mala, Connie, Suzanne, The Pineapple Ladies – more women who bolster me daily and inspire me through their resilience and hope.

About the Author

Kel O'Connor lives with her husband in the mountains of North Carolina. They have two young-adult offspring and many animals – both wild and tame. In addition to reading and writing, she adores coffee, loud rock music, the smell of old books, and subversive humor. You can find her online on Twitter, Facebook and at keloconnor.com.

www.ingramcontent.com/pod-product-compliance
Lightning Source LLC
Chambersburg PA
CBHW020921110726
47900CB00001B/245